CORNERED

"Don't try to go anyplace," he said softly. "I can outrun you."

The color had faded from her face, leaving it even more sallow.

"What do you want?"

His lips twitched. "Come back in and close the door."

She swallowed again. He'd seen that look in eyes before, and it excited him, as it always did. She weighed her chances of getting away—he could see it, read it in her face as if it were written there in block letters—and then she complied.

He didn't say anything. Between the dark day and the trees that pressed close to the cabin, it was murky enough in here to turn on a light. Except that he didn't need one for what he was going to do . . .

A LONG TIME TO HATE

WILLO DAVIS ROBERTS

AVON
PUBLISHERS OF BARD, CAMELOT, DISCUS AND FLARE BOOKS

A LONG TIME TO HATE is an original publication of Avon Books. This work has never before appeared in book form.

Afterword reprinted from *The Oakdale Leader*, a publication of Live Oak Publishing Co., Oakdale, California.

AVON BOOKS
A division of
The Hearst Corporation
959 Eighth Avenue
New York, New York 10019

First Avon Printing, February, 1982

AVON TRADEMARK REG. U. S. PAT. OFF. AND IN OTHER COUNTRIES, MARCA REGISTRADA, HECHO EN U. S. A.

Printed in the U. S. A.

WFH 10 9 8 7 6 5 4 3 2 1

To my sons, Dave and Chris Roberts,
writers in their own right

The author wishes to express sincere appreciation to Sergeant Harold "Lucky" Reed of the Humboldt County Sheriff's Department for his advice and assistance.

Redwood County and the town of North Bend are imaginary. The characters in this book are fictitious, with the exception of Russell William Jory, who is a composite of several actual criminals whose stories have recently appeared in the newspapers.

At the time of this writing, it was possible in the state of California for a man who had been convicted of kidnapping, rape, and murder to serve seven years of a so-called life sentence and then to be released upon society. *A Long Time to Hate* is my commentary on the laws and the judicial system that allow this to happen.

The defense rests.

W.D.R.

.... Thursday, January 17

The item in the *San Francisco Chronicle* was brief. It stated only that Russell William Jory, age thirty-three, had been released from San Quentin after serving seven years of a life sentence for murder, kidnapping, and rape.

The article did not appear in the paper until two days after Jory had been freed.

By that time it was already too late for a number of people, including Morris Westbein, M.D.

"It's quite possible, Mr. Jory," the physician said, "that the condition is operable."

A pallor heightened the contrast between skin and the straggly facial hair the patient had already started to grow. Almost imperceptibly, Jory's head began to make negative movements.

"No. No way anybody's going to cut into my head."

Westbein smiled gently. He'd been through this before. "I can't say without more tests and further observation, of course. But if the growth is removed you could go on to many years of healthy life. There is, at this point, every reason for optimism." He had noted the pallid skin—hospital, prison? He looked into Jory's pale blue eyes and guessed: prison. "What is your occupation, Mr. Jory?"

The blue eyes were flinty. "I'm unemployed."

"No insurance, then."

"No insurance," Jory agreed. He had an oddly roughened voice; it needed lubricating, Westbein thought—or use. "Not that it matters. Nobody's cutting on my head."

"You might consider applying for assistance. Medi-Cal was designed for people who are unable to meet medical bills, you know." Westbein took a sudden stab, to satisfy his own curiosity, nothing more. "San Quentin, Mr. Jory? How did you get out without anyone finding out about this terrible pain in your head?"

A muscle bunched along the unshaven jaw, and Westbein knew he'd scored.

"But of course—you were afraid if they knew they would put you into a hospital rather than turning you loose, wasn't that it? But there's nothing to be afraid of, Mr. Jory. This sort of surgery is done all the time. It will only get worse, you know, if you leave it alone. The pain will increase as the thing grows."

13

Jory had a wide, thin-lipped mouth. The lips barely moved. "Give me something for the pain, then."

"But I can't do that. Oh, I could give you enough for a short time, but I can't provide narcotics indefinitely. And eventually it will kill you, you know."

It was unnerving, staring into a face that revealed so little. It made Westbein uncomfortable; indeed, he was feeling pain of his own, an increasing pressure in his chest that was oddly familiar. It had happened several times over the past weeks. He put up a hand and began, absently, to massage his sternum.

"How long?" Jory said at last.

"On the basis of a single examination I've no way of determining that. I don't yet know the rate of growth. It could be months. But there's no reason for it to come to that; I think it can be removed. The sooner we do it, the better your chances."

The discomfort in his chest increased; it became a pain that radiated out along his left arm, and comprehension of the symptom finally registered in his conscious mind. *Jesus Christ—*

He lost interest in Russell William Jory. He reached out for the intercom button that would summon his nurse, but the pain felled him before he could reach it. He sprawled across the desk, an expression of fear and agony contorting his features as his fingers scrabbled helplessly between the charts.

Jory watched the clutching hand, saw it slacken as the man slid slowly down behind the desk. The floor was carpeted; the impact made only a dull thud.

Westbein's office nurse was trained in cardiopulmonary resuscitation. If Jory had called her at that moment, she might possibly have saved the doctor's life.

But Jory, for several minutes, did nothing. Then he got up and crossed the room to the adjoining cubicle, which was filled with glass-doored cases containing various instruments and medications.

There were too many, and all the names were unfamiliar to him. Anger again bunched the muscles along his jaw. The pain would get worse—there must be something here for pain.

Codeine, that was for pain, wasn't it? There wasn't much, though, hardly enough to be worth taking. Christ, the man was a doctor, didn't doctors keep painkillers anymore? The names were a jumble, meaningless—he swept a row of them off onto the carpeting, scattering them beneath his feet.

He turned back to the elegantly appointed office, stepping over the legs of the fallen Dr. Westbein to jerk open the drawers of the oversized desk.

Ah, this was better. Two prescriptions, newly refilled—no, three; another rolled forward as he watched. Percodan, what the hell was that? For pain, it said. Every four hours for pain. He dropped it into his pocket.

"For Alice Westbein," the next one said. Lincocin; was that a painkiller? It didn't say, only that it should be taken four times a day. An antibiotic, or what? Anyway, it didn't say for pain. He picked up the last vial. Again for Alice, and this one said Darvon. There was a red cautionary sticker on it, stating that it could not be refilled, and this one, too, stated that it could be taken every four hours for pain. It joined the first container in his pocket.

The phone rang.

Jory closed the desk drawer, kicked Westbein's legs farther behind the desk so that they would not be visible to anyone who did not actually enter the room. Then he walked out into the corridor and paused at the front desk.

"The doctor says not to disturb him for the next ten minutes, please," he told the gray-haired woman there.

She cast a startled glance behind him, then nodded. "Very well. Are we to make another appointment for you, Mr. Jory?"

"Yeah. But I'll have to call you back. I don't know yet when I can come in."

She nodded again, and he walked past her and out the door and directly to the elevator. Five minutes later, he came out on California Street and began to walk up the hill.

It was a shabby house, one of dozens similar to it; they crowded close together, each two and a half stories high, narrow, with tall windows facing matching windows across the steeply inclined street.

Jory found the number, 1743, with the seven dangling upside down from its one remaining nail. There were eight mailboxes at the top of the steps, and he bent his head to read the scribbled names.

Hawker. Number three. That was it. He pushed open the door into a dirty vestibule. Two doors, bearing the numbers one and two, opened to his right. On the left, a stairway rose to the second floor. There was the smell of urine and some cleaning compound that combined to make each odor worse than it would have been alone.

He climbed the stairs, wondering why the hell they didn't leave a light on, stepped in a dog's dropping, and swore.

It was a long time since anybody'd painted the place. The sick-chocolate doors were scarred and warped. He rapped his knuckles on number three.

She opened the door, a thin plain woman of twenty-eight who looked older than that. Everything about her was mouse-colored: her unwashed hair, her eyes, her wrapper. She still wore a wrapper, at nearly two in the afternoon. She stared at him, unwelcoming.

"Hello, Wanda."

The mouth so like his own tightened. "Whatta you want?"

"Is that any way to greet the brother you ain't seen in seven years?"

"It's okay by me if I don't see you for another seven," she said, and started to close the door, but he got a foot in it.

"Come on. Blood's thicker than water, ain't that the way it goes?"

16

She looked down at his foot, then resignedly stepped backward, opening the door. "Whatta you want?" she asked again, but not as if she really cared.

The apartment was reasonably neat, but everything in it had been worn out years earlier. Linoleum, sofa, recliner with the stuffing coming out of it. The curtains were limp and needed laundering.

She pushed back a greasy strand of hair. "When did you get out?"

"Yesterday. Nice of you to ask. As nice as all the visits you paid me while I was in Q. Nice as all the Christmas cards and birthday presents. Real nice."

"Oh, shit." Wanda Jory Hawker turned away from him and walked to the hot plate on the table, lifting the coffeepot. She poured two cups, shoving one toward him. "Look, don't expect to lay any heavy guilt trip on me about that, Russ. You got in there by your own actions, and you got us run out of our own neighborhood, because who wants to live next to a killer's mother and sister; so don't come whining to me now. How did you find me?"

"Went back to the old place. Mrs. Smithers knew where you'd gone. Where's Ma?"

"She died two months ago."

His jaw jutted, then relaxed. He rubbed at his day-old beard, which itched. "Nice of you to let me know. What happened to her?"

"She got run over by a bus. Down on Mission. They cited the driver. Anything else you want to know?"

"Where's Hawker?"

"We split over a year ago."

She sipped her coffee, remaining on her feet, not offering him a seat. Bitch, he thought. Same as she always was. A bitch. He ignored the second cup of coffee.

"I need a car, and some money."

Her laughter was harsh, choked. "Oh, that's a good one! You came to me for a car and some money? Look, Russ. I had my gallbladder out in November, and I been on welfare ever since, because I lost my job. I haven't got a car and I haven't got any money, and I wouldn't give them to you if I had. Anybody that'd rape little girls, just kids—what kind of shit are you, anyway? And killed that boy, why'd you have to kill that boy? I don't owe you nothing, Russ. Nothing."

17

He hit her, open-palmed, across the face. He knocked her back into the edge of the table and the coffee spilled and burned on the hot plate.

She put down her cup, the imprint of his hand red on her cheek.

"Okay. That make you feel better? That's always your answer to everything, isn't it? Hit somebody, shoot somebody, rape somebody. Well, I haven't got anything for you to take. There's my purse, over there, I think it's got a dollar and sixteen cents in it. That's it until I get my next welfare check, which will be a week from Thursday. I don't have an extra bed, so I don't guess you'll stick around, waiting for that."

He picked up the purse, a worn black one with a broken clasp, and dumped its contents onto the couch. He took the dollar and the change, dropping it into the pocket with the plastic vials. His head was beginning to ache again.

His sister stared at him, hatred naked in her colorless eyes. Jory kicked the empty purse toward her, then turned and walked out of the apartment.

San Francisco's beauty failed to touch him. Jory got on the bus and rode through the streets toward the Mission District and the bus station. Christ, he didn't even have enough money to buy a bus ticket for any distance.

He watched his fellow passengers, wondering if it would be worthwhile to follow one of them when he got off the bus. But they all looked as poor as he was, mostly old people. A couple of more prosperous-looking matrons eyed him suspiciously and clutched their handbags. The hell with it.

The bus station was even worse than he'd remembered. Someone had vomited in the men's room and nobody had cleaned it up. There were used paper towels everywhere.

He stood in line at the window, waiting his turn, as a man bought a ticket for Willits, and an older man one for Portland, and a fat black woman purchased passage to L.A. When it was his turn he passed over his only twenty-dollar bill and asked for a ticket to Stockton.

He was oblivious of fellow travelers as he waited for his bus. As oblivious as he had managed to be, most of the time, of San Quentin. All he thought about was getting back to Redwood County, and the pain behind his eyes. There was always the pain behind his eyes, even after he'd taken one of the capsules from Dr. Westbein's containers.

Always the pain.

It was raining in Stockton.

It was only a light drizzle, but it was enough to make a man uncomfortable when he had no overcoat and no place to go to get out of the weather.

Jory had left the bus on the edge of the city and jogged along half-remembered streets to the house where Joe Ropas had lived, seven years ago. Joe Ropas, who might help him. Might loan him some money or a car.

But Joe Ropas no longer lived there, in the battered old house with four rusting vehicles in the front yard. The new tenant was perfectly willing to talk about it.

A slatternly woman of fifty, she leaned against the door-frame, pulling a ragged sweater around her for warmth. "They come with guns in the night, a whole bunch of 'em. Cops. They said he had drugs hid in the house, and they swarmed all over, lookin' for the stuff. Bullets in everything." She gestured at the holes in the doorframe beside her. "Joe, him and the other guys with him, they lost their heads and started shootin', and the cops killed two of them."

He was already turning away; all he'd cared about was a contact who could help.

"Not Joe, he's still in the hospital. Shattered a kneecap. Probably won't never walk right again," the woman said, with as much satisfaction as if she'd disabled him herself. "Bad for the whole neighborhood, having a place full of drugs. Only good it done was I got the place for less rent. Damn cops shot the locks off all the doors, and the landlord wouldn't replace 'em. Had to do it myself."

Jory wasn't listening. He was already walking back toward the street. A crippled Ropas was of no use to him.

He'd eaten in the bus station, one of those papery sand-wiches out of a dispensing machine, along with what purport-ed to be coffee. The Percodan had helped his head for a

20

while, but it was already beginning to fade. He knew that before long the pain would be back, deep inside his head, behind his eyes.

Before that happened he intended to find a place to hole up for the night. Get something decent to eat.

He walked quickly along the nearly deserted street. The houses were scattered and poor; he expected the pickings here would be lean. He didn't recall where he had to go to get to a better neighborhood; things had changed a lot. Buildings gone, new ones built, businesses changed.

The world hadn't waited for him.

He was going in the wrong direction; the street was petering out in countryside. Jory cursed without energy. He'd have to retrace his steps.

And then he saw the little brown house, the last one on the street, almost hidden behind overgrown shrubbery. There were three rolled newspapers on the concrete step.

Three. The place had been empty for at least three days.

Jory looked around and saw no one. It was dusk and lights were coming on; behind some of the windows he saw flickering TV's as the housewives watched one more soap opera or game show before starting dinner.

He went quickly up the broken walk and stooped to pick up one of the papers. The *Stockton Record,* including today's. Jory pushed the bell.

He heard it ringing inside, but no one came. He tried the door, knowing that it would be locked, and then he went around the side, looking for windows that might have been overlooked. Actually, on the far side from the neighbors he could probably break the glass without anyone taking notice.

There was a garage he hadn't seen from the street, and when he peered inside he saw that there was a car in there. An old one, but maybe it ran. The garage was locked, too.

He worked around to the back of it, however, and found a rock to put through a window that looked out over an open field. A moment later, he was inside the house; the door between garage and kitchen hadn't even been secured.

It was a crummy little house, smelling of age and mice and the peculiar body odor of its inhabitant. He hated body odors.

Jory moved methodically, checking out the refrigerator, which was virtually empty, and then the cupboard, while it was still light enough to see. Plenty of canned goods; he took down a tin of corned-beef hash and found a frying pan to put on the gas stove. That, and a can of peas, and one of peaches—an ample meal.

There was the kitchen, a tiny living room, and an even tinier bedroom, besides an antique bathroom. He went through the medicine chest, dumping everything into the sink that he didn't want. Christ, the guy must be a hypochondriac, all the junk he had. Aspirins, Anacins, Tylenol—he wondered if that was any good, any stronger than aspirin? He took it, just in case. Old antibiotics, one capsule left to a vial. Diuretics. Burn ointment. Antihistamines. Tranquilizers. FOR PAIN. He didn't know what that was, part of the label was torn off, but he took that one, too. And Empirin Compound, wasn't that a painkiller?

The smell called him back to the kitchen. His hash was scorching and the peas had boiled over. He ate moving around, too restless to sit. There was no pleasure in eating; it was simply a matter of taking on the necessary fuel.

He rifled the closet, looking for anything of value, and withdrew wrinkling his nose. The dresser, then, although there wasn't really much hope whoever lived here had had any money to leave around.

There was a bonus, though.

In a dresser drawer he found the .38 and a box of shells.

Kevin Rutledge was eighty-two years old, and he'd just been to his sixth funeral in two months.

He got off the bus carrying his suitcase and plodded along the wet street toward home. It was nearly dark, and since the heat had been turned off for three days the house would be cold. He couldn't stand cold anymore, not since they'd put him on that rat poison stuff after his second heart attack. If he didn't have the temperature at eighty degrees or above, his bones ached.

They ached now.

Maybe the next funeral would be his own. Only he wasn't having a funeral, and he'd made arrangements to be cremated. Cheaper that way. Not that it was going to matter to *him*, what it cost. And the more he paid the undertaker, the less there'd be for that worthless son of his.

Little enough, no matter how they sliced the pie. The house was so run-down they'd probably have to give it away. TV needed a picture tube. Jack might get a few dollars out of the car; it still ran, after a fashion. He wished he'd dared to take the car to old Tilton's funeral, but the doctor had warned him not to drive.

"Could kill yourself," he'd said.

Well, small loss that would have been. Only he didn't like the idea that he might kill someone else along with himself. Maybe some of the other people on the highway wanted to live.

He didn't much care, himself. He was old, and he was tired. There wasn't anybody left anymore, not Maisie nor Hal nor Bernie nor Fred—what the hell did he have to live for? If he had any guts, he'd load up that gun Jack had left here and put a bullet in his brain. But he supposed he'd muff that, the way he'd muffed everything else in his life. He'd heard of a

23

guy that shot himself in the head and lived through it, just lost his sight in one eye.

Yeah, with his luck the gun would probably misfire.

He went up the broken walk and put his suitcase down to get out his key, and picked up the newspapers. He'd forgotten to tell the boy to hold up delivering them.

He unlocked the door and then found he could hardly make himself turn the knob. He didn't want to walk into an empty house, to stand around shivering while it warmed up, to go to bed alone. Jesus, he thought drearily, I'll never have anybody to go to bed with again, not ever.

He opened the door and went into the house and something hit him over the head, but it didn't seem to hurt very much. He sank down, and down, and down, and the last thing he thought was, I'm not cold anymore.

If the old fool hadn't diddled around there on the front porch, Jory thought, he'd have been caught off guard. Now the old man was out of the way, though, there was no reason he couldn't stretch out and rest a few minutes before he started driving.

He'd checked out the car and found that with a little coaxing it could be persuaded to run. But he didn't want to attract the attention of the neighbors by driving out in it, not yet. He'd wait until later, when they were all watching their televisions, but before everybody went to bed.

There was less than half a tank of gas. Nowhere near enough to get him to North Bend. The old man's wallet yielded twelve dollars, his pants pocket another eighty-five cents. It was better than nothing.

He set his mental alarm clock and stretched out on the bed that had the same musty smell as the body of the old man crumpled just inside the front door.

Lying there in the darkness, he thought about them all. The girls whose testimony had sent him to Q; that big redheaded cop; the jury who convicted him; the judge who had so coldly pronounced sentence: *life in prison*.

Seven years they'd stolen from him. Seven years, and now with this son-of-a-bitching thing in his head he didn't have seven more. Months, maybe, the doctor had said. Months, in exchange for seven years.

Jory's fingers closed around the weapon beside him on the bed, and he thought about what he would do to them.

Wanda Jory Hawker stared at her image in the cracked mirror. She'd washed her hair and wrapped it in a towel; she wished wearily that she could afford a permanent, she looked so crappy it'd be a miracle if she ever found another job now that the doctor had released her to go back to work. But even one of those do-it-yourself jobs was beyond the reach of her pocketbook.

Her pocketbook. She snorted in derision, remembering the pathetic thing that still lay on the floor, stripped of its contents by her brother Russell. A bruise was forming on her face where he'd slapped her.

God, how could the authorities have been so stupid as to let him out of prison?

He was a psychopath. He had been, all his life. She wondered, not for the first time, what had made him that way.

The Jorys had always been borderline poverty, as far back as she could remember. Clifton Jory worked, when he could find work, but he wasn't trained for anything and he never made much money. He didn't start drinking until Wanda was in school; after that, things went downhill. He and his wife began to fight about the drinking and the lack of funds. It ended when Clifton got into a brawl and cracked his head on the base of a bar stool; he died two weeks later, no great loss to anyone.

Rosie Jory kept right on doing what she'd done before, cleaning other people's houses and coming home too tired at night to do much about her own. Too tired to do much about controlling her kids, either, Wanda remembered.

By the time Russ was fifteen, she doubted that anyone could have controlled him. He and Rosie used to have some violent shouting matches, which didn't change much of anything. Russ was man-sized, beyond the reach and strength of his mother.

Wanda herself, five years younger, had been Russ's victim as long as she could remember.

He stepped on her fingers when she was creeping, ran over her with a tricycle when she was learning to walk, put spiders down her dress, pinched her with pliers, and threw one of her new shoes into the trash burner two days after she got them.

Oh, he got whipped for things like that. Clifton Jory used to pull off his worn broad belt and apply it liberally to Russ's backside, but it never did any good. The minute his father was out of sight, he'd be back in Wanda's orbit, finding a new way to torment her.

She learned to stay out of his way as much as possible, and it was a relief when he started running around with boys his own age and older, leaving her alone.

He was first arrested when he was twelve, for joining a gang of other boys to rob a pawnshop. But Wanda knew he'd been stealing for a long time before that. Money, food, small items like radios and tape recorders. After the first time he was caught removing money from Cliff's pants pocket while his father presumably slept, Russ was smart enough not to steal at home anymore.

The cops brought him home and turned him over to his parents. Cliff whipped the boy and promised dire things if the episode were to be repeated.

Russ changed gangs, running with older boys who were up to more interesting things. He was thirteen when he raped the little Seegar girl.

Wanda hadn't understood what had happened, only that it was something terrible. Rosie had cried, and Cliff beat the boy almost senseless; Wanda had looked in on her brother as he lay on his cot, nose bleeding, eyes blackened, his scrawny chest rising and falling with each rasping breath, and wondered if her father would really kill him as he'd threatened.

Cliff died before the second rape. The first one never got as far as the police. Mr. Seegar had come over and told them about the first one, but the next time the girl was from out of the neighborhood, and her family called in plenty of cops.

They took Russ away and put him through all sorts of tests with doctors and psychiatrists, and they kept him in juvie for a while.

Wanda hadn't missed him. Home was a better place without Russ. She dreaded the day when he would come home.

When he did, there was a new toughness about him. He didn't argue with Rosie anymore; when she yelled at him he simply stared into her face with those blank pale eyes, and when he'd had enough he got up and walked out.

He acquired a gun, which he kept under a loose board in the cubby that served as his room. Wanda didn't know if he shot anyone with it, but every time they heard on TV about an armed robbery she wondered if her brother had been involved.

He had been arrested twelve times by the time he was eighteen. He spent a total of less than six months in detention, which never seemed to bother him a great deal. Each time he came out his mouth was flatter, his eyes colder. Wanda used to spend the nights with various friends whenever she thought he was going to be around home, which wasn't so often by then.

From the time she was fourteen until she was seventeen, Russell disappeared altogether.

She didn't know if he'd been in prison in some other part of the country, or not. He never came home again, not to live, although he showed up once in a while to eat or appropriate any money that might be available. Rosie and Wanda both learned not to have any cash on hand, and Rosie hid even her checkbook for fear he'd force her to write checks for him.

They knew he was in and out of the old neighborhood, and Wanda sometimes heard that he'd been involved in various crimes; on the few occasions when he was picked up, however, he invariably got off with a suspended sentence or no more than thirty days in jail.

Until he'd killed the Fitzpatrick boy, up in Northern California, and raped those two girls.

That time they gave him life—seven years.

It wasn't enough, Wanda thought, turning away from the mirror. Her jaw ached and she wondered if it was only bruised or if there might be a cracked bone.

They should have locked him up and thrown away the key. He'd hurt somebody again. Really hurt them. She knew it.

But what could she do about it? If the stupid parole board didn't know Russ was a psycho, they'd find it out soon enough.

The next time he killed somebody.

He didn't get away from the old man's odd-smelling little house until more than an hour later than he'd planned. Jory stood, fuming, behind the old-fashioned curtains, watching the activity down the street.

Some stupid old biddy had set fire to her mattress and the neighbors had called the cops. The smoldering bedding was scattered on the lawn, where it could hardly do any damage considering the way the goddamned rain was beating down on it. Why the hell didn't they all go back to bed and forget it?

They didn't. The fire engines—two of them for crissake, for one crummy cigarette in a mattress—were still there. People in their raincoats over their pajamas stood around watching—what?—and talking.

The car ran. He revved it up to be sure. But how the hell was he going to drive it out of here with all those idiots standing around out there in the street?

Another siren sounded, and he craned his neck to see what was going on. The garish red lights on the fire department vehicles gave the scene a surrealistic effect, and there was a small flurry of activity.

An ambulance. The old biddy must have been burned, or inhaled the smoke. Well, load her up and get her the hell out of here, he thought.

Even after the ambulance had gone, and the gawkers mostly returned to their homes, one of the fire engines stuck around until the mattress no longer emitted even a trickle of smoke.

Now. Was it safe now? There were still lights on, still people up and around. The neighbors probably knew the old man had been away; maybe they knew more than Jory did, as to why the old geezer hadn't driven the car but had apparently traveled on the bus. Would they be nosy enough to investigate if he pulled out now?

His own adrenaline drove him out. He hoped they were all absorbed in television and wouldn't notice the old car leaving. But at least the street was no longer blocked. His departure might be less obvious now than if he waited until they were in bed, when the neighborhood was quiet.

Jory dropped the curtain and moved through the darkened house, the streetlight the only illumination, and opened the door into the garage.

He had a flat tire before he'd gone fifty miles. Then the engine overheated and he had to stop for water. There was something wrong with the heater, and Jory was uncomfortably cold.

Christ, the amount of narcotics he'd taken, you'd think he wouldn't notice the cold.

It had been a waste of time, the side trip to Stockton. Ropas gone, and only an old man to rob of a few dollars and this shitty excuse for a car. He'd have been better off to have bought a ticket for as far north as he could afford, and then to have stolen a car along the way. He couldn't possibly have gotten a worse one, not if he'd taken it from a junkyard.

He wanted to make time toward North Bend. The pigs were going to learn he was loose and they'd be watching for him. The more warning they had, the more likely it was they'd spot him.

But hell, why should they spot him, unless he was driving an obviously stolen car? He was just an ordinary citizen, going about his business.

And he was going to finish that business before this thing in his head got to him.

First he'd find that judge, His Honor Horace Verland. Damned little creep, all swelled up with his own sense of importance, just because he wore a black robe and sat up there behind the bench.

Well, Jory'd told Verland what he'd do to him when he got the chance. Cut his damned balls off, he'd told him. He could still remember how the guy got bright red and then went fish-belly white. Cut 'em off and feed 'em to him.

He'd do it, too.

And then he'd find those girls. Kay Richards and Donna Malloy. He remembered all their names, even all the jurors.

He stared through the driving rain that slashed across the

windshield; now the wipers were faltering, and they'd been squeaking ever since he started.

He'd definitely have to get another car. There was a gas station ahead, and he started to slow down, sliding on the wet pavement. The goddamned brakes were shot, too, and probably the tires were bald as well.

Just before he pulled in under the canopy, the station lights went out.

Jory swore. There were two attendants, and something else he hadn't noticed when he started to pull in.

A black and white Highway Patrol car rolled out from behind the building.

The young station attendants came out into the rain, heading toward their cars parked on the far side of the lot. One of them bent to speak to the CHP officer through the open window.

Jory rolled down his own window to speak to the other one, who had turned in his direction.

"You need gas, mister? We just closed. And once we lock up the pumps we can't do nothing about it until the boss comes in the morning. Sorry."

"Yeah, me too," Jory said. He had half a tank; it wasn't gas he needed.

"Okay, see you at Marty's in ten minutes," the other kid said, and the cop agreed and waved a hand.

Jory watched the diminishing lights of the patrol car, then let his gaze rest on the kids getting into their vehicles to leave. If they were meeting a cop, he'd better not try for either of these cars; he didn't want a goddamned pig coming looking for them when they didn't show up as scheduled.

He didn't drive out of the lot, though. The engine sputtered and died before he got more than halfway across it.

He swore, an obscene litany against the old man who had owned the broken-down old car.

He didn't want to just walk away and leave it here. It was too soon to have anyone asking questions, tracing the car.

He didn't want to spend the night in it, either. He coasted downhill into the area where the attendants had parked. Maybe if he left a note on it, saying that it had conked out and he'd be back for it, they'd leave it alone for a few days.

Nobody, Jory thought in disgust, would think he'd stolen such a piece of shit.

31

Twenty minutes later, fairly well soaked, he gave up trying to hitchhike. Every damned car had kept on going past at high speed. He couldn't even see any other lights, no motel, no restaurant, nothing. Not so much as a stray house.

He crawled into the backseat, carefully locking the doors in case some goon got funny ideas; forcing himself to ignore his physical discomfort, Jory went immediately to sleep.

.... Friday, January 18

Lieutenant Patrick McDuff was a big man. Six-three, two hundred thirty pounds, fighting a losing battle with his waistline although he still looked fairly decent when he remembered to suck in his gut.

His reddish hair was fading now, at forty, but his eyes were as bright and sharp a blue as they had been when he joined the Redwood County Sheriff's Department seventeen years earlier. They kept him mostly behind a desk these days, which he didn't like, although his wife Molly was delighted. It would keep him out of trouble, she thought.

Mac was no stranger to trouble. Giving it, or taking it. It was all the same to him. If he hadn't become a cop, he'd probably have been a hood. Sometimes he wondered how successful he'd have been. He thought he'd have been smarter than the creeps running around today, but then, they all thought they were smart. Until somebody locked the barred doors behind them.

He would never have allowed anyone to put him behind bars. He knew, from a couple of experiences in the drunk tank when he was just a kid, that he'd have killed somebody before submitting to that. No, it was just as well old Whaley had got hold of him and straightened him up before some cop put a slug into him.

It was raining. Not unusual in Redwood County, even in a year like this one, which had been the closest thing to a drought year he could remember. Not as bad as farther south, in the interior valleys, where it had been dry last year and this summer was expected to burn to a crisp. But dry, for Northern California.

The drought was breaking, they said. A little snow in the mountains, and if it didn't warm up too fast so that it all came down at once, they'd be saved for this year. He hoped so.

35

Redwood was a depressed area, only two industries—logging and fishing—and both seasonal. They didn't need any more reasons to boost the crime rate.

He slid his black-and-white into the slot reserved for it in the basement of the courthouse, and flipped a hand in acknowledgment at the uniformed officer getting out of the next car.

"Morning, Lieutenant."

"Morning," McDuff echoed. "Have a quiet night?"

"Pretty much. Broke up a brawl at Murphy's around closing time. Had a head-on just north of the bridge before that, two dead, four in St. Luke's. Damned drunk. *He* was only slightly hurt, naturally."

They walked together toward the elevator, and McDuff punched the button for the sheriff's offices on the floor above. Sandy Moennig, slim and pretty in spite of the uniform, walked ahead of them along the corridor to Mac's office, and both men were silent, observing the taut tan material across her bottom and wishing the department hadn't given the females a choice between skirts and pants. Most of them had chosen pants; women didn't have legs anymore. But there was nothing wrong with bottoms, McDuff thought.

Andy Sleder looked up from his desk. He was a twenty-year veteran of the department, a few years older than McDuff and not much over half Mac's size, a wizened, swarthy man who would have a higher rank than sergeant now if he hadn't had such a temper and if he'd learned to brownnose it a little.

"Hi, Lieutenant. Just made a fresh pot, I'll get you some coffee."

McDuff nodded. "Clue me in, Andy. Strope told me about the head-on. Anything else interesting?"

"Nah. Couple of kids got caught breaking into Penney's; they tried to go down through the roof and the rope broke, and they couldn't get out of the store. One of 'em's Shaw's kid."

They exchanged looks of resignation. Shaw would have the kid out before the booking officer finished his paperwork, and that'd be the last anybody would hear of it. Slap his wrist and turn him loose, Mac thought. What the little bastard really needed was for someone to beat the shit out of him. The way old Whaley had done to him, when he was seventeen; Jesus, he could still remember that!

36

But Edmond T. Shaw would never allow anyone to lay a finger on his precious brat, and while papa wouldn't defend his own son in court, he'd see the kid was sprung, all right.

"Waste of time booking him," Andy said, reading his mind. "Here, I picked up this morning's *Chron*. You want a doughnut?"

McDuff sighed. "No, just coffee. You think we're going to get any work out of that girl?"

They both glanced toward the front counter where Sandy was talking to two uniformed officers and a third who looked like a bum but was really a narc. The men were all grinning, animated.

"Oh, *she* works all right. It's *them* that don't," Andy said. "Can't hardly look over there but what some young dog is hanging over that counter trying to look down her neck. Can't blame 'em, really. It's worth looking."

He placed the steaming cup on the desk and returned to his own. He was typing out a report with two fingers, something he accomplished only with a good deal of Ko-Rec-Type and profanity.

McDuff didn't have to look to see that the desk in Dan Evers's office was vacant. It had been for three days, ever since the sheriff got the news that his wife had terminal cancer. Terminal, at forty-eight, he thought. Christ, that's only nine years older than Molly. They probably wouldn't see much of Evers for a while.

And Captain Bill VonDorn was falling so far inside a bottle most of the department didn't care if he ever came out of it. But he was close to retirement, and Evers wouldn't tie a can to him. He'd give him his damned pension.

He opened the *Chronicle* and read the headlines. Depressing. Reading a paper was a hell of a way to start a day, it was always so depressing. He flipped back to the green section, looking for the comics. Hell, even the funnies weren't funny anymore, although *Doonsbury* had a wry humor that he usually found entertaining.

The name jumped out at him from the page, a name he hadn't even thought of in probably five years. He set the coffee down so hard it slopped onto his desk pad.

"Son of a bitch!" he said between his teeth.

Andy stopped typing. "You say something, Lieutenant?"

"You read the paper yet?"

"No. I get indigestion soon enough drinking the coffee in

this place, without pushing my luck reading the paper. What's the matter?"

"They're paroling him. No, they already did it. Russell William Jory. Remember that son of a bitch?"

"Killed the Fitzpatrick kid, sure. Raped those little girls, what were they, sixteen, seventeen? Got life, didn't he?"

"Life," Mac agreed. There was a bitter, metallic taste in his mouth and he didn't know if it was the coffee or the prospect that Jory was again loose on society. "Seven years, that's what it's worth to kill a boy and rape two girls."

Andy got up to come over and stare at the newspaper. "No doubt they *re-hab-il-i-tated* him," he said, exaggerating pronunciation of the word. "He didn't kill or rape nobody while he was in San Quentin, so what else could they do but turn him loose? We shoulda shot him the day we took him in, Mac. We shoulda put a big one right between them ice blue eyes."

"But he didn't reach for the gun," Mac reminded. "He didn't give us any excuse, remember?"

"Nobody there woulda told. We could've always said he went for the gun. It was right there beside him on the bed, and it was the gun that killed that boy. God, you remember that guy's eyes?"

McDuff nodded. "Pale blue, and cold. Coldest eyes I ever saw. Well, he's out. Served out his *life sentence*, and he's out."

"You think he'll come back here?"

They looked at each other.

"He said he would," Mac remembered.

"Son of a bitch," Andy commented, and Mac didn't contradict him.

Tim Fitzpatrick was one of the first people in Redwood County to read the *Chronicle* that morning. He was the next, after Pat McDuff and Andy Sleder, to see the notice of Jory's release.

For a moment he did not credit his eyes. He stared at the words, until they blurred and blended, and he had to blink and begin again.

Released. A madman he was, and they'd turned him loose. My God, how could they have failed to see how dangerous he was, like a mad dog that has to be shot. Rabid. That's what he was, rabid, like a mad dog.

Fitzpatrick was only fifty-two years old, but he looked at least sixty. He had always been a vigorous man; he'd worked in the mills for nearly thirty years, and pulling greenchain builds muscle. Of course he hadn't been on the chain in a long time, and the muscle was less firm than it had been. Especially since he'd damned near crushed his foot six months ago, he'd been going downhill. He'd been a hard worker all his life, and now that he couldn't work anymore—the doctor said he'd probably *never* work again—he didn't know what to do with himself.

If Larry had lived, there might have been grandchildren by this time. He and Sara might not have been alone, with nobody but each other to talk to, to look at.

But Larry was dead. The life had run out of him onto the pavement on the fifth of June almost eight years ago, and soaked into the ground beside Svenson's front pasture, and the house that had been intended for a big family held two aging people with nothing to live for.

They'd expected to have a family, he and Sara, and they'd

been happy as clams the first few years they were married. But the expected babies didn't come along, Sara couldn't even get pregnant the first six years. And then she had four miscarriages, one right after the other, so they thought they'd never have one.

And then there had been Larry. God, he'd been a ray of sunshine! A beautiful blond little boy, always bright, always asking questions. Couldn't wait to go to school, to learn to read. Tim had never been much of a reader, but by God that kid of his sure was. Read everything he laid his hands on, and got straight A's in school, and was going to be the valedictorian of his graduating class on the seventh of June.

Only on the fifth of June a madman gunned him down, there beside the road, and there was only Tim and Sara left, and they nearly as dead as Larry.

Fitzpatrick made a rasping sound, clearing his throat, and stared out across his backyard into the rain. It wasn't right. It wasn't right, they shouldn't have turned that killer free again—

"Tim? Something the matter?" Sara was looking down at him, his plate of eggs in one hand.

"That Jory. That Jory, they've turned him loose."

Sara had been a pretty woman, once. Funny, he couldn't even remember now what she'd looked like, but he knew she'd been pretty. Now the blond hair was faded and even her eyes looked washed out, as if she'd cried all the color right out of them.

She brought her tongue out between her lips, moistening them. "Jory? But they sentenced him to life in prison."

He shoved the paper toward her with violent motion. "Right there it is, they turned him loose! What do they think, he's going to be a useful citizen now?" He pushed his chair away from the table, the sight of the fried eggs causing his stomach to churn.

"Where are you going?" Sara demanded.

"Is there any ammunition for the thirty-aught-six?"

Sara's mouth formed a horrified circle. "You don't think he'll come back here, do you? Tim—"

"If he does," Tim Fitzpatrick said, "I'm going to shoot the son of a bitch."

His wife stood looking after him long after he had vanished

up the stairs of the farmhouse. Gradually the plate tilted in her hand, and the eggs, now cold in congealing grease, slid off onto the floor.

Sara looked down at the eggs and then she started to cry, the silent, hopeless tears she thought she had long since exhausted.

Ordinarily Kay Salvetti liked to sit with a cup of coffee and read the paper when she put Denny down for his morning nap. He was getting so he didn't want to sleep until afternoon, however, and sometimes she didn't get to the *Chronicle* until after dinner.

Today, she thought with a surge of irritation, she wouldn't have a chance to see it even then. Not with that damned dinner coming up tonight.

She ignored her year-old son, whimpering in the playpen in the corner of the big kitchen, and loaded the dishwasher and the washing machine. Why the Salvettis always had their big family dinners when she had so many other things to do remained a mystery, but they always did.

For the most part she liked the family she had married into, for all that they were so different from her own. The Richards crew enjoyed one another on holidays, and they exchanged news over the phone, but they weren't eternally gathering at every little excuse for an enormous dinner.

Not that tonight was a *little* excuse. It was Angela's birthday, and everybody in the clan would be on tap with flowers and gifts, and Angela's own daughters would have made an elaborate cake (never a store-bought one!). At times like this, Kay thought more warmly of her own mother, who was perfectly happy to be remembered with some small gift and didn't want all her kids coming home to dinner just because she was now a year older.

Denny clung to the braces inside the netting of the playpen, emitting a wail that could not be ignored. She scooped him up and went to answer the telephone, wishing as she caught sight of herself in the mirror that she'd had her hair done yesterday.

"Kay?" It was Wally's sister, Jeanette. "It's me. How's everything?"

Kay shifted the baby to her other hip and readjusted the phone. "About as usual. Denny's fussy. I think maybe he's cutting some more teeth or something. I'd call Dr. Pappas but I hate to bother him unless it's really an emergency."

"Ah, no need for a doctor with teeth," Jeanette said comfortably. Jeanette had four children and although they constantly ran around inadequately clothed and ate junk, none of them ever seemed to get sick. "What I called for, sweetie, is to see if you'd bring about four more chairs. Those folding ones. I count thirty-two for dinner."

"Yes, sure. Anything else you need?"

"No, everything's under control. Connie's got the cake done, it's gorgeous. Even Ma will be satisfied. Wally's taking off work early, isn't he?"

"I think so." Denny uttered a piercing shriek, and Kay flinched. "I hope so. I've still got so many things to do—"

Jeanette took the hint. "Okay. Bring the four chairs, and we'll see you tonight. 'Bye."

Kay hung up the phone and shifted her son around so she could look at him better. "What's the matter, honey? Don't you feel good?"

A hand on his cheek revealed a suspicious warmth. She sighed and headed toward the stairs and the thermometer in the nursery. All she needed was for him to get really sick.

It was a big house, an old two-story farmhouse she and Wally had bought against the advice of the entire Salvetti clan, and they loved it. They had remodeled and redecorated, and while they weren't quite finished, even Angela now had to admit that it was a very attractive place.

The stairs were recently carpeted, in the same pale gold Kay had chosen for most of the first floor—an impractical color, Angela said, but elegant—and she liked the lush feel of it beneath her feet. Denny was crying in earnest now, his sobs rising to angry resistance when she inserted the thermometer.

The nursery was, on fine days, a lovely sunny room. Today, of course, it was raining, but the colorful yellow and white tile flooring and the bright colors in pictures, curtains, and spread made it a cheerful place. They already had the youth bed, although Denny wasn't nearly ready to be moved out of his crib. She bent over him there, holding him until his temperature registered, putting her face close to his, patting him, whispering loving words.

With Denny's first birthday a few weeks past, she knew it

43

wouldn't be long before someone in the Salvetti clan asked when they were going to have the next one. Her stomach tightened, thinking about it. Her own family, while they might speculate among themselves, would never come right out and ask if she was trying to get pregnant.

So far she hadn't been able to tell anyone, except Wally, of course, that there weren't going to be any more babies. She could hardly bear to think about it, let alone put it into words.

The big house had been planned for a family. Not the big family the Salvettis had, nobody in their right mind had eight kids these days the way Angela had, but two at least. Or maybe three.

Only there wouldn't be any but Denny. Wally had begun to suggest, very tentatively, that they adopt. But so far she hadn't been able to cope with that idea, either. For one thing, adoptable children were few and far between, because so many unwed mothers decided to keep their babies and raise them themselves. They knew one couple who'd been waiting for nearly two years for a baby.

For another thing, she wasn't sure how she'd feel about raising a stranger's child. Wally said after they'd had it a few months it would be just like their own, but she wasn't sure of that. After all, it was important that a child be loved, as she loved Denny, but he was her *own*. She wasn't certain that she could feel the same way about a baby that had grown inside someone else.

If she hadn't been raped seven and a half years ago, there might have been other babies.

She hadn't thought about Russell William Jory in a long time. She didn't want to think of him now, she decided, withdrawing the thermometer and wiping it on a tissue. The doctors said they couldn't be sure that it was the injuries she'd suffered when she was raped that had made it so difficult for her to carry Denny full term, that had necessitated the surgery that meant there would be no more babies.

But she knew.

One hundred two point six.

She stared at the silver line on the slender glass tube.

She knew Jeanette wouldn't panic about a little thing like a temperature of a hundred and two. Well, closer to a hundred and three. Sometimes she wondered if Jeanette would worry if one of her kids fell out of a tree and broke his neck; she'd

44

probably nod complacently and say, "Ah, well, he'll get over it."

She stared down at her crying son. His blond hair clung damply to his head; the blue eyes were screwed up so tightly she couldn't see them most of the time. He was such a beautiful baby. Sometimes she wondered if Wally was sorry Denny wasn't dark like all the Salvettis, but he'd never indicated he was anything but pleased that his son had Kay's looks. Even if he was the only one—she thanked God for him, for the joy he brought to their lives.

She picked up the baby and jiggled him against her shoulder. Maybe he'd take some juice or something.

She glanced through the open doorway into the master bedroom as she passed it. The dress she was intending to wear tonight was spread out across the foot of the bed, awaiting a final adjustment to the hemline. If she were going anywhere but to Angela's, she'd simply wear her green silk and let it go at that. But everyone else was wearing new dresses (for a family birthday party? her mother would have asked, astonished) and Angela was quite capable of embarrassing her in front of all those people by demanding, however jovially, "What's the matter, Kay? Isn't the old mother-in-law good enough to dress up for?"

She sighed. She hoped Denny would let her put him down long enough to hem the dress.

She got the liquid aspirin from the upstairs medicine chest and carefully measured out the proper dosage. Denny swallowed it, then immediately began to whimper again. Dear Lord.

She put apple juice into a bottle and then rocked him while he drank it.

The *San Francisco Chronicle* lay unopened on the hall table.

Judge Horace Verland read the paper on his mid-morning break.

He was in a poor state of mind, since he'd had an argument with Edmond Shaw the first thing he got out of bed that morning; Shaw was undoubtedly the highest-paid lawyer in North Bend, in all of Redwood County, and he was a good one. But the man was an absolute son of a bitch personally, Verland thought. And now his secretary told him that Shaw's son was one of those arrested for breaking into Penney's. The boy was under eighteen, so at least Verland wouldn't have to make any ruling about *that*, thank God; he didn't envy Judge Marston, who handled the juvenile cases. There was no doubt in his mind how Marston would rule—if he were going to make an example of anybody's kid, it wouldn't be Edmond Shaw's—but he was glad it wasn't anything *he* had to feel guilty about.

And then this case he was trying this morning—the case itself didn't bother him, it was routine enough, but the attorneys for both sides were new, inexperienced, and so enthralled with the sounds of their own voices, and impressed with their own vocabularies, that the jury sat in an uncomprehending stupor; he himself had to keep interrupting counsel and getting them to drop their convoluted sentences long enough to get a point across.

He wished he had time to go home for lunch. His wife was a superb cook and a remarkable woman; he always felt better just to walk into the house where she was.

He dug into his desk drawer for his Tums and wished he had a martini instead of the poisonous beverage that passed for coffee from the court house cafeteria.

46

He ignored the front page and moved directly to the Sporting Green to see what the basketball scores were. And then he read the comic section, and after that he'd read Herb Caen's column, and then his recess would be up and he'd have to cope with those idiot attorneys again.

He sighed, and then held his breath for a few seconds.

Russell William Jory—released.

My God.

Had it actually been seven years since he'd sentenced Jory?

He could no longer bring to mind a clear image of Jory's features—he remembered him as a rather nondescript fellow except for those incredibly cold, pale eyes—but he recalled well enough what the fellow had said to him after he'd pronounced sentence.

Even after all this time it brought a flush of anger to Verland's face. Nobody said words like that in his courtroom, nobody. Except that Jory had. And what could he do about it? Contempt of court, when the man was already sentenced to life in prison?

Well, nobody could say he'd chickened out on *that* sentence; if it had been within his power to make it a *real* life sentence, to lock the man up forever, he'd have done it without a moment's hesitation. He'd sentenced a number of killers, but none that he remembered more vividly than Jory.

The man had threatened him. He had not only used language fit only for the gutter, but he'd threatened the judge, and the jury, and those two girls who testified against him.

Verland shifted uneasily in his chair. One of the conditions of parole had undoubtedly been that Jory remain out of Redwood County. But what did that mean? How were they going to stop him from coming back here? How would they know if he did, until it was too late?

He popped another Tums in his mouth and reached for the phone. He hoped they'd put every cop in the county to watching for him, so they'd know if Jory came back.

But the thought was cold comfort. For although an ignorant, cold-blooded sadist, Jory was smart enough to know that the police would be watching for him.

He wished to God the sheriff's deputies had shot the bastard when they arrested him.

The thought was unexpected and it astonished him. What was he thinking? He, a judge for over twelve years, and sworn to uphold the law.

Still, he'd feel better if Jory was safely dead. And that's the only way the man could be rendered harmless. To kill him.

Turned him loose. Jesus Christ, he thought.

By four o'clock Denny's temperature was 103.2°.

He had stopped crying and lay listlessly across her chest, quiet so long as she rocked him, but protesting when she tried to put him down.

She hated the idea of taking him out tonight. The weather was miserable, and she didn't want him to catch a cold on top of whatever he already had.

Wally wasn't home yet when it was time to feed Denny his supper. She'd hoped he would be, because she still hadn't hemmed her dress. Kay heated baby food in the little glass jars and tried to feed the baby, but he refused everything but his milk. He took his bottle, being rocked while he drank it, and this time he was exhausted enough so she managed to carry him upstairs and put him to bed without setting him crying again.

She stood for a moment looking down on him with a frown, then went to the telephone in the master bedroom and called Dr. Pappas. She got the answering service, though, instead of his office.

"He's doing emergency surgery," the operator said. "I don't expect him to be available before about eight o'clock. Shall I have him call you back then, Mrs. Salvetti?"

Kay sighed. "No, I won't be here by then. If I have to, I'll call him from my mother-in-law's."

It was a temptation, a tremendous temptation, to tell Wally to go on to his folks' place alone, and she'd stay with Denny. It was really a sensible idea, because a sick baby belonged at home, not in a houseful of noisy people, half of them smoking, and all of them celebrating with the wine that was sure to be urged on them by Sy, Wally's father.

Wally wouldn't go. Not by himself. And if they both stayed home, the entire Salvetti clan would be all over him.

"You couldn't get over for Ma's birthday? You know how

much it means to her. Kay really didn't want to come, did she? What's the matter, Wally, you getting henpecked?"

But Denny was sick.

"A little fever? Kids always run fevers when they're cutting teeth," Wally's sisters would say. "Rub his gums, I've got some of that stuff for teething infants. Or ice, haven't you got one of those teething rings that you put in the freezer? That'll feel good to him."

Kay stood looking down at the unhemmed dress. Wally wouldn't go without her, or if he did his family would drive him crazy (although they didn't affect him nearly as badly as they did *her*), and yet the more she thought about it, the more foolish it seemed to wake up a sick baby and take him out on a night like this.

Again she picked up the phone, consulting the list in the back of the phone book for the number.

"Hello, Mrs. Malloy? This is Kay Salvetti. May I speak to Stacy, please?" She'd do the next best thing. She'd go with Wally and leave Denny home with a sitter. Stacy would keep a close eye on the baby, and if he seemed worse they'd come home. Surely if the sitter called to say he was sicker, the family wouldn't raise a ruckus if the two of them left.

But Stacy wasn't saying, "Sure, Mrs. Salvetti," the way she usually did.

"I'm sorry, but I've got a date tonight. It's the junior prom, and I've got a date."

"Oh." Taken by surprise, because she'd never known Stacy to date, Kay couldn't think what to say next. She didn't know anyone else, nobody she'd trust with Denny when he was sick, except her mother. And she knew her mother had guests of her own tonight, a couple who regularly played bridge with the Richardses.

"Hey, I know. Maybe my sister would do it," Stacy suggested brightly. "I don't think Donna's doing anything. Shall I ask her?"

Kay hesitated perceptibly, then agreed. "All right. Would you?"

Now, why had she hesitated?

She hadn't seen much of Donna in a long time. They'd been best friends once, and they had gone through that terrifying experience eight years ago—

And that was it, of course. Somehow they'd never felt quite the same with one another. You'd think sharing such an awful thing might have drawn them together, but it hadn't. They didn't want to talk about it, yet when they were together they couldn't think about anything else. Maybe that was why they'd stopped running around together. It was too painful for both of them.

But Donna was just as responsible as Stacy. She was twenty-four, Kay's own age, and a first-grade teacher, and she had all those younger brothers and sisters. She knew about babies.

Perhaps Donna hesitated as well, because it was some minutes before Stacy came back on the line.

"She'll do it, Mrs. Salvetti. Six-thirty?"

"Six-thirty," Kay agreed. She should have been relieved, because if there hadn't been a sister available she'd have had to take Denny along to Angela's. Why, then, did she feel uneasy?

She'd see Donna for only a few minutes before they left the house, and a few minutes when they came home. They wouldn't talk about Russell William Jory.

"Hey! Anybody home?"

Wally had come in the back door. A tall, well-built young man, he was the best looking of the entire Salvetti family. His father and two older brothers had put on weight through the middle—the way Angela and the girls cooked, how could they help it?—but Wally was trim and flat-bellied. He'd grown a small mustache and at first Kay hadn't liked it, but now she did. It brushed softly against her as he bent to kiss her.

"Hi, kid. Have a good day?"

"Well, not really. Denny's sick."

"Oh? You call Pappas?"

"I tried, but he's in emergency surgery. It's only a fever, one-oh-three point two, but I don't think I ought to take him out tonight. So Donna Malloy is going to stay with him."

"Good. Break Ma's heart if we missed the dinner. Guess I better grab a shower right away, huh? Do I have to pick up Donna?"

"No. Hurry, will you? I still haven't had mine, Denny's been so fussy I was afraid to bathe until you got here. And I still have to hem my dress. I'll start that, but yell when you're out, will you?"

"Will do." Wally whistled on his way upstairs. He felt good. Why shouldn't he? He was only twenty-seven, was buying an interest in the family pharmacy, enjoyed being a

51

pharmacist himself, had a gorgeous wife, and the house in the country that he'd always wanted. And a son. A beautiful son. What more could a man ask?

His gorgeous wife was also efficient. She'd laid out fresh clothes for him and towels in the bathroom. On his way there, he peeked into the nursery. Denny slept on his stomach, rump up in the air.

Probably he was just teething. Wally wished Kay could be as relaxed about raising Denny as his sisters were with their kids, but maybe that was asking too much. Kay was a good mother, loving and concerned. He had no complaints.

He had his shower and was half-dressed when Denny began to whimper. Well, there went any possibility of getting a look at the paper before they left the house. He'd have to entertain Denny while Kay got ready.

So Wally didn't see the *Chronicle* either.

If Russell William Jory had believed in God, he would have thought He was deliberately preventing his progress toward North Bend.

Jory woke in the morning, stiff and hungry, when a different young man arrived to unlock the station. Jory unfolded his legs and climbed out of the car, walking toward the other man.

"Good morning." The words sounded stiff, unnatural. They were not words he ordinarily used.

"Hi. You spend the night here?" The guy acted a bit suspicious, and that wouldn't do.

"Yeah. Car quit. Can you take a look at it?" It might be something simple, something easy to fix.

"I'm no mechanic, just a gas jockey. Buff will be here by ten, he's the mechanic."

"Ten?" It couldn't be more than eight now, on another gray and rainy day. "There anyplace else along here that might have a mechanic?"

The youth shook his head. "No. We're sort of isolated here. I don't even know why I'm opening up this morning, no more traffic than there'll be until they clear away that wreck."

Jory stared at him. "What wreck is that?"

"Two miles north. Blocking all lanes. Guy driving a gasoline truck had a heart attack or something, they don't know for sure; he's dead. Rolled over his truck and took a couple of cars with him. A real mess."

Jory's lips barely moved. "The whole road's blocked?"

"Yeah. That's why Buff won't be here until ten, he lives the other side of the wreck, and he called me. They said maybe two hours to clear everything away."

Jory's pale eyes assessed the younger man and decided he was on the level.

He looked up and down the rain-swept ribbon of asphalt.

There was a ditch on the other side of the road, beyond which lay a fenced field with a few cows in it. There were scattered trees, but no buildings visible in any direction.

"Hell of a place to build a gas station. All alone out here."

"Yeah." The youth unlocked the station door and opened it. "Actually, we do a pretty good business most of the time. We're the only station for about fifty miles, and there's a turnoff going east five miles up, nothing that way for seventy miles. There used to be a restaurant here, too, but it burned down a couple years ago."

"So there's no place to get anything to eat," Jory said sourly.

"No. I got my lunch pail, though. I can let you have a sandwich, I guess. You been here all night with nothing to eat."

So he sat in the tiny station, letting the oil heater dry the remaining dampness from his clothes, and ate a tuna fish sandwich, washed down by a can of cold pop from the dispenser.

It was a quarter after eleven before the mechanic showed up. If Jory had fingernails, he would have bitten them. As it was, he sat, tight-lipped, while absolutely nothing happened. The police must be rerouting traffic, or holding it up farther south, or something, because very few cars passed, and only three stopped for gas the entire morning until the road was opened again.

"Clogged fuel line, I think," the mechanic said. He was a man of about thirty-five, brawny, hirsute, muscular. "Let's see if we can't blow it out."

Jory sat in stoic silence while this was accomplished, handed over a minimal amount of money, and once more took to the road with the old man's car.

The girl was standing beside the road, holding out a hopeful thumb. From a distance he wasn't sure of the hitchhiker's sex; jeans, an old jacket, waffle-stompers. The car ahead of Jory's passed her by, and when she turned, the wind blowing open the jacket, the bustline was definitely female.

He slowed before he even had time to think about it. There was a moment, only a moment, when he remembered the urgency of his mission. And then he braked in full and stopped only a few yards beyond the girl.

Seven years in prison is a long time.

She ran toward him and slid in, gasping, flipping water off her hair. "Oh, wow, I was about to give up hope. Jeeze, what a rotten day!"

She turned and grinned at him, wiping her palms on her jeans.

Nineteen or twenty, sallow skin, a wide mouth and slightly crooked teeth. Not pretty, Jory thought, but his disappointment was minor. She had dark eyes and her hair was almost black.

"You going far?" she asked.

Jory permitted himself a slight quirk of the lips. "All the way," he said. "How far you want to go?"

For a moment uncertainty made the grin flicker, and then she decided he was being gallant. "I've got a place about thirty miles from here. Two miles off the highway. You know where Subsy's is? Tavern?"

Jory shook his head.

"Well, I'll tell you when you get there. Thanks for picking me up. I got so damned wet."

"Maybe your coat would dry if you took it off. I'll turn up the heater," Jory offered.

"Yeah. Maybe that would help. It's wet through now, so it's not much warmth, anyway." She shrugged out of the jacket and draped it over her knees, spreading it out so the heat would reach it. She wore one of those ribbed knit shirts, wine-colored, that hugged her breasts. Jory took one quick look, aware of the heat beginning in him, in no hurry, savoring it.

"My name's Joe," he said. "Joe Ropas."

"Glad to know you. I'm Lucy Olivera." She held out her hands to the heater, strong, slim fingers. Ringless. "God, that feels good."

"How long you been standing there?"

"I don't know, maybe half an hour. Seemed longer. I usually get a ride with a friend, but she didn't work today."

"You on your way to work?"

"No, on the way home. I'm not working now. Well, I'm looking for work, actually. You job hunting too?"

"Right," Jory said. He watched the road, but he was aware of her, of the odd but not unpleasant scent of her. "You know of anything around here?"

She shook her head and the water flew off her hair. "No.

This is a depressed area, I guess. Not many jobs, unless you're trained for something special. Only thing I've ever done is be a waitress, and I haven't done that for two years. I didn't think I'd have to go back to it, but I guess I will."

He looked at her then, and she took his glance for a question.

"I just split with the guy who was supporting me. I mean, he paid the bills. The cabin's mine, it belonged to my grandfather, and he left it to me. It's not so much, but it doesn't cost me anything, you know? Dan left four days ago, and I've been trying to find something to do for eating money. He took every cent with him."

"Tough," Jory said. The warmth was increasing, spreading through him as if he'd had a stiff shot of whiskey. Only this was better than whiskey. Nothing that came in a bottle ever felt this good.

"My folks are vacationing in Hawaii," Lucy Olivera told him. "Would you believe that? My dad's an insurance broker. Plenty of money, and they'd be happy to support me if I'd live the way they want me to. Why does everybody have to put so many strings on their generosity?"

Jory grunted. "I don't know. Nobody's been very generous with me lately."

"I mean, they want me to go to school and get a degree. And what for? I had a year at U.C. in Berkeley, and it was a bore. I guess I'm not brainy enough. But what really gets me is that three-quarters of the kids I know can't get jobs even after they get their degrees. I know two Ph.D's who are washing dishes in a restaurant and parking cars. Who needs to study for years for that kind of crap?"

"Nobody," Jory agreed.

"Yeah. That's what I thought. They think I'm crazy for moving into the cabin. It's only two rooms. But it's got electricity and an inside bathroom. Not fancy like home, but decent, you know? And if I don't take their money I don't have to listen to their lectures." The grin flashed again, showing the crooked teeth. "Like, they'd have flipped if they'd known about Dan. There's a guy who works for my dad, they'd like me to marry somebody like that, and live the life my mother lives. You know, entertaining clients, presiding over business dinners, keeping house. No way, not for me."

Excitement, in fine tremors, heightened his senses until it was almost like being high—almost, hell, he *was* high, and he didn't need any expensive stuff to get that way, either. He'd found out a long time ago, when he was thirteen to be exact, what gave him a high. And he'd never paid a cent for it.

"That's Subsy's," she said, leaning forward. "On the right, where the cars are parked."

Obediently, he slowed. "And where's your place? I might as well give you a ride all the way, only take a few minutes more."

"Would you? That'd be swell. Turn right, and it's just a little ways back in the hills."

"Don't it bother you, living out in the country alone? Or do you have close neighbors?"

"Nobody real close. There's a guy lives about a quarter of a mile away, miserable old creep who yells at me if I cut across his lot even though it saves me a good walk and there's nothing there but weeds. Some people are so selfish."

It was a narrow dirt road. The few houses were small and dreary looking. There was no other traffic.

"Next turn to the right," Lucy said. "The house on the corner is the one where the old guy lives. See how much I cut off the walk by going across? My place is up there on the left, under the trees."

They coasted into the yard and Jory took it all in without being obvious about it. A small frame cabin, it was, with wild berry vines all around it, and trees that shielded it completely from observation except from the road directly in front.

Lucy began to shrug into her jacket. "Gee, thanks. I really appreciate this."

"Any time. I wonder, before I push on, could I use that indoor plumbing of yours?"

For the space of seconds there was hesitation in the narrow face. And then she nodded. "Sure. Why not? Come on."

He followed her into the house, stepping over dog droppings along the path. The front door wasn't locked; Lucy pushed it open and met the assault of a small fluffy-haired dog.

"Get down, Taffy. This is a friend, wants to use our bathroom." She gestured with one hand while stroking the dog with the other. "It's through there." She stood on one foot and began to unlace a boot.

The living room–kitchen was furnished simply yet with a good deal of color. Wild art prints on the walls, a gaudy rug on the board floor, an afghan of multicolored granny-squares on a sagging couch and red and yellow pillows in a bean-bag chair. Books spilled out of the board-and-brick shelves onto the floor, and there were stacks of newspapers.

Jory walked through the clutter and found the bathroom, which consisted of a shower, a toilet, and the tiniest lavatory he'd ever seen. Across from the bath was the bedroom, with an unmade bed and clothes strewn across the foot of it.

He turned back to the main room. Lucy was putting out food for the dog, talking to it as if it were a child, and it barked excitedly and leaped against her legs. She was in her sock feet.

"Feed the dog outside," he said.

For a moment the girl didn't move. Then she straightened and looked at him.

"Outside," Jory repeated.

"Hey, look. It's my dog, and my house," she said.

"I don't like dogs."

Her hesitation was perceptible. "Nobody asked you to like them. You gave me a ride, and I thanked you, mister, but maybe now you'd better leave."

He didn't move. In the half-light his lips scarcely moved, yet his voice carried clearly. "If you don't want me to kill it, put it outside."

She swallowed. For a few seconds it seemed that she might defy him. And then she swept up the small animal in one hand, and the dish of dog food in the other, and placed them both outside the door.

"Don't try to go anyplace," Jory said softly. "I can outrun you."

The color had faded from her face, leaving it even more sallow. "What do you want?"

His lips twitched. "Come back in and close the door."

She swallowed again. He'd seen that look in eyes before, and it excited him, as it always did. She weighed her chances of getting away—he could see it, read it in her face as if it were written there in block letters—and then she complied.

"Look, mister, I'm not a whore. I lived with a guy, yes, but I'm not a whore. There are plenty of them around, you don't need me."

Jory didn't say anything. Between the dark day and the trees that pressed close to the cabin, it was murky enough in here to turn on a light. Except that he didn't need one for what he was going to do.

Her tongue snaked over dry lips. "Don't."

"Take off your clothes," Jory said.

She didn't move, and in a savage gesture he grabbed the front of the knit shirt and ripped it to her waist.

She wasn't wearing anything underneath. Her breasts were small but high and firm. He put a hand on one of them and twisted, squeezing, until she cried out in a high, choked voice that stopped when he put the other hand behind her head and forced his mouth over hers.

She tried to drag herself away from him, tried bringing up a knee, but he blocked that and bit her lip until he tasted blood. He let go of her breast and jerked at the waistband of the jeans, hearing the fasteners pop and the rasp of the zipper. The girl made a gurgling sound, her fingernails raking his face, trying for his eyes.

"Bitch! Don't do that again!" He knocked her backward over the bean-bag chair and bent to jerk the jeans off her. She struggled to kick him. Her dark eyes were wide and terrified, her breath was harshly painful.

Jory hit her, an open-palmed slap that jerked her head around and left her momentarily stunned. He ripped the pants off her as she began to fight again.

He enjoyed the struggle of getting her into the bedroom, onto the unmade bed. Lucy Olivera was a fighter, but she was no match for him. He'd had nothing to do for seven and a half years but exercise to keep in shape.

Her left eye began to discolor and puff up, and a trickle of blood ran down her chin. Her breasts heaved from the exertion, flattening now that he had her on her back; he pinned her legs with his body, her wrists with his hands, as he deliberately bent and bit her right nipple until it bled.

Lucy screamed. It was a high, anguished sound that reached her little dog outside, making it scratch madly to come in and cry in its turn.

"Okay, bitch," Jory told her softly. "Now you're going to get it."

A blow with his fist to her abdomen, totally unexpected, left her white-faced and retching.

Vitality flowed through him like adrenaline. This was a practice session, for when he got to Kay Richards Salvetti and Donna Malloy, and he was going to enjoy every minute of it.

Outside, the frantic small dog clawed at the door, yapping wildly. Nobody heard it.

Inhaling deeply, Jory stood up and began to rearrange his clothes. Lucy lay sprawled in her own blood on the disordered bed, her dark eyes glazed in pain and shock. Her chest scarcely moved except for a crimson trickle from her right nipple to the sheet beneath her.

Jory bent to pick up his jacket and withdrew the .38 from its pocket. He fired from a distance of five feet.

The girl's body jerked and flopped, her head rolling from one side to the other as he emptied three rounds into her chest.

Then he went into the bathroom and washed his hands and put his jacket back on.

There was one of those push-button latches on the door. He twisted it and stepped outside.

Immediately he was assailed by the tiny dog; it leaped at his ankles, nipping with incredibly sharp teeth, and Jory kicked it as hard as he could.

The animal yipped once and lay where it had fallen. Jory hesitated for a moment, then picked it up and flung it inside the cabin, closing the door behind him.

A part of him knew that he shouldn't have allowed himself this diversion, that he'd increased his chances of being stopped before he could do what he intended to do.

But what the hell, the girl was alone, her parents were in Hawaii, and who was there to tie her to him?

He walked to the old man's car and got in, hoping to Christ nothing else would go wrong with it for a while.

He lost another tire an hour later. He was able to buy a recap for it. It took too much of his funds, but he didn't dare do anything else at the moment. Broad daylight, Highway Patrols all over the place because the weather was causing accidents, no doubt. First town he came to, he stopped and had a decent meal. There wasn't even a radio in the car so he could hear a newscast. Not that he expected anyone would be onto him, yet, but it paid to listen to the news, just on the off chance.

Luck was something he wasn't exactly having, though. By

late afternoon the engine began to splutter again. Rage surged through him in a hot flood. By Christ, he'd had it.

At least this time it happened before he was all the way through a town, not out in the goddamned woods.

He pulled into the nearest station and sat for a minute before he felt calm enough to open his door and get out.

"Fuel pump," the station attendant stated. "This one's leaking bad."

"What would it cost to fix it?" Jory thought of the slim fold of bills in his pocket.

"I don't know. I don't have anything to fix it. We don't stock anything like that. Nearest auto parts is back the way you came, about two miles. But they close at six." The clock in the window stood at 5:45.

Jory swore. "I wanted to be in Grant's Pass by morning."

"Don't look like you'll make it with this car. Not unless you can scout around and find a junkyard that might have one. Place back off the highway about four miles might have something."

And how was he supposed to get there? Jory wondered sourly. Walk, in the goddamned rain? He probably didn't have enough money for a fuel pump, anyway, and even if he replaced that some other fucking thing would go wrong. The car was of no more use to him.

"Would it be all right if I left it here? If I can hitch a ride?" It wouldn't do to simply abandon it, not where anyone would start checking on it. Not yet.

The attendant shrugged. "I guess so, if you move it over there to the back of the lot. I mean, just for a few days, you know."

"Might be a week before I can get back," Jory told him. A week, he shouldn't need more than a week. By then they could check anything they wanted.

He ignored the first two cars that pulled in to gas up. There were two men in the first one, a man and a woman in the second. The third was more likely, a skinny blonde of about thirty, driving alone.

He approached the car diffidently, bending his head to look into her window as the attendant unlocked her gas tank.

"Would you be willing to give me a lift?" he asked. "My car's broke down—" he gestured with a thumb toward the ancient vehicle, "and I have to get to Grant's Pass." He didn't

61

mention North Bend. He didn't want to be associated with North Bend, if anyone started asking questions.

She stared at him. Stupid bitch. She reminded him of his sister Wanda.

"If you're not going all the way, any distance would help," he said.

"No. I'm sorry, but I don't pick up hitchhikers. Nothing personal, you know, but it's too dangerous these days."

He looked down at her, hatred roiling his guts. Stupid bitch. He wanted to throttle her, right there, but the attendant was watching.

"Sorry," the woman said again.

Jory stepped back from the car. "Yeah," he muttered, and moved back out of the wet wind. "I'm sorry too."

The next car was a bunch of old ladies, all wearing corsages. He stared impassively as they all got out and used the restroom and then divided between them the price of five gallons of gas. Christ.

The next car was it.

Jory knew it immediately. The driver was in his early twenties, wearing jeans and a sweater and a big cross on a long gold chain. The car was a two-year-old T-bird.

The boy got out of the car and used the restroom, then hesitated before a pop-dispensing machine. He glanced at Jory. "Rotten night, isn't it?"

"Rotten," Jory agreed. Excitement prickled through him. This kid was *it*.

"Too bad they don't have a coffee machine. More to the point than Pepsi when it's so cold." He put his coins in and took out the can, though. He drank deeply and shivered.

"You heading north?" Jory asked. "I'm looking for a ride. Fuel pump went out on my car." He gestured once more at the disabled vehicle. "The guy here says I can't get a new one before Monday, and I wanted to be in Grant's Pass by morning."

The kid was already nodding his head. "Sure. Why not? I'm going as far as Garberville. Maybe you can catch another ride from there."

Jory stretched his mouth into a smile. "Thanks. I appreciate it."

The T-bird was in good condition, and it had a full tank of gas. It hummed through the night, snug and warm. The kid was a good driver, relaxed, cheerful. He smiled a lot.

"Going up to my sister's wedding," he said. "My whole family lives in Garberville, except for a few over at Fort Bragg. My sister's the first one of our family to get married, and everybody has to be there. About fifty of us, I guess, just the relatives."

Jory didn't say anything.

"You got family in Grant's Pass?"

"Yeah," Jory said. "Not a big family, though. Just my folks."

"My name's Jerry. Jerry Hornecker."

"Joe," Jory said. "Joe Ropas."

"Glad to know you, Joe."

The radio played softly on a country music station. Jerry yawned and stretched. "Guess I need some hot coffee and a hamburger, maybe. You hungry?"

"Wouldn't mind a bite," Jory allowed.

"There's a little place up the road a ways that stays open late. I usually stop there when I'm going home. I drive up every few months. I'm going to U.C. at Berkeley."

Jory said nothing. Small talk didn't interest him, except insofar as he had to do it to get what he wanted. What he wanted now was the car. It didn't worry him. He had all the way to Garberville to get it.

They stopped and ate. Jerry kept talking, handing out gratuitous bits of information about himself and his family. Finally, as they returned to the car, he asked a question.

"You married, Joe?"

"No."

"I'm not either, yet, but maybe I'll get married next summer. My girl says she'll keep on working so we can do it. She's a real sweet girl. Pretty, too. You got a girl?"

"No," Jory said. Jesus, why did everybody always try to talk him to death? What was wrong with a little peaceful silence?

The country music station went off the air. Jerry twiddled the dial but couldn't find anything else. They were getting too far away from the cities, and the hills cut off the reception, too. A sign appeared for a few seconds in their headlights—REDWOOD HIGHWAY—then vanished.

Redwood Highway. They were moving into big trees. Pretty soon, now, Jory thought. He began to watch for a place for it to happen.

Donna Malloy approached the Salvetti house unwillingly, maneuvering her Pinto off the gravel road and onto the long drive that led to the rambling two-storied structure.

She was annoyed with Stacy for putting her on the spot this way. She was even more annoyed with herself for having submitted to being roped in as a sitter for Kay.

It wasn't that she had anything else to do. It wasn't even that she disliked baby-sitting. It was simply—well, what was it? she wondered.

She didn't want to see Kay. Didn't want to see her handsome husband and her pretty baby and her beautiful house. But most of all she didn't want to see Kay.

There. She'd finally brought it out in the open. She could look at it.

She hadn't been to Kay's house before, although they'd lived in it for over a year now. She had visited, a few times, the little tract house they'd moved into when they were first married. But Donna had been so uncomfortable she'd managed to avoid continuing the relationship; any relationship.

In the summer this would be a pleasant place. The house was well back off the country road and was surrounded by big trees and a nice yard. A good place to raise a family.

She turned off the ignition and sat there, not wanting to go in.

Why had she and Kay been so close during those last two years of high school? They were totally unlike in so many ways. In looks, most noticeably. Kay was stunning, a tall, willowy natural blonde. She'd never been much of a student, but that hadn't mattered. She passed everything, she was popular, she had a lot of fun.

What did she see in me? Donna wondered. Had it been that she was bright enough to help Kay with her math and do the stickier parts of the biology experiments? Or was it that the contrast between them, beautiful blonde and mousy brunette, made Kay all the more the princess the other kids considered her to be?

That was unfair, Donna told herself immediately. What was the matter with her tonight? She wasn't usually nasty. And Kay had never been condescending, never unkind. They'd had a lot of fun together, and, face it, if Kay hadn't dragged her along on double dates Donna probably wouldn't have dated at all.

If Kay hadn't dragged her along to Smithy's party that night, she wouldn't have seen Larry shot and killed; she wouldn't have been raped, either.

Oh, God. Why did she allow herself to start *that?*

Donna groped for her plastic rain hood and tied it under her chin, although her straight brown hair was worn short and uncurled, so getting it damp didn't make all that much difference. She'd used to curl it, to try to look as nice as Kay did, but she was too busy to fuss with hair anymore.

She slid out into the rain, wincing at the chill of it on her face. Was she supposed to go to the back door, or the front? Most of the country people she knew used primarily the back doors, but she had a notion that Kay would expect her at the front. She ran up the walk and stuck her finger on the doorbell button.

It was Wally who opened the door, smiling. "Hi. Come on in, and let me take your coat." Donna noticed with dismay that she was stepping onto pale gold carpeting, leaving wet spots. She should have gone to the rear of the house.

"I think I'll take my shoes off; I don't want to make tracks."

"Put them over the register, there. They'll be dry pretty fast," Wally said.

She didn't really know Wally. She'd been invited to their wedding (although not as Kay's maid of honor, as they had once promised to be for one another), but by the time Kay and Wally met, Donna had already drifted away from the old gang.

"Sure was good of you to take Stacy's place," Wally was saying. "Come on in here where I've got a fire going. Kay will be down in a minute. Denny's asleep and he's been fussy all day, so we didn't bring him downstairs. Rotten night, isn't it?"

"Rotten," Donna agreed. She followed him into a living

room every bit as lovely as she'd expected—pale carpeting, softly flowered slipcovers, a big color TV, hanging plants, bookcases, and a white brick fireplace with a welcoming blaze. She took off her glasses and polished them dry with a tissue.

"I brought in enough wood to last through the evening, I think. There's central heating, but we keep the thermostat fairly well down most of the time and enjoy an open fire. There's a rocker if Denny's fussy when he wakes up." He gave her an apologetic smile. "Extra duty, rocking him, I guess. But it seems to help when he doesn't feel well."

She wished she'd changed out of her jeans and sweater. She felt out of place here, a sandbur among the roses. "What's the matter with the baby? Anything serious?"

"We don't think so," Kay said from the doorway, "or we wouldn't be leaving him. Probably his teeth, he's running a fever."

Kay was wearing a long dress of some soft blue stuff that did great things for her hair and skin and eyes. Not that Kay needed any help in that direction.

"Hey, you look great," Wally said, and bent to kiss his wife. There was no reason why he shouldn't have, but it made Donna uncomfortable.

Kay was smiling. "I've made a list for you, there by the phone. We'll be at Wally's folks', probably not very late. I hope we can start home by eleven or so. I tried to call Dr. Pappas—his number's there, too—but he's in surgery. If you think it's necessary, you can check with him after eight. And call us, of course, if it seems more than you want to handle. Come on, I'll show you where everything is."

It was a beautiful house. They didn't have everything finished, Kay said; they were still working on what would be the study, and it was a mess. They had the door closed and it wasn't heated. Denny would probably want a bottle when he woke up; he hadn't eaten much, but if he acted hungry there were prepared baby foods in the refrigerator. Also stuff to eat if Donna herself got hungry; she was to help herself.

They went up the stairs to look in on the sleeping baby. He was sweet-faced, Donna thought, but pink with fever. A moist thumb trailed from one corner of his mouth.

Kay showed her where the baby aspirin was, and the thermometer, and the spare diapers.

"Don't hesitate to call us if you need to," Kay said.

"Sure," Donna agreed.

And then they were gone, and she felt more relaxed. Why had she made such a big thing about coming over here? So it was a nice place, and Kay was as lovely as ever—that didn't detract anything from Donna herself, did it?

She prowled around the living room, hoping she'd hear the baby easily if he woke up. Maybe she ought to stay upstairs, but she hadn't seen anyplace to sit up there, to read or anything.

Saturday's *Chronicle* was lying on the coffee table, as if someone had just brought it in. Maybe she'd read the paper if the baby kept on sleeping. On the other hand, it wasn't even unfolded yet. Maybe Wally was as particular as her father was about reading an unblemished newspaper; at the Malloy house no one touched the paper until Jack Malloy was finished with it.

She didn't see the paragraph about Russell William Jory.

He wished he remembered better what the terrain was like. Too bad the kid wasn't going all the way up the coast. Or that here Highway 101 was so far from the ocean. Between North Bend and the Oregon border there were some good places to get rid of a body; shoved over a cliff, it might never be found. But the kid was going only to Garberville and Jory didn't want to push his luck by waiting until they got too close to it.

It had been all narrow, winding two-lane road the last time he'd been over it. The time they took him down to San Quentin, seven fucking years ago.

Now they were apparently making a freeway out of it, right through all those big trees. Everything was different. He didn't know what the hell he'd find up ahead, and that made him nervous.

He didn't like being nervous.

"Uh, Jerry."

"Yeah?" Jerry turned his head, the light from the dashboard glinting on the big gold-colored cross that swung on his chest. "Something wrong, Joe?"

"Yeah. I think that hamburger I got musta been bad. I'm getting sick."

Immediately Jerry eased up on the gas. Sure way to make a guy stop without much argument, threaten to puke all over his nice clean car.

"I think we can pull off here, there should be a wide spot—there it is. Truckers use it for sleeping, sometimes." The T-bird hit gravel and rolled to a halt.

Jory unbuckled his seat belt and bailed out into the rain. It wasn't ideal, but it would have to do. There was a level place and then a fairly deep ditch; he could hear the water gurgling through it. Trees on the bank above, none along the ditch that he could see, but maybe the ditch itself was deep enough.

He had left the car door open behind him, so the light was on. Jerry leaned toward him across the seat, his curly head outlined in gold. "Joe? You Okay?"

"Help me," Jory said, and he didn't have to fake it, the thickness, the tension in his voice.

"Sure," Jerry said, and unbuckled and was out his own door, coming around the front of the car, lit up perfectly in the headlights.

Jory fired two shots.

Jerry took the first slug in his chest, the second in the face.

He staggered backward, eyes wide, his mouth open and blood pouring out of it, drowning the words. He fell, still moving, trying to speak.

There were headlights far up the road.

Son of a bitch.

Jory grabbed the twitching ankles and jerked, hard. Get the sucker out of the light, at least, get him into the goddamned ditch—

Jerry was making noises, choking, bubbling sounds. Jory let go of his feet and moved around to put his hands under the younger man's arms; he was well muscled himself, but it took all his strength to heave Jerry into the ditch.

It was too dark to see anything, but he heard the splash and the sounds stopped. Maybe he was lucky, the water was deep enough to cover a body.

He moved at a trot, back toward the car, staying out of the full glare of the headlights but visible to the oncoming driver at the side of the vehicle. Just another guy taking a leak. Nothing to investigate.

The car swept by and red taillights vanished in the opposite direction.

Jory was calm. He slid in behind the wheel of the T-bird, which throbbed smoothly with power and welcome warmth. He didn't even have to worry about the trail he'd left, dragging the stupid slob to the ditch. The way it was raining, nobody'd notice anything ten minutes from now.

He reached over and pulled the right-hand door closed, then turned up the heater before he put the car in gear.

The road unrolled before him, black and eating up the light

except for the Botts Dots that curved gracefully down the center-line, bright yellow and easy to follow.

He didn't recognize anything about the son-of-a-bitching road, it was all changed.

But it didn't matter now. He had a car, and a gun, and he wasn't far from home.

Donna held the thermometer under the nursery light, twisting it until the silver line appeared. One hundred three point four. Up two-tenths of a degree from what Kay had reported.

Not high enough to run to the doctor with, she decided. But she'd give the baby some more of the liquid aspirin.

Denny accepted it without interest. His face was flushed, the fair hair standing in damp wisps, blue eyes shiny with fever. He pushed irritably at the bottle she offered, and Donna put it aside.

"Poor little boy. You really feel tough, don't you?" She scooped him out of the crib, picking up a blanket to wrap around him. "Maybe you'd just like to be held and rocked, how would that be?"

She carried him downstairs, hearing the wind that whipped around the corners of the big farmhouse. For a moment she thought it was hail against the windows, but it was only rain driven by a furious wind off the ocean. They were too far from it to hear the surf, but the breakers would be spectacular tonight.

Usually she didn't mind storms, but for some reason she felt uneasy tonight. With the baby on her shoulder, she walked through the lower floor of the house, checking on all the doors.

Wally had locked them before he left. She knew he had. Yet she checked them all again. The kitchen door opened onto an enclosed back porch. Double-locked there. There was also a new sliding patio door from the dining room onto a side veranda. Locked, and the pale gold draperies drawn over it.

The front door was secured, as she had known it was, but she fastened the bolt-and-chain thing, too. That was all the doors, unless they'd done something off the study, too?

She opened that door and was immediately chilled by an icy current of air. Kay had said they weren't finished working on that room, and it wasn't heated—that was an understatement.

She didn't turn on the light; enough came in from the hallway to assure her there were no doors to the outside. There was another fireplace in there, and a roll of carpet ready to go down, and a ladder where they'd been painting.

Donna shivered and closed the door.

There was a key in it, one of those old-fashioned skeleton keys that probably fit every interior door in the place. They had a bunch of doors and locks just like it at home.

On impulse, she turned the key and tested the door to make sure it had locked.

And then, feeling slightly foolish, she went back into the living room and sat in the rocker with the baby.

After a time he fell asleep, but it was an uneasy rest; if she stopped rocking he squirmed uncomfortably and whimpered. She wished she'd turned on the television, but she didn't want to disturb him by getting up now to do it. He smelled nice and she liked the feeling of the small body against hers.

The paper was almost within reach on the coffee table. But she couldn't manage the paper and the baby at the same time.

She rocked, and she thought.

She thought about her life, and Kay's, and how different they had become. Kay had everything she wanted. . . .

And Donna, what did she want? She liked teaching first grade. She liked little kids, before they got old enough to think they knew more than you did, before they were disciplinary problems. Some of those kids in Sally Johnson's fourth-grade class—boy, she was glad she didn't have any of *them*. They used words Donna's father and brothers wouldn't have dreamed of using in front of females. Once Sally had tried to separate two boys who were fighting and one kicked her in the shins and the other bit her arm so that she had to have medical attention for it.

The way things were going, eventually even the first-graders would know all the four-letter words. And nobody let you wash out their mouths with soap anymore. That had been very effective in the Malloy household.

Once, she thought, I wanted just what Kay has now. A husband, and a home of my own, and a baby.

Well, didn't she still want those things? She enjoyed

teaching, but was it enough, all by itself? Didn't she want a personal life as well as a job?

She did, and she didn't. Up to the point where some man actually wanted to make love to her, she did. And then after that, she didn't.

Oh, she knew it was all in her head, this total lack of response to a man. All in her head, although it affected everything else, too, because of Russell William Jory, who had appeared out of the night and shattered her mind and her body and her life.

Why in God's name was she thinking of him again? He was in jail, she hoped he stayed there until he rotted, and there was nothing to be gained by going over any of it again.

She sat there, in Kay's dimly lighted and charming living room, rocking Kay's baby, who was warm and heavy against her breast, and she remembered Russell William Jory.

There had been a party at Smithy's that night, the fifth of June, just a few days before graduation. A pregraduation celebration, Smithy called it, because nobody would allow them to do it right on the actual night. The parents had planned a party at the country club then, but there would be only pop to drink and there would be chaperones. So the entire class was invited to Smithy's on the fifth, while his parents were on a trip to San Francisco.

Donna didn't have a date, it wasn't that sort of thing. The entire senior class was invited. Kay had been more or less going with Larry Fitzpatrick then, so they all went in his car. Donna and Kay and Dick Trencher and Jimmy Hale.

It was a pretty good party up to the time Smithy's parents came home unexpectedly.

Smithy's mother seemed a bit put out, but after all, no one was drunk (it was only 10:30) and nothing had been spilled or damaged in her house; Mr. Smith thought his son pretty clever to have thought of having a party while his folks were supposedly several hundred miles away, even if they did break into his supply of booze.

Mr. Smith told them to go ahead and have a good time, but somehow the party sort of petered out; by eleven Larry said, "Let's go home," and they all piled into the car.

Larry took Dick and Jimmy home first. Not because they lived the closest, but because he wanted to have some time alone with Kay, of course. The town was full of high school seniors, all of them pretty happy, filtering out to their homes in outlying areas.

Donna sat in the front with Kay and Larry. She'd only had two beers (which was two more than she'd ever had before) and she felt good and sort of lazy and glad to be a part of a crowd like tonight's. Dick Trencher had paid attention to her, in fact when Smithy's mother walked in Dick had Donna in a secluded corner and she was debating how far to let him go. It had been a near-miss, exciting without being frightening.

Larry left off the boys, and then they cut across on the River Road to take Donna home. They were singing, laughing, having a good time.

When they saw the lights behind them, blinking a signal, Larry thought it was some of the other kids from the party.

"Probably Stutzy," he said. Larry was a tall, good-looking boy with blond hair only a little darker than Kay's; they made a spectacular couple. "That Stutzy—have you ever seen anybody funnier when he's had about four beers?"

"What's he want?" Kay wondered, twisting her head to look back.

"Probably he swiped some of old man Smith's booze and he's willing to share it. After all, it ought to be worth something to him that I kept him from failing math for two years." Larry eased his father's car over onto the shoulder and turned off the ignition. The lights came on when he opened the door, and the girls both swiveled to look back at the car that had pulled in behind them.

Larry got out and started walking back to where the other driver was emerging from a car that remained only headlights. There wasn't even an interior light in it.

Kay frowned. "That isn't Stutzy," she said, "he's too tall," and then it happened. The nightmare began.

They told her, later, that it might help to talk it all out. Tell someone—the psychiatrist, the police, her mother, anybody —all about it. Every detail. She might purge herself of the memories if she talked about it.

Curiously, though, Donna didn't remember all of it. It was like one of those old-time movies, that flickered and jumped from frame to frame, with some of the motion lost between.

It was all there in her subconscious, they told her; she'd put it out of her conscious mind because she couldn't bear to think about it. Yet it was only by retrieving it from her subconscious that she could be relieved of the burden.

She would never be relieved of that burden, not if she lived another hundred years.

Those first few minutes were indelibly imprinted on every level of her mind.

Larry had stepped out of the car and took a few steps toward the rear of it. The stranger stepped out, too, and brought up a gun—a shotgun—and fired.

There had been an explosion, so near it deafened them, and a burst of flames in the summer night. Larry staggered and put up his hands to his face and then fell on the ground between the two cars.

Kay screamed, and Donna strangled on her own cry; they were frozen in the front seat of Larry's father's car, and the shotgun blasted again, so that Larry's body flailed with the impact.

After that a few seconds were lost. She remembered the killer saying, "Get out of the car," but had no recollection of doing so. She stumbled against Kay and nearly fell, and the man prodded her with the muzzle of the shotgun. The girls huddled together, staring down at Larry's body.

He had taken the first blast in the face, the second in the chest. Most of his face was blown away, and from the great gaping hole below that the blood gushed and ran onto the pavement.

Shock held them rigid, unmoving, unable even to breathe until the pain reminded them.

"Unless you want the same thing to happen to you," the man said, "you're gonna do just what I tell you."

"There were two of you," Jory's lawyer had said later in court. "Why didn't you resist? How could he control *you* while he was assaulting your friend?"

He hadn't been there. He hadn't seen Larry. He hadn't heard the deadly voice, nor the words that spilled like venom from the thin-lipped mouth, poisonous, terrorizing.

Jory had taken Kay first. The unspeakable things he did to her—even when Donna closed her eyes she was aware of them. She wasn't much aware of her own tied hands nor of the pain where the shotgun had been jabbed in her ribs, but she heard Kay. Begging, pleading, then screaming, on and on into the uncaring night.

Somewhere there were people, but none of them came. No one heard them.

There on the ground beside two vehicles with the lights left on Jory subjected them to every vile thing it was possible for a man to do to a woman.

No, she didn't want to remember it all, no matter what they told her. For months afterward Donna would waken in the night, gasping, drenched in sweat, crying, as she relived it.

There was pain, searing, tearing pain, and she remembered that. But it wasn't as bad as Jory's voice, Jory's words. "Suck it. Go on, you bitch, suck it." Kay's sobbing in the background, Larry's body, now mercifully still, only a few feet away, and those terrible words. "You like it, bitch? You like it?"

For a few seconds, before Jory left Kay in a bleeding terrified heap and turned to her, Donna had prayed. *Dear God, don't let this happen. Let someone come. Please God, please God.*

It was one of the times God wasn't listening.

The agony went on and on.

Had she fought? they asked her. Couldn't she have gotten away while he was raping Kay, couldn't she have escaped into the darkness?

She remembered the prosecutor's angry face at Edmond Shaw's turn of questions, the intervention of Judge Verland, who had put an end to them. And she remembered Russell William Jory.

He had been the calmest person in the courtroom. He looked at her with those cold blue eyes and his thin, flat lips moved slightly; she knew he was saying it to her again. *Bitch. Bitch.*

It made her throat ache yet, remembering how it had felt to scream and scream.

She felt as if she had been literally torn apart—being drawn and quartered, it must have been something like what Jory did to them.

And at last it was finished. The act of breathing was almost more effort than she could make, and the agony seemed not to have diminished at all.

Her hands were sticky with her own blood. She felt as if she were choking on it, but no, she had vomited into the grass, it wasn't blood . . . and when the hands touched her she flinched and tried to cry out.

76

"Donna! Donna," Kay said, talking and crying at the same time. It was Kay's hands on her, bloody hands—God, the entire world was bloody—

She never remembered hearing Jory drive away. He left Larry's car where it was, the lights streaming into the darkness, and they crawled to it. Kay couldn't stop crying. "Where are the keys? Where are the keys?"

They couldn't find the keys. Maybe Larry had taken them out of the ignition when he stopped the car. Maybe Jory had taken them. But they were gone.

"Can you walk?" Kay asked. "My God, we'll bleed to death—"

Walked, crawled, she wasn't sure. She guessed they'd done quite a bit of both. Certainly among the injuries listed when they eventually reached a hospital were *"abrasions and contusions, both knees,"* those were the minor things. Donna didn't even feel them.

There were lights, far away across a field. Had they crossed the field or gone around by the road?

Neither of them remembered.

Stan Case found them.

He'd been out in the barn late that night because he had a Jersey heifer calving for the first time, and he expected trouble. She'd delivered by herself, though, and Casey was on his way back to the house when he heard the peculiar sounds and went to investigate.

Donna literally fell into his arms, leaving bloody handprints on his blue chambray shirtsleeves.

He swore in astonishment and scooped her up, then paused to listen to what she said: "Get—Kay. She fell."

"Christ almighty!" Casey raised his voice, bellowing so that those in the house would hear him. "Dad! Dad, call an ambulance, then come help me!"

The older Casey appeared on the back porch. "What's the matter?"

"I don't know if it was a wreck or what, but there's a girl here, hurt bad, and she says there's somebody else! Hurry!"

Donna retained only a vague impression of being wrapped in a blanket against the Northern California chill that pervaded the air even in June. Casey's face appeared above her, concerned, kind.

"You'll be all right now," he assured her. "Take it easy."

"Kay," Donna croaked.

77

"We found her. She's okay. We've got an ambulance coming, and the police." For he had realized, by then, that their battered condition wasn't the result of an accident.

Casey's young wife loomed over his shoulder, near tears herself. "My God, who would have done this to them? He must have been crazy. Crazy!"

"They'll get him," Casey said. He had an ordinary, unremarkable face, but Donna thought he was beautiful. "I hope they shoot the bastard when they catch up with him."

His wife leaned forward to dab tentatively at the trickle of blood at the corner of Donna's mouth. "Poor things. Do you know who it was, honey? Did you know him?"

"Don't," Casey said. "Leave her alone, don't make her talk." His hand closed around Donna's in a firm, reassuring clasp. "You'll be all right," he said to her. "I hear the ambulance coming. You'll be all right."

But she wasn't, Donna thought now, rocking, cradling Kay's baby on her shoulder. She was still suffering because of that night. It had crippled her, made it impossible for her to have a normal relationship with a man.

How had Kay managed to overcome it? She'd married Wally and had his baby, and she seemed perfectly normal, perfectly happy. Yet the same things had happened to both of them. Why had it crippled *her*?

Maybe they were right about talking it out. Maybe Kay'd been able to do that, to get it out in the open, so the wound had healed from the inside out, the way it should have.

Donna had no visible surface scars. But deep inside the wound was still raw and oozing.

The trucker blinked against fatigue, hoping he could last until he got to the good turnout before he had to pull over. He had a full thermos of coffee, and a couple of sandwiches, and they both sounded good. But what he really needed was sleep.

It was a losing battle, but if he could make it another two miles—and if there wasn't already some other son of a bitch taking up the space—he'd catch a nap. Half an hour would put him in good shape again, and he'd make it the rest of the way home with his load of insulation for the new housing project. And Sunday night he'd be on his way back south with a load of lumber, his regular twice-weekly loop from North Bend to the Bay area.

Christ, he was tired. Nothing doing even on the CB except that hag who called herself One Tit. He didn't believe driving a truck was a job for a woman in the first place, and one who called herself One Tit—Jesus.

The turnout loomed ahead, a black spot in the blackness around it; he knew by instinct more than by sight that it was there, and it was empty. Great. Half an hour, and he'd have enough energy to put him over the top.

He pulled in with a wheezing of the jake brake, locked his wheels, and shut it down. Sleep first, he thought. Then the coffee and maybe a sandwich. First, though, he had to answer a call of nature. That was the trouble with driving long-line, you had to drink so damned much coffee to stay awake and then you had to stop every fifty miles to drain the tank.

He dropped down from the cab and walked away from the road. He had relieved himself and rezipped his pants when he heard the sound that brought the hair up on the back of his neck.

A low moan issued from somewhere off to his left.

He froze. He thought about the wrench he kept under his

79

seat in the cab, and he remembered a buddy who'd taken to carrying a .357, the hell with what the law said. A guy'd got a right to protect himself, and some of the places you had to take a load, late at night and by yourself—

The moan came again. Over that way, in the ditch, for crissake? He'd seen plenty of deer hit along here, and a truck could have tossed one that far, but he'd never heard one make a sound like that.

He took a few steps in the right direction and then stopped as several cars swept by, headlights streaking across the turnout, illuminating it in intermittent flashes.

A hand came out of the ditch and clawed at the gravel almost at his feet.

The trucker didn't hesitate then. He bent over and grasped the wrist attached to the hand, and pulled.

The kid came out of the water, blood streaming by the gallon in the passing headlights—out of his mouth, out of a hole in the side of his face, out of the corner of one eye.

The cars had gone and the trucker stood in darkness with his grisly discovery.

For a few seconds horror practically brought his scalp off his head. Then the trucker eased the boy to the ground and ran for the truck. He grabbed the CB before he was even into the cab.

"Breaker seventeen for a ten-thirty-three. At the turnout in Rattlesnake Canyon, an ambulance and the cops. There's a man been shot and he's in bad shape."

Judge Horace Verland was spending a rare evening alone. His wife had gone to a Stanley party, whatever the hell that was. Women were amused by the strangest things. Even the cat wasn't there, they'd taken him to the vet's because of a badly torn ear. He should be neutered, so he'd stop fighting, Midge said. Maybe she was right.

He ate the supper Midge had left, then settled down to watch television. Reception was poor; they were having trouble even with the cable stations, no doubt because of the weather.

It was hard to keep his mind on the program, anyway. He kept thinking about Russell William Jory.

After a while he gave up on the TV and picked up the phone to speak to Glen Witwer, on night duty at the sheriff's department. He liked Witwer, felt he was a sensible man. Not hostile or a hothead like some of them.

"Evening, Judge. What can I do for you?"

"Just checking, Sergeant. I saw in the morning paper they've released Russell Jory. Remember him? I just wondered if your men were keeping an eye out for him. There's a chance he may be heading this way."

There was a moment of silence. Then, "Hold on a minute, Judge."

Verland waited. He'd turned off the TV and the place was abnormally silent, except that somewhere in the house a board creaked. God, he was as jumpy as an old woman.

"Yes? You heard something, Sergeant?"

"Came in a few minutes ago," Witwer confirmed. "Could be Jory. A trucker pulled into a rest stop south of Garberville and found a young fellow lying in the ditch; he'd been shot in the jaw but it missed anything vital, and the other shot—lucky son of a bitch—hit a heavy metal cross the kid was wearing. Bent it all to hell and bruised his chest but deflected the slug, or it would have killed him, sure. He's going into emergency surgery shortly, but the CHP man was there and managed to communicate with the boy. Kid picked up a hitchhiker who conned him into thinking he was sick, so he'd pull over. Then he shot the kid and took off with his car, a light green T-bird. We've got the license number and we're looking for it. Sounds like the kind of thing Jory might do, don't it? To get a vehicle?"

Verland's guts tightened in a spasm of pain. "And he's got a gun, too."

"He's got a gun," Witwer confirmed.

"Maybe you better get through to Dan Evers," Verland suggested.

"The sheriff's on emergency leave, sir. His wife has terminal cancer."

It was as if someone were stabbing at his innards with an ice pick. A red-hot ice pick. "VonDorn, then."

In the slightest of pauses, Verland knew VonDorn must be drinking heavily again. He liked VonDorn, but there were limits to what a man could drink and expect to retain his job, damn it.

"I think Lieutenant McDuff should know, sir," Glen Witwer suggested.

"Yes. Good. Ah—" He didn't want to come right out and ask for police protection; he knew they didn't have any extra men. Good God, if a judge asked for protection every time some small-time hood threatened him . . . But Jory was somehow different. "He's a dangerous man, Jory."

"Yes, sir. I'm sure the lieutenant will take all necessary precautions."

"Yes. Yes, of course he will. Thanks, Glen."

He hung up, knowing he had accomplished nothing. There was no proof it was Jory who'd shot the young man, no evidence that Jory was headed back to Redwood County. Yet Verland felt in his bones that it was so.

The psychiatrists had said Jory was sane. He hadn't believed it seven years ago, and he didn't believe it now. A sane man might have some aberrations, but raping and indiscriminate killing weren't among them.

He prowled the house, getting a beer out of the refrigerator, checking the plants on the kitchen windowsill, watering several of them. He missed Midge. She seldom went out without him. It was a miserable night, and she didn't like night driving. He wished she'd stayed home.

He pulled back the draperies to look out into the street. It was hard to believe, after the long dry winter they'd had, that it could rain so hard. The drains were clogged with dead leaves and debris, so that the gutters overflowed to the middle of the street and would soon be over the sidewalk, from the look of things.

He'd better turn on the outside light for Midge, so she wouldn't get out and step into a deep puddle. Across the street his nearest neighbors, the Harleys, were leaving. He wondered where they were going this time of night.

He wasn't friendly with any of his neighbors. The homes in this section of North Bend were set well apart, in broad lawns, with plenty of trees and shrubbery for privacy. Except for the Harleys, he couldn't even see anyone else's house.

He turned on the light over the front door and went back into the living room, looking for something to read. There were some new books from a book club on the coffee table, something Midge had ordered. A novel and a biography of some obscure military man. He wondered why she'd ordered that, and he took it over to his chair and settled down to read it.

"It's Glen Witwer," Molly McDuff said. She passed the phone to Mac, her expression watchful. Members of the department didn't often call him at home unless they wanted him to do something.

McDuff accepted it without comment. Molly was a good cop's wife, as good as it was possible to be. She didn't bug him, and she did her worrying on her own time. Sometimes it showed in her eyes, but mostly she managed not to let him know that every day when he went off to work she wondered if he'd be coming home again.

Oh, it probably wasn't so bad anymore, since he'd been promoted and gotten into the administrative end of things. He wasn't so likely to get shot at. She even resisted the urge to call and check on him when he was really late. To even it up, he tried to have someone call her, if he couldn't do it himself, so she'd know he wasn't hurt. Being a cop's wife was undoubtedly one of the more difficult things for a woman to be.

"Yeah, Glen," he said into the receiver, and mentioned for Pete to turn down the sound on the TV.

The kids, all three of them, moved closer so as not to lose the thread of the program they were watching. Molly returned to her chair, but although she faced the set, her attention remained on him. Waiting.

"Yeah, hi, Lieutenant. Got something I thought you ought to know about." Witwer related the facts as they'd come in. "I thought it could be Jory."

"Sounds like his M.O., all right," Mac agreed. "Well, if you've got an APB on the vehicle that's a step in the right direction. If the kid was shot say within fifteen or twenty minutes of the time the truck driver found him, the son of a bitch could be nearly to North Bend by this time."

He saw Molly turn her head and remembered the kids were

listening. He got up and carried the phone on its long cord into the den, closing the door behind him. Immediately the sound came up on the television.

"Yeah. We're watching for him. There's another thing, Mac. Judge Verland called. I think he's really spooked. He didn't come right out and ask for a guard, but I think he wants one."

McDuff exhaled slowly. "Sure. He would. Not that I blame him, but he's not the only one Jory's interested in, if it is him and he's heading our way. Those two girls are in every bit as much danger as he is. And probably everybody on the goddamned jury. That's fifteen people." He had 130 men to cover three shifts and almost six thousand square miles; there were just fewer than one hundred thousand people in that area and all of them were potential victims if Jory went on a rampage. Still, some of them were more likely to be targets than others. "Posting an officer with each of those people is out of the question. But maybe we should warn them. Why don't you get hold of a list of those jurors."

"Christ, Lieutenant! Where am I going to get a list of jurors on a Saturday night? For a trial that took place seven or eight years ago?"

"Call Judge Verland," McDuff said with a certain grim humor. "He'll unlock some doors for you, I'm sure."

"And what do I tell him to do about himself? If we don't offer him protection of some kind he's going to ask for it. What do I tell him?"

"He could always get a reserve officer out. Pay the guy himself, the same as everybody else. Hell, we haven't got any men to spare, have we?"

"No," Witwer said reluctantly. "There's something else shaping up that may keep us busy, too, Lieutenant."

"Oh, great. What?"

"The rain. Rivers are rising. They're predicting flood stage before dawn on the Hupa, the Big Bend, and Little John Creek."

McDuff gnawed on the inside of his cheek. "Sweet. Oh, really sweet. First we have a goddamned drought and then we have a flood. Lovely."

The door swung slowly inward and Molly peered in at him.

"The National Guard started broadcasting ten minutes ago, putting their people on alert," Witwer said.

"Good. Why don't you have them alert their men to our

friend Jory, too. Tell them he's armed and he's dangerous and for them not to get any wild ideas about being heroes, but if any of them spot him, let us know."

Molly's mouth went slack at the mention of Jory. She stepped into the den and closed the door behind her.

"Okay, Lieutenant. I'll be in touch."

"Yeah," Mac said, and hung up the phone.

"Jory?" Molly echoed. "Russell William Jory? Has he escaped?"

"They paroled him. The stupid bastards paroled him. We don't know for sure, yet, but there's a chance he's the one who shot a guy and stole his car tonight, headed toward North Bend."

Molly's breathing was audible in the quiet room. "I suppose you're going down there."

"I suppose I am," Mac said, and gave her a quick kiss. "Don't wait up for me, babe."

She didn't reply, but her dark eyes said it all.

The Salvetti family dinner was noisy and genial as usual. Angela, radiant in a new pink dress that encased her uncorseted fat like a tent, presided over all. Her husband, Sy, moved about, replenishing wine, speaking in turn to each member of his family, of which there were thirty-two present including children, grandchildren, sons- and daughters-in-law, and Angela's brothers and sisters.

The Salvettis loved to entertain. They lived in a large two-story house in a good section of North Bend, the same house where they had raised their large family. Sy had always made a good living, having inherited the drugstore from his father and enlarged and improved upon it himself.

The house, which had been somewhat shabby during the child-rearing years, was now freshly painted, carpeted, curtained. The colors were brighter than Kay would have chosen—the living room, vast enough to seat almost the entire clan without bringing in extra chairs so long as the kids sat on the floor, was carpeted in bright red, a shade picked up again in the cushions on the oyster-velvet sofa and love seat—but they suited Angela. And Kay had to give her credit, Angela allowed her house to be lived in. There was no fussing about kids eating in the living room or anyone putting down a glass on her tables; she was relaxed, enjoying the house and the party without restraint.

Kay herself sat in a big chair in a corner, watching with a half-smile as Jeanette's little girls played "mother" to Connie's two-year-old, Stephie. Stephie was as dark as Denny was fair, a cheerful, chubby little girl who raced around jabbering at anyone who would listen.

Maybe they were right, it ought to be possible to relax more with your kids, she thought. Certainly none of the youngsters here tonight looked anything but healthy and happy.

Wally was across the room, deep in earnest conversation with Sy and Sy's brother, Tony. Wally enjoyed his family, as much as all the rest of them enjoyed one another. If there'd ever been a fight, or even a serious argument, in the Salvetti clan, Kay wasn't aware of it.

Connie edged through the room, scooping up her youngest to divert her from a dish of salted nuts, and deposited her with older cousins with an admonition, then dropped onto the arm of a couch beside Kay.

"Ah, thank God for dishwashers. The second load is in, one more to go, and they're all rinsed. Ma looks good tonight, doesn't she?"

Connie was still slim, although there was a hint of things to come in the roundness of her chin and bared arms—she was handsome, if not pretty. Probably, with her dark hair and eyes, she was much as Angela had been twenty-five years earlier. She grinned at her sister-in-law. "You're looking good, too, Kay. Lovely dress. Too bad you couldn't bring Denny. He's such a love. I like watching the babies, and they grow up so fast. When you going to have another one?"

So, there it was. Kay's throat tightened. Well, she wouldn't hedge. "The doctor says I'm not," she said.

Connie's smile faded. "Oh, no! Kay, what a shame!"

Kay swallowed. "Yes, we think so, too. We never planned on Denny being an only child, but that's the way things go, I guess. Still, we *do* have Denny. And it's not as if it's impossible to raise one child without ruining him. Lots of people elect to have only one these days."

"True." Compassion showed on Connie's face. "And Denny will have lots of cousins, so he won't really be raised alone. Not in this family, where we all get together so often." Her mouth formed a rueful smile. "Sometimes it drives me nuts—and Charlie thinks we're all crazy, but fortunately he likes us—the way Ma wants us together every time anybody has a birthday or an anniversary. Seems like we seldom have any time to ourselves. But I'd rather be like the Salvettis than like Charlie's folks—they can't stand each other, and even on Christmas they'll get in a fight about something. They can't even play Monopoly without somebody punching somebody else in the mouth, or at least getting mad enough to go home." She laughed. "I'll bet we came on pretty strong for you at first, too, didn't we?"

Kay had to grin in return. "Sometimes," she admitted.

"Still?" Connie prodded, then laughed aloud when Kay reluctantly nodded. "Well, I'm sorry about the babies. I guess we've quit, Charlie says three is enough for one man to try to support, but if it weren't for that I'd have a couple more, population explosion be damned. We *want* ours. And Stephie's not a baby anymore. I miss having a baby. The boys, though—" She glanced across the big room to where her older offspring were engaged with their cousins in a four-party wrestling match until Angela reached over, without a break in her conversation, and thumped the nearer two on the head, toning things down. "Well, if you ever want to borrow a couple of kids, let me know."

"I will," Kay said, and then Connie got up and took off after Stephie, who was escaping into the dining room.

There. She'd done it, she told one of the Salvettis, and it hadn't been so distressing after all. At least, no more distressing than it was to know she couldn't have another baby. Connie had been as warmly understanding as anybody in her own family could have been. And the chances were that Connie would tell the others, and she wouldn't have to go through making the announcement again.

It was a relief to have given out the information.

Laughter broke out among the men gathered in front of the fireplace; two of Wally's brothers were slapping him on the back, and they all grinned. She wondered what they were talking about.

When they were first married, Kay had stuck close to Wally's side at these gatherings. Now, though, she realized that he enjoyed the man talk, and she wasn't as intimidated by his female relatives. She could be left to shift for herself with the other women, and on the way home they would compare notes, laughing, comfortable in their solidarity.

Stephie came hurtling through the mob, flinging herself into Kay's lap. She clutched a tattered copy of *The Tawny Scrawny Lion.*

"Read me," Stephie ordered. "Read me, Auntie Kay."

Someone across the room turned on the television; for a moment it blared as the announcer's face, badly adjusted to a magenta hue, stared out from the screen. ". . . are rising

89

rapidly. No primary highways are at present endangered, but some secondary roads may be—"

"Turn that thing off," Jeanette ordered, and her oldest disgustedly flicked the switch back the other way.

"Read me," Stephie urged, and Kay hauled the child into a more comfortable position and began to read.

He was getting sleepy. When the red neon blinked up ahead Jory swung the car over, jouncing onto the unpaved parking area behind two trucks headed south loaded with redwood and a third, heading north, hauling bags of something tarped down against the weather.

He slid the .38 under the seat, then locked the car when he got out. The gun had been a bonus, more than he'd expected to find so easily. It wasn't the weapon of his choice—he liked a shotgun—but it would do until he could lay hands on something else.

A black-and-white, red light blinking a warning, roared out of the night, going south, rain briefly visible in its headlights, rain that slashed at Jory as he looked after it. No siren, but in a hurry. Accident, maybe. Right kind of night for it.

He turned and made for the café, stepping in a puddle he couldn't see, cursing as the cold water closed over one shoe. Stupid hicks, why the hell didn't they level the place off? Or put in better lights, so you could see where the holes were?

A pair of trucks, southbound, swung around the corner, lights blinking signals, and pulled in alongside his stolen car. Jory hustled into the café, feeling the squish of water in his left shoe.

The place was overwarm, the windows steamy. The waitress was fifty, skinny, and cheerful. Obviously she knew all the truck drivers by name. They joked and called her Maisie.

The two at the counter were eating hamburgers and fries, two more in a booth having coffee and pie. Jory slid onto the stool nearest the door.

The waitress smiled. She had bad teeth. "Good evening. What'll it be, sir?"

"Make it coffee. Black," Jory said.

A blast of cold air came in with the two drivers who entered, shaking moisture from their clothes, loud, cheerful.

Everybody knew everybody else. Jory scowled into the cup Maisie brought him.

The newcomers took over a booth and gave their orders, then one raised his voice to carry over the jukebox. "You guys hear about the murder attempt? Clayton found him in Rattlesnake Canyon, guy'd been shot and thrown in a ditch."

Jory froze, his fingers cramping on the handle of the mug.

"No kidding! Dead?"

"No. Jaw shot away, Clayton said he's a hell of a mess, but it sounds like the kid was conscious. Guy shot him twice, but one slug hit a metal cross the kid was wearing, so it didn't kill him. The CHP is out in force, man. Looking for a stolen car."

Jory's guts crawled. The truck headlights had outlined the T-bird only moments earlier.

"Got a description of the car?" one of the truckers asked.

"Nah, not yet. Kid was hurt bad enough so Clayton couldn't talk to him, but he figured soon's they got him to the hospital they'd be able to communicate with him. He still had his wallet on him, no money but his driver's license and his credit cards were there. They'll have a description of the car and the license number on the air before long."

Christ. They must have found him almost as soon as Jory drove away. Not dead? Jerry wasn't dead? Shattered jaw, but able to communicate? Jory picked up the cup and drank, scalding his mouth. He wanted to bolt, but he knew better than that. He sat, *must finish the coffee, don't panic.*

"By God, Christensen's got the right idea," one of the truckers said. "Carry a goddamn gun, and don't pick up no hitchhikers."

So little time had passed. How did the word get around so fast?

"Clayton said the kid was bleeding like a stuck pig. But he got a CHP car there within a few minutes, and they didn't wait for an ambulance, just loaded the kid into the police car. I tell you, my old lady screamed like a bitch when I wanted to put in that ole CB, but like I told her, you only got to save one life and the thing has paid for itself."

"Oh, man, is that ever right. It don't even have to save somebody's life to be worthwhile," one of the newcomers stated. "Just gettin' a mechanic out and savin' me a walk in the rain makes that radio worthwhile."

"Just saving my sanity makes it worthwhile," his partner contributed. "Not to mention spreading the word about the

92

smokies lurking in the bushes. I ain't had a ticket since that CB went in the cab. Have to admit, though, I bet Clayton was glad to see a cop tonight. Glad I didn't find the poor sucker."

Their conversation flowed around him, no longer heard. CB radios. Shit. It sounded like they all had them. Which meant that if Jerry *could* communicate—nod to answer questions? Write on a pad?—it wouldn't be any time before everybody up and down the highway knew every goddamned detail of everything—description of the car, even a description of him, Jory.

The profanity went on and on in his mind. It didn't seem possible that he hadn't killed Jerry. Yet it must be so. Jory drained his cup, ignoring the way his mouth burned, and stood up.

Nobody paid any attention to him except the waitress, who took his money.

He walked out into the night, his pleasure in the T-bird spoiled now. He'd have to ditch it, and fast.

It was a bad omen. He shouldn't have blown it with Jerry, it should have been so easy. The kid should have died, drowned in the ditch if nothing else.

Gravel spurted when he pulled out of the parking area, heading north, and his mouth was set in a flat uncompromising line. Well, he wouldn't muff the next step, Jory thought, and bore down on the accelerator.

It wasn't enough to get another car. He had to dispose of
the T-bird in such a fashion that the authorities wouldn't
know what he'd exchanged it for.

His head was beginning to ache again. Christ, it wasn't
even three hours since he'd taken the last of those capsules.
Didn't they make anything to kill pain any longer than that?

Jory drove fast, on a two-lane road now, between towering
trees that closed over his head. The asphalt absorbed the light
so that he was hurtling through a narrow tunnel with a
visibility of only a few yards.

He rounded a curve too fast and skidded, fighting for
control of the T-bird. He hadn't driven for a long time; his
reflexes weren't as good as they'd once been, although he'd
worked out every day in his cell, trying to stay in good
condition. But you couldn't practice driving a car from a
prison cell.

The car went off the pavement, narrowly missing one of the
gigantic trees that looked, in the headlights, as if they were
made of concrete. And then Jory straightened around and
began to move again, more slowly, and he saw the sign.

REDWOOD INN. Under it hung a smaller sign: CLOSED FOR THE
WINTER. But there were lights, Jory saw. Maybe the place was
closed, but there were people living there, way off the
highway. He backed up and eased the T-bird into the
driveway.

It was a sort of lodge, a big, rustic building with a circular
drive in the front and outbuildings looming beyond it. Jory
stared at the single lighted window on the second floor.

There was a Volkswagen parked at the side door, a
battered little sedan.

He cut the motor and got out of the T-bird. Here under the
heavy trees the rain was scarcely noticeable, although everything was sopping wet. He checked out the Volks, found the

keys in it and three-quarters of a tank of gas when he slid into it and turned on the ignition.

For all its vintage, the little car purred silkily. It would do, Jory decided. He left the motor running and approached the side door, banging his fist on it.

Above him, the window creaked upward. "Who's there?"

It was an elderly voice, a man whose white hair haloed around his head when he leaned out to see.

"I got car problems," Jory said. "Could I use your phone?"

"Phone ain't working. Been out all day," the old man said.

"Well, then, could you run me into the nearest town, where I could get some help?"

"I got arthritis, can't hardly get around. I can't go out this time of night," the old man said. "I'm just the caretaker here. You'll have to go out on the highway and flag somebody down. Lots of trucks going by."

"They won't stop," Jory said. "I already tried that. Isn't there anybody else here could help me?"

"No, there's only me, and I can't do nothing for you, mister." The old man drew in his head and started to close the window.

"Well, hey, can't you at least let me inside out of the weather, then, until morning. Maybe in the morning somebody will stop."

"Highway Patrol comes along every little while. They'll stop for you." The window slammed shut.

Jory stared up at the lighted window, as angry as if he'd been telling the truth and been denied assistance. Damned old fart, what did he expect a man to do, stand out in the pouring rain for hours in the hope that a cop would come along?

Above him, the light went out. So that was that, the old turd was going to go to bed and let him drown out here.

He could just take the Volkswagen and go. But then the T-bird would be here in plain sight, and when the phone was fixed—or the old man realized his own vehicle had been stolen—the caretaker would contact the police on his own. No, he had to do better than that.

He thought Jerry would have had a flashlight in the T-bird; he found it in the glove compartment, and moved around the outside of the lodge, looking.

He cut the phone wires, just in case the old man was lying. Then he opened the doors on the double garage and ran the

T-bird into it. It didn't look as if anyone ever used the place; there was so much junk stored in it he had trouble getting the car inside and had to run over a couple of bicycles to do it.

The lower windows and doors were all locked, as he'd expected. Jory swung the light around, looking for a big rock. There weren't any, but he found a broken piece of concrete off a rear walkway. He hefted it, then threw it through a window and brushed aside the remaining shards of glass before he climbed over the sill.

Inside, the elderly caretaker had turned out the light but he had not climbed into bed.

Jeb Tupper recognized the sound of his own car engine, and he recognized the menace in the stranger's voice, too. Up to no good, that one was. He'd driven in here all right, nothing wrong with his car that Jeb could tell.

He hastily put on his trousers and pulled a thick sweater over his pajamas, thrusting his feet into sheepskin-lined slippers. The owners didn't want him to heat the entire place in the winter, so it was always drafty.

The intruder had a flashlight and was poking around out there. What the devil?

Jeb Tupper observed from his second-floor bedroom when Jory put the T-bird into the garage.

God Almighty! What was going on?

The old man turned and made his way as quickly as he could down through the darkened building. He knew his way, he'd lived here for nearly fourteen years, caretaker in the winter, doing odd jobs during the tourist season.

Didn't get any TV reception here, but he read the papers. He knew whatever the devil that guy was doing out there, he didn't mean any good by it.

Jeb emerged from the back stairs into the kitchen. The light was bobbing around out there again. He groped for the wall phone, but it wasn't going to help him. He'd lied about the phone being out of order—he knew enough not to let anybody in—but the damned phone was sure enough dead now. It wouldn't surprise him if the stranger had done something to it.

The chunk of concrete crashed through the window on the other side of the room, showering him with bits of glass.

Jeb had told the truth about his arthritis. He was seventy-two years old and he was stiff and sore. He couldn't outrun a young feller; he doubted if he could make it to his car ahead of the younger man. He hadn't seen him, but he could tell from his voice. A young punk. That's what he was, a young punk. Might even have a gun.

Too late Jeb thought of the guns the owner left here when he went back to Santa Rosa for the winter.

There wasn't but one thing for it.

Jeb heard the cautious hand knocking glass out of the window frame and he moved as rapidly as he could. The cellar door opened silently, and Jeb slipped through it, tottering for a moment on the steps as he reached behind him to latch the door. Not that latching it was going to be enough, though.

He groped in the darkness and found what he sought. Firewood, stacked inside so that he didn't have to haul it from the shed in back, cut in long lengths to fill the big fireplace in the room where guests sat around on chilly evenings. With any luck he'd find a chunk long enough to wedge against the door, the ends held by the studding on either side of the narrow stairway.

Many a time Jeb had cursed that stairway, because he was overweight and his girth nearly filled the space, making it difficult to manuever when he was carrying anything. Tonight, though, he was grateful for the lack of width; he shoved the split log into place and grunted with satisfaction when it held. Let the devil move that if he could. Not without bringing the entire house down, he wouldn't.

Light swept across the kitchen; it showed in the crack under the cellar door. The knob above him turned audibly and the door gave until it jammed against the wedged slab of wood. Not far enough for the feller to get his hand through the crack, not far enough for him to move the wedge.

"Come on out, old man," Jory said.

Jeb Tupper didn't answer. He edged on down the steps, puffing with his exertions, careful not to fall. He didn't want any broken bones, not at his age, he didn't. He encountered a wooden box and sat down on it to catch his breath.

The intruder threw his weight against the door, but it held. Thank the Lord there were studs only six inches in from the doorframe, Jeb thought. Any more than that, and the wedge wouldn't have worked. But it was holding.

"Come on out," Jory said again.

Jeb sat in silence. It was cold down here; he was glad he'd grabbed the heavy sweater and wore his sheepskin-lined slippers. With any luck the feller would steal whatever he'd come after and leave.

He was an old man. He'd spent a lot of his life waiting. He could wait a little longer.

Above him Jory ground his teeth when the door failed to give. Damned old fart had jammed it some way. Well, if he wanted to stay in the cellar, let him rot down there. Jory jerked the door shut again and slid the bolt that made the old man a prisoner.

Then he made his way through the lodge, looking for anything of value.

He found thirty-six dollars in the wallet beside the bed in an upstairs room. But the most valuable thing was the shotgun.

It was there in a case in the upstairs sitting room that probably served for the people who ran the place. A case that held four weapons, among them a shotgun. The case was locked, but he smashed out the glass, telegraphing to the old man below that he'd found the guns.

The shells were in the drawer below the gun rack. Getting into that took a little more time, but he pried it open and took all the shells that were of any use to him.

He thought about shooting through the cellar door, shutting the old man up for sure. But in the end he decided not to bother. He didn't know how far away they were from another house, and he didn't want anybody investigating shots this time of night, or calling the cops to investigate.

Besides that, the old guy couldn't get out. There were a couple of windows in the cellar, but so small no full-grown man could crawl through them. The caretaker was locked in, and from the look of things he lived here alone without much in the way of company.

He could burn the goddamned house down around the old man's ears, but that, too, could attract attention, even more quickly than gunfire would. No, the old man was no threat. Let him starve down there.

He let himself out the back door and slid into the waiting Volkswagen.

The sheriff's department offices were only partially staffed at night; across the big open room where the clerical work was done a lone typist and two file clerks shared an area where, during the day, several dozen people would have been busy.

Glen Witwer looked up when Pat McDuff pushed through the swinging gate and approached his own desk.

"Little John's over its banks," Witwer greeted him. "Hupa's three feet from flood stage, Big Bend expected to crest within the hour. The National Guard are moving people out of the Salmon Creek area, alerting everybody along the Bend. Warnings going out on radio and TV, too."

McDuff poured himself a cup of coffee. "I suppose it's too much to hope that our friend Jory will get held up by the storm, if it was him who shot that kid."

Witwer was thin, with glasses for reading. He wore them now. "Yeah. There was a car caught in a rock slide north of Leggett half an hour ago, but we weren't lucky enough to catch Jory, just a nice young couple trying to go to Santa Rosa."

"Hurt?" Mac asked. The coffee had stood too long. It tasted terrible.

"No. Just scared the hell out of them. They had rocks in front and in back of them, one that skimmed their Volks that was three feet in diameter, but they weren't hurt."

"Close the road?"

"Only for about twenty minutes. We're going to have some closed around here, though. There's water over East End Road already, they expect it to be cut off before long. The Guard is out there, too."

Mac drank and then gave up on the brew. "How'd you make out on the list of jurors?"

"I got a list, okay," Witwer said. "Judge Verland's secre-

99

tary got it to us about ten minutes ago." He indicated a sheet of paper on the desk. "What do you want me to do with it, Lieutenant? We going to call them? Tell them Jory's out and may be moving this way? We can't send anybody out on fifteen or twenty stakeouts, waiting for him to show up. And we don't want to start a full-scale panic."

Mac snorted. "More likely we'll have half the county getting out their deer rifles, ready for him. Save us the trouble. Except that Jory's a foxy, cold-blooded bastard. He'd probably get them first."

Witwer looked down at the list. "There's another name ought to be on here, Lieutenant."

"The girls, what were their names? Malloy and Richards— didn't the Richards girl marry young Wally Salvetti?"

"I was thinking of Pat McDuff," Witwer said. "Seems to me Jory offered to rearrange your anatomy, too."

The big man made a noise that might have indicated amusement. Both officers turned to see Andy Sleder letting himself through the gate.

"What are you doing out this time of night, Andy? Thought you put in one shift already today."

"Might say the same of you, Lieutenant. I heard they was calling out the Guard, figured maybe I ought to check in and see what's going on before they mobilized all the rest of us, anyway. Crazy, ain't it? First we nearly dry up and blow away, and now it sounds like we got a goddamned flood lickin' our ass."

"That may not be all we've got," Mac told him. "Somebody shot a kid and left him in a ditch alongside the road in Rattlesnake Canyon a few hours ago. Would have killed the boy except that the kid was wearing a heavy metal cross on a chain around his neck that deflected one of the slugs. Whoever it was got his car."

Sleder paused in the act of lighting up a cigarette. "You think it was Jory?"

"Could have been."

Sleder inhaled and coughed. "Ah, shit. Those stupid assholes, turning him loose. Russell William Jory is about the best argument in favor of capital punishment that I know of. Get some of those bleeding hearts off the parole board and restore capital punishment. . . ." He inhaled and blew smoke out through his nostrils.

They'd all heard it before, but Witwer made the expected rejoinder, the one they got poked down their throats all the time.

"There's no proof capital punishment acts as a deterrent to crime."

"The hell there ain't. You execute a guy, and he sure don't kill nobody else. That proves it to *me*. I said we shoulda shot the bastard when we caught him."

"I thought about it," McDuff admitted. He'd made a lot of arrests, but few of them remained more vividly in his mind than Jory's. There were more homicides per capita in Redwood County than in more densely populated urban areas to the south—possibly due to the fact that the unemployment rate here was so high and that they had so damned much rain, which tended to be depressing—and McDuff had participated in the investigations of a major share of them. Anything that happened within the city limits, of course, fell within the jurisdiction of the North Bend police force; anything else was sheriff's department territory.

He hadn't been a lieutenant the night Jory killed the Fitzpatrick boy. He'd been a sergeant, and he'd seen his share of dead bodies. Wives beaten to death by drunken husbands, husbands shot by wives they'd mistreated one time too many. Neighbors who took out their shotguns because they couldn't agree over a property line, or the control of a dog, or because Jones's leaves fell into Smith's yard. And there were always the knifings and shootings in various bars, and the whores down on First Street every so often picked the wrong john.

A cop saw those things all the time. If the victim of an assault was still alive, even if his throat was cut and you knew damned well he was going to die, you relied on basic first aid and got him to the hospital as fast as you could. Once in a while one of them fooled you—even with a nearly severed throat—and lived, so you made the effort. If you had to go home and knock back a few stiff jolts of whiskey in order to sleep, well, that was part of the job.

But the part of the job McDuff had never gotten used to was the kids. Battered kids. Redwood County had a high rate of injuries there. Most of the time the goddamned judges would ignore the reports from the investigating officer and the welfare department and the kid's teacher who said he often came to school with burns or bruises or whatever; when it came time to dispose of the case, the judge would decide that the kid was better off with his natural parents, and put him right back in the home until the next time the old man either killed him or permanently crippled him.

And then, once in a while, there would be somebody like Larry Fritzpatrick.

McDuff remembered standing there on a summer night, between two vehicles with the lights on, looking down at the body of a seventeen-year-old boy who'd taken a shotgun blast in the face and another in the chest.

His own son was only seven years old then. But he'd looked down at what was left of Larry Fitzpatrick and felt sick to his stomach. This could happen to Pete, or to one of his daughters, one day. There were always madmen running around, and one of them could pick his kid next time.

He remembered Andy Sleder standing beside him over the bloody body. "Oh, Christ, what a thing," Andy said, and for all his years as a cop, there were tears as well as anger in his voice. Andy had a son the same age as the dead boy.

When the word came in that Jory was cornered, McDuff took charge of the arrest with a fierce, white-hot determination. An hour before Jory shot and killed young Fitzpatrick, he had attempted to assault a middle-aged woman. He had forced her car off the road, but when he approached on foot, she nearly ran over him getting away.

She hadn't gotten the entire license number of the car that blocked her way, but she had the first letters of it—BET—which she remembered because her own nickname was Bette. And she said the car was an old red Ranchwagon. A Ranchwagon was one of the few cars she could identify, because her brother had one just like it except for the color.

And she struck the left rear end of the wagon when she drove away. Hard enough, she thought, so it probably crumpled a fender on the assailant's car as well as on her own.

She could even describe the man in general terms. Young, she thought. In his twenties. Wearing jeans and a white T-shirt.

When the call came in a few hours later that two girls had been raped, and the girls also described a male in his twenties, wearing jeans and a white T-shirt, they went looking for a red Ford Ranchwagon with a license plate number beginning with the letters BET.

The arrogant bastard had simply gone home to bed. The

car was parked in the driveway in front of the small duplex where Jory lived.

The patrolman who spotted it was a rookie, but he had the good sense to call for reinforcements. Four of them went into the house, and there were four more officers outside.

The roommate who opened the door was a tall, skinny kid with thick glasses, his straw-colored hair standing on end. He stared at them uncomprehendingly, still half asleep, his shorts drooping.

"Yeah?" Behind the heavy lenses, the eyes widened as he realized he was facing a small army of cops. "What's the matter?"

"You own that red Ranchwagon out there?" McDuff asked.

"Me? No, I don't have a car. That belongs to a guy who's staying with me for a few days. Name's Russ Jory."

"Where is he?"

The kid's Adam's apple bobbed. "Sleeping. In there." He gestured with one thumb. "What's he done? He's done something bad, ain't he? What's he done?"

"We'd like to come in and talk to him," McDuff said.

The kid swallowed again. "All of you?"

They left him standing there in the shabby little living room, blinking, under the overhead light.

Jory, half-rousing at the sound of voices, pushed himself up onto an elbow when McDuff flicked the light switch. The shotgun lay beside him on the bed, but he didn't reach for it.

McDuff kept his voice level. "What's your name, fella?"

"What the hell's going on?"

"What's your name?" McDuff repeated. Beside him, Sleder's .38 didn't waver.

"Jory. Russell Jory. What's the matter?"

"You own that Ranchwagon in the driveway?"

"Yeah. Why?"

"Where were you this evening? From about six o'clock on?"

"Right here," Jory said. The sheet slid down, exposing a pale chest without hair. The arms were muscular and the hands had broad, blunt fingers.

"Anybody verify that?"

"Tris can. Hey, Tris! Tell 'em! I was right here, all evening," Jory shouted.

The skinny kid's voice quavered. "Hell, I wasn't here after

103

seven, until about an hour ago. He was here when I left, and he was here when I came home. That's all I know about it. Whatever he's mixed up in, I didn't have nothing to do with it! I don't even know the guy, he's somebody my brother met in a bar, said he was looking for work and needed a place to stay for a couple of days. He's using my brother's room, but I don't know nothing about him."

"Ah, shit," Jory said. "I was right here, the whole evening."

"You better get up," McDuff said with deceptive softness, "and put your pants on. We'd like to ask you some questions."

"Well, ask them. I don't have to get up for that, do I? Christ, it's the middle of the night," Jory objected.

"You put on your pants," Andy Sleder said, "or we'll fix it so you don't need pants anymore."

"We'd like you to go down to the courthouse with us," McDuff said. "Right now."

For a few seconds the words hung in the small room. They saw Jory's fingers twitch, on the hand nearest the shotgun, and four officers suspended their breathing while he made up his mind.

Reach for it, you fucking bastard, McDuff thought, twitch once more, and save the state the expense of a trial.

"Ah, shit," Jory said again, and rolled over. Away from the shotgun. Toward the pair of jeans that hung over the foot of the bed.

He'd changed his pants, and they never found the ones he'd been wearing when he killed the boy. But the girls identified him, picked him out of a lineup with no hesitation whatever, although the little dark-haired one threw up once she'd done so.

Most of them knew there wasn't all that much you could do to them. A trial, sure. And a prison sentence. If he got caught.

Most of them didn't give you any excuse to shoot them.

The phone rang and Witwer reached for it, identifying himself, then listening. They saw his jaw tighten and waited for him to hang up.

"We got a good one, Lieutenant. The dam's going on the Big Bend. Just cracking, so far, but the debris is building up behind it and they don't expect it to hold for long. They've got

104

the Guard out there evacuating the flats, and they want traffic rerouted and roads kept clear for emergency vehicles."

"I knew they'd need us," Sleder said with sour satisfaction, and McDuff cuffed him on the shoulder.

"Come on, let's go check it out," he said.

Behind them, Witwer was moving toward the radio.

The list of names lay forgotten on the desk.

Jory could find them all, every one of them. Judge Verland, that big redheaded cop, the girls who had testified against him, the jurors. Even the bailiff who'd nearly dislocated his shoulder getting handcuffs on him when the judge started yelling.

He'd kept track of them through the seven years he'd been away.

Or, rather, Mousy had kept track of them for him.

He'd met Mousy in jail. Not San Quentin, but the county jail, where they'd held him until he went to trial.

Ordinarily he wouldn't have given Mousy the time of day. Mousy was a real turd, a ferret-faced little creep who couldn't steal a hubcap without getting caught.

But Jory had done him a favor and Mousy had returned it. Big damned bruiser of a cop had had the kid shoved into a corner and was going to teach him a lesson, and Jory got in the middle of it with something pretty close to a karate chop.

He didn't even know why he'd done it, except that he hated cops. One of them had kneed him in the balls, of course, and flattened Mousy, too. But it had created a bond of sorts between them.

So when Jory asked a favor of Mousy, the little guy had agreed. Sure, he'd keep track of them. Hell, he spent most of his time in jail, anyway. He had nothing to do but read the local papers, which was all this crummy place provided.

North Bend wasn't such a big town that a guy who tried couldn't keep track of fewer than twenty people. Especially when they were such dull people. None of them even moved out of the county while Jory was in prison, although a few of them had changed addresses.

Mousy had faithfully recorded the moves. He'd reported

when Kay Richards married some guy by the name of Salvetti, and when they'd moved to a house in the country.

Stood off by itself, Mousy reported. Nice house. Salvetti must be making good money as a druggist.

Richards was one of those cool-looking blondes, but she'd fought him like a tiger. And spoken out, clear and firm, looking right at him in the courtroom, when she identified him.

There wasn't one of those jurors who didn't believe her. After that Richards, they didn't even need the testimony of the other one, the Malloy girl. Kay Richards said Jory was the one, and she described what he'd done to her until the women on the jury squirmed uncomfortably.

It had only taken them two hours to bring in a verdict of guilty.

He'd get to her early on, Jory had decided. Right after that little piss-ant of a judge, who was on Jory's way to the Salvettis, with only a small detour.

The rain continued so it was all the windshield wipers could do to cope with it. There wasn't much traffic passing through the town. North Bend was strung out along a few miles of a shallow bay off the Pacific. The main highway ran north and south; only a few miles back from the bay the flatlands faded into foothills, then climbed a mountainous ridge that effectively cut off any east-west traffic except across Chilton Summit.

Jory had a little confusion in finding Judge Verland's place, mostly because they'd made several of the main streets one-way since he'd been there. He wasn't familiar with the area where Verland lived, but he had a city map; Mousy had provided everything, with only a little prompting.

Nice neighborhood, Jory thought. Even in this stinking rain he could see enough to tell that. Not laid out in neat rectangles like ordinary people had, but with curving streets that followed hillsides or avoided stands of redwoods or cedars and gulleys. Country living, right there ten minutes from the courthouse.

Verland's place was a big one. Expensive. Private, too, set well apart from all its neighbors except for an impressive Tudor directly across the street. The Tudor was dark. Jory grunted in satisfaction.

Verland had even left his outside light on, so that the

number was clearly visible from the street. There was a light inside the house as well, in what he judged might be the living room, its glow muted by drawn draperies.

He'd check out the rest of the street, he decided, make sure it wasn't a dead end, that he could tie back into an easy exit. It took only a few minutes to orient himself.

When he returned to the Verland place he picked his parking spot carefully, well in the shadow of a stand of trees, far enough from the streetlight so he wouldn't be noticed unless someone drove right past him, but where he could watch Verland's front door. The Volkswagen was out of place here—the cars that weren't garaged were a Cadillac and an Oldsmobile—but he didn't see how to get back into an alley.

He had become almost impervious to physical discomfort; he was no longer aware of the wind or the rain or the cold. One of the things Jory had learned to do while in prison was to disassociate himself from his surroundings, and he did it now. If it hadn't been for the lingering ache behind his eyes, nothing would have disturbed his complete concentration upon the task at hand.

The light over the front door meant either that a member of the family was out or that they were expecting a guest. He decided to wait awhile and just watch the place.

He was not at all nervous. On the contrary, the hand resting on the wheel was steady, controlled. He knew it was a weakness not to keep his cool. You made mistakes when you couldn't keep your cool.

He'd kept his cool when those pigs arrested him. The shotgun had been right there beside him on the bed, but he hadn't gone for it.

They'd wanted him to. He'd read it in all their faces, the big redheaded one, the little dried-up one, the whole damned bunch of them. They were looking for an excuse to blow him to hell.

But he hadn't moved. He hadn't reached for the gun. So they'd read him his rights, and they'd been polite—kept their hands off him—when they took him to jail, and they'd got him a lawyer. Not that the stupid son of a bitch had done him much good. But at least nobody'd shot him.

They might yet, of course. With this thing growing in his head, the idea didn't bother him as much as it might have done. Maybe better a bullet in the head than having it split open from the inside out by some goddamned tumor.

Well, he'd take as many of them with him as he could.

He settled lower in the seat, relaxing, one hand resting on the shotgun, the other beating a tattoo on the wheel.

He waited.

With the wind banging things around the way it was, Verland couldn't tell what was normal noise and what wasn't. He resisted the temptation to check with Witwer again, to see what was going on.

It was stupid, to get so jumpy about one convicted felon out of so many. A man couldn't be any use as a judge if he were intimidated by the people he had to sentence. He'd known of cases where a judge had disqualified himself from a case, gotten out of it because he was afraid. If things came to that pass, though, he'd retire, quit being a judge, if he couldn't function except in fear.

He wished Midge would come home. He would ask her to make them each a cup of hot chocolate before bed, and she'd entertain him with the latest gossip she'd picked up at the Stanley party. Amazing, the things women said to one another at those gatherings.

Horace Verland loved gossip. He seldom passed any of it along, except to his wife, but he loved to listen to it. It was one of the reasons he'd kept his secretary on for so many years. In spite of the fact that she was horse-faced and had thick ankles. She had an ear for the type of story he most enjoyed, and she regaled him endlessly with juicy bits of information about everybody from the lawyers to the police to the secretaries. He was a moral man himself, he would never have dreamed of a sexual relationship with anyone but his wife. It gave him a sense of superiority to hear about the lapses of all the others.

A car turned into the driveway, the headlights sweeping across the front windows for a moment before he heard the sound of the engine. He moved to unlock the front door for her; Midge had trouble getting the car in and out of the garage without scraping something, so she preferred to park on the drive and dash for the front door even when it was raining.

He swung the door wide and waited, silhouetted in the light, as his wife got out of her car.

"Good party?" he called.

"Oh, I bought almost fifty dollars' worth of stuff. I brought home the refreshments that were left over. Can you help me carry it in?"

"What did you bring? Cake? Chocolate cake?" Verland asked, moving out into the weather, ducking against the stinging rain.

He had his hands full of the promised goodies when the shotgun blast took him in the back.

For a moment he seemed to hang, suspended, although it could not have been more than seconds. He saw Midge turn, her mouth open and eyes wide, and then a scarlet flower blossomed on the front of her yellow coat. He did not hear the second blast.

He did not see his wife crumpled on the concrete drive, nor the door of the house standing wide open, the light making a welcoming stream across the front steps.

His sightless gaze was fixed on the chocolate cake, dumped from its container, which quickly began to disintegrate in the rain.

Sophie Garabaldi was a small brisk woman of sixty-seven. She had been widowed for twelve years, and she lived with two cats named Eloise and Henry and a dog named Percy in a three-room apartment. The building was an old one, in a part of town where she was afraid to emerge after dark, but it was the best she could afford.

She spent the evening of January 18 watching television on her small black-and-white set. She hoped the poor reception was due to the weather (she didn't have cable; she couldn't afford it) and not to a tube going out. She didn't know how she'd replace a tube unless she gave up eating. The way those repairmen charged, it would probably take a week's grocery money.

Percy looked up at her hopefully when she turned off the set, tipping his head to one side, his eyes bright. He was a little mongrel she'd taken pity on when some boys were teasing him over a year ago. It had taken the cats a while to get used to him, but he made a welcome addition to her family. You could talk to Percy.

"You don't need to go out," she told him severely. "I took you out before dark."

Percy wagged a tail that was oddly connected somewhat off-center on his small rump. He whined softly, and padded to the door, scratching at it, then turning once more to look back at her.

Sophie stared down at him. "Didn't you see that last program I watched? The girl went outside at night and she was attacked. It happens all the time. A woman isn't safe anywhere."

Percy barked.

"Not even with a dog, she isn't safe," Sophie insisted. "Believe me, the papers are full of cases. Men who have

112

nothing better to do than rob somebody, or rape them. You'd think they'd rape only the young, pretty ones, but sometimes they even attack someone my age."

Percy jumped at the door, leaving claw marks in the varnish.

"You don't believe me, do you? Well, I was on a jury once, the trial of a man who attacked two girls. Nasty fellow, he was, we voted unanimously for conviction. And another time a friend of mine was knocked over the head and someone snatched her purse when she was right on her own doorstep. That's one of the reasons why I gave up my own little house and moved into an apartment, so I'm not all alone."

Percy barked again, more urgently. Sophie sighed.

"Do you really have to go? It can't wait until morning?"

Usually Percy was very good. She took him out just before dark, and then as soon as it was light in the morning. She was an early riser anyway, so that didn't bother her. But this time of year, when it got dark so early, and stayed that way for so long—she wondered if Percy was getting too old to go so long. Maybe he, like herself, had to relieve himself more often because of age.

She didn't know how old Percy was, but there were a few white hairs on his muzzle. It might denote age. And he was quite determined to go out.

He'd never wet in the apartment. The management tolerated her pets because she was a good tenant, and she didn't bother anybody. But she had no illusions about how long the pets would last if they created a mess.

"It's a pity you don't know how to use the cat box," she told him, relenting. "But I suppose if you must go out, you must."

Percy raced in circles around her as Sophie buttoned herself into the coat she'd bought at St. Vincent de Paul for five dollars. They had been asking seven-fifty, but she pointed out that one of the buttons was missing and there was a rip in the lining. It was a good, warm coat, just the thing for Northern California in January. Strangers who came here were amazed at the climate. Some of them thought all of California was like Los Angeles. They didn't know that in Redwood County a winter coat sometimes was most welcome even in the summertime, late at night, when the cold air came in off the ocean.

She tied a scarf over her head and tucked her door key into her coat pocket. Eloise stood up on the sofa, and stretched, meowing.

"Be good while we're gone, you two. I'm going to turn off the lights to save electricity, but we won't be gone long," she promised.

Percy had his own little harness and leash. He loved having it put on him, because it meant they were going outside. He trembled in excitement while she fastened it.

It wasn't really so very late; she could hear the television in the Bateman apartment across the hall, and classical music playing in Lottie's rooms next door to her own. Sophie closed the door behind her, tested it to make sure it was locked, and began to walk slowly toward the stairs.

There were voices behind Lottie's door.

Sophie paused, listening. The music was loud, but it didn't drown out the voices. There was a man in there with Lottie.

Lottie always seemed very nice when Sophie met her in the hallways. But sometimes Sophie had a suspicion that Lottie brought men home with her. Not just friends, but strange men, who only stayed a short time and then went on their way. She seldom saw any of them, and as badly as the halls were lit a body wouldn't recognize her own father at a dozen yards, but Sophie suspected there were quite a lot of men.

She heard Lottie's laughter through the thin door, and kept on going to the stairs.

There was an elevator, but it was old and creaky and Sophie expected that one day a cable would break and the thing would fall. Besides that, everyone else used the elevator, and she didn't like to take Percy on it; people looked at him with hostility, and she didn't want anyone to complain about him to the management. It was only one flight down; she could still manage that. The exercise was probably even good for her.

Percy ran ahead as fast as the leash would allow. She heard the elevator moving while she was on the stairs, so it was a good thing she hadn't summoned it. No, better to stick to the stairs and keep Percy out of sight as much as possible.

The tiny lobby of the apartment house was empty and the front door stood ajar.

Sophie frowned at it. They didn't lock it until midnight, which she thought was poor policy. No telling who would walk in off the street. Still, she had to admit she didn't want to contribute toward one of those intercom systems, so they could keep it locked all the time and a prospective caller could call a tenant to have the lock released, the way they did it on television. It was too expensive to do here, Mrs. Barrows had told her. The building was old and there wasn't much profit anyway.

Percy scampered toward the fresh air, which was not nearly so invigorating to Sophie as it was chilling. She was thankful she had the good coat.

"Raining cats and dogs," she said to Percy as they stepped out onto the sidewalk. "You'd better do your business in a hurry; I don't want to get soaked."

Percy knew when to take advantage and when he was wise to tend to business. He lifted his leg over the rhododendrons against the front of the building, holding it long enough to convince his mistress that his need had been genuine.

Sophie was not, she told herself, a nervous person. But she was sensible. The sooner she was back inside her own apartment, the better off she'd be.

The Tates came in just behind her, and they took the elevator. The Tates were a rather disagreeable couple who thought they were better than the rest of the tenants. Sophie had never discovered what they based this belief upon, and she had no desire to ride up to the fourth floor with them, nor to endure their unspoken disapproval should she delay their journey for a moment by disembarking on the way up. The stairs it was, again.

She had to stop a couple of times to rest on the upward climb. Percy sat, patiently waiting, a few steps above her each time, his tiny tongue hanging out.

At the top she opened the door into the second floor corridor and heard the voices. A man's voice, and Lottie's.

Lottie's friend, she thought. She stopped in the shadows, waiting where she could see the elevator, curiosity overcoming her good manners.

"What's all the racket?" Lottie asked. "If she hasn't answered by this time, it's because she ain't home, mister."

Not Lottie's friend, then. Sophie edged forward to peer around the corner, and saw that a man stood at her own door.

"I got an urgent message for Mrs. Sophie Garabaldi," the stranger said. He had an odd voice that was, even more oddly, vaguely familiar, although she couldn't place it.

"Well, like I said, if she didn't hear *that*, she's not there.

Come to think of it, I ain't seen her around for several days. I think maybe she said something about taking a trip—someplace warm, where was it? Bermuda, someplace like that." Lottie laughed. She was standing in her own doorway, dressed in a rather low-cut red dress that might have excited Sophie's interest more if she hadn't been concentrating on the man. "I think her son's treating her to a trip, so she's gone. Slip your message under the door, she'll find it when she gets home."

"For crissake, come on back in here," a man's voice said from within Lottie's apartment.

"Well, I will, if this ape will stop pounding on doors. I told you, man, the old lady's gone on a trip."

What nonsense. Lottie knew perfectly well she didn't have a son, and couldn't afford a taxi across town, let alone a trip to Bermuda. Sophie stayed where she was, scooping up Percy so she could keep him quiet. She didn't know who the man was, but this was a peculiar time of night to be calling on anybody.

Lottie remained in the doorway, her dress vivid in the lamplight, blonde head tilted. She simply stood there and the man turned and walked away.

Sophie had often deplored the way bulbs in the building were allowed to burn out and go unreplaced, but tonight she didn't mind the fact that she stood in an unlighted alcove. Something about the man made her uneasy, so that she didn't step out and identify herself. Something . . .

She closed her hand around Percy's muzzle, holding him against her chest.

The light over the elevator was working. The man jabbed angrily at the button and Sophie had a good look at him while he waited. Early thirties, medium height, rather nondescript. Not a Western Union man; they wore uniforms, didn't they? Caps, anyway. And besides, they usually telephoned messages these days, and she was sure they didn't work at night. So who was he? What was the urgent message he'd mentioned? If there really was a message, she ought to know what it was.

The elevator rumbled down the shaft. The doors slid open, and the stranger stepped inside; for a few seconds he was bathed in a brighter light and again he seemed familiar, although Sophie still couldn't identify him. Jeans and jacket—unshaven—young men all looked alike these days.

Then he was gone. The man bellowed from inside Lottie's apartment. "Will you come in and shut the goddamned door?"

"Damned bill collectors," Lottie said, turning. "I thought there was supposed to be a law against harassing people in the middle of the night. Poor old gal, she hasn't got enough income to feed herself, let alone the cats and that puny little dog. Did you see his eyes, hon? Coldest eyes I ever saw. Such a pale blue they were almost white."

"God dammit, Lottie!"

Sophie put Percy down and trudged past Lottie's closed door. Nice of Lottie to care, she thought, if it *was* a bill collector. She couldn't think what bill it would be, though. There was only the pharmacy bill, and she'd told them she would take care of it the first of the month. They'd never sent anyone to pester her for money before, not even the time she had to let it go for four months because she had pneumonia.

Pale eyes, Lottie had said. Sophie unlocked her door, reached in for the light switch, and closed and relocked the door, remembering to slide the bolt as well. Pale eyes. So pale a blue they were almost white.

It seemed to her she'd seen eyes like that somewhere. She tried to remember and then gave it up. It didn't matter. If there was a genuine message, the man would be back in the daytime. And if it was some sort of con game, she was just as well off not to have answered her door. An older woman was at the mercy of people like that.

Henry twined around her ankles, purring. Eloise echoed from the back of the sofa.

"Yes, yes," Sophie said. "It's time for your snack. Come along, come along."

They trailed her into the kitchen, all the family she had.

She couldn't remember where she'd seen the man before, the one with the pale blue eyes.

117

Sara Fitzpatrick turned restlessly in bed, reaching out for her husband, but her hand encountered no familiar warmth.

She became aware, then, of the light sifting faintly through the open bedroom door. Tim was up, moving around the kitchen. She heard small sounds, the ones that must have awakened her, but she could not identify them.

"Tim?" She sat up, peering at the clock beside her, which was set to go off at six even though there was no longer any necessity to arise at any particular time. It was only a quarter after eleven; she'd been asleep less than an hour.

There was no reply from the kitchen. She got up, shrugging into her robe, and padded barefooted through the darkened house.

Sometimes Tim was in pain, and he couldn't sleep. At such times, he often sought release in a shot or two of whiskey. Tonight, however, it was not the bottle of Jack Daniels that was before him on the kitchen table.

Sara stopped in the doorway, apprehension tightening the pit of her stomach.

"What are you doing?" she asked, although it was perfectly obvious that he was cleaning and oiling the thirty-aught-six. A new box of shells sat at Tim's elbow, ready for loading.

"I couldn't sleep," Tim Fitzpatrick said. He didn't look at her, his hands busy with the rag and the gun. "I watched the late news after I got up. Turned it down low so it wouldn't wake you up."

"What are you doing with the gun, this time of night?"

"Getting it ready to shoot. I saw a thing on the news, some poor young feller was shot and left to die in a ditch, while the guy that shot him stole the car."

Sara was aware of the cold of the linoleum under her feet, and an even greater coldness radiating from her midsection,

118

throughout her body. "There's always things like that on the news."

"Feller didn't die. They're operating on him," Tim said. "It sounds like the kind of thing that Jory would do. Killing an innocent boy, just to get his car. The way he killed Larry, to get at those girls."

He ran the rag along the barrel of the gun, in almost the way he would have caressed his wife in a tender moment. Sara swallowed hard and painfully.

"There's no reason to think it was *him*. That Jory."

"Could have been," Tim Fitzpatrick said. "He ain't in prison no more. A man like that, he's like a wild animal. He did that kind of thing before, and he'll do it again. Killing people, raping young girls. A man like Jory, he don't change."

Her heart was beating audibly. Sara pressed the heel of her hand against her chest, as if she could lessen the force of it. "But he won't come here, Tim. There's no reason he'd come here."

"He'll come back to Redwood County," Fitzpatrick said with conviction, and he finally looked at his wife. "He said he'd come back. You heard him that day in the courtroom. You heard what he said he'd do to that judge. Well, he meant it. He'll come back. And when he does, I'll be ready for him."

He broke open the gun and began to load it. "Go on back to bed."

Sara stood for a moment longer, looking at him, at this man she had loved for as long as she could remember. He'd never said so, but she knew he thought he was less a man since he'd been hurt, since he couldn't work anymore. It didn't matter to her, it didn't change the way she felt about him. He would always be the strapping fellow she had married, all those years ago, no matter what happened to him physically.

What was happening to him now wasn't physical. But it was more frightening than the accident had been. She didn't know anything about mental illness, but it seemed to her that Tim was unbalanced on the subject of Russell William Jory. Surely there was no reason to think that Jory would come anywhere near them; they were no threat to him, he probably didn't even remember them. They would be of no significance to him at all.

Yet Tim was going to kill him. He meant it, she could see that. Tonight he was sitting in the house, preparing to do that. How long would he be content to wait for Jory's appearance? What if, her mind raced on, he mistook some perfectly innocent stranger for Jory, and shot him?

My God, what was she thinking? Tim wasn't crazy, and he'd have to be crazy to do a thing like that.

She withdrew from the lighted doorway, but she didn't go back to bed. She was shivering, unaware of it, thinking only of Tim. Ever since he'd seen that little piece in the paper he'd been obsessed with the idea that Jory would come back to North Bend. Yes, that was the word, obsessed.

Jory had threatened the judge, she did remember that. Not his exact words, but they'd been shocking, ugly. The judge had been furious, and they'd put handcuffs on Jory and removed him from the courtroom.

Impulse, born of a growing fear, turned her toward the living room. She made her way by instinct and the faint illumination that filtered through the dining room from the kitchen.

The telephone was there. She didn't know who to ask for help, but she recognized that she needed advice. If Tim shot anyone, even Jory, they'd lock him up. You weren't allowed to shoot anyone, even the man who had killed your son. Perhaps someone else could talk to Tim, get some sense into him.

Who?

Maybe the minister, if old Pastor Holman had still been there. But that new young fellow, Tim couldn't stand him, wouldn't even go to church anymore.

Dr. Barnes? Sara hesitated, feeling for the telephone book in the darkness. She doubted that he would take her seriously. He'd offer her some platitude and tell her Tim would get over it.

The judge, she thought. That judge, he'd know if it was likely that Jory would come back here. If anybody had reason to be afraid of him, it would be the judge. And maybe he could tell her what she ought to do about Tim. She might get her husband in trouble, so they'd take away his gun or something. If that happened, Tim would be furious with her.

But if they took the gun, he couldn't shoot anybody. And they wouldn't lock him up. He'd be safe, even if he was

120

angry. He'd been angry lots of times, and he always got over it.

She had to turn on a light, then, of course, to find the judge's number. She remembered his name, it was in the paper often enough to have kept it in her mind. Horace Verland. They'd had a goat once, when she was a child, named Horace. Childhood, and Horace the goat, seemed light-years away.

She ran her finger down the column of names until she came to the number, and then she dialed.

The phone rang and rang. She counted it: ten times, twelve, fifteen. On and on in an empty house.

Horseshoe Road, where the Salvetti house stood, was to the east of the north-south freeway, in an area of smallish farms. The name was descriptive, for the unpaved road made a six-mile loop off the more heavily traveled River Road some two miles apart, and each of these ends passed over Little John Creek.

Ordinarily Little John was innocuous enough, an attractive small creek where the kids fished and swam in the summertime. On the night Jory arrived in North Bend, however, it had been raining for days. As temperatures rose in the mountains, melting snow joined the rivulets and became rushing falls and streams.

Little John began to overflow its banks, encroaching on farmland and roads, and backing up in drainage ditches.

Jory's mind wasn't on his surroundings, except that he was watching for the sign indicating Horseshoe Road. He was thinking about that dried-up little old lady, that Sophie Garabaldi. Imagine the old bitch being able to go to Bermuda!

He didn't know why he'd deviated from his plan of going right down his list, with the judge and the two girls first. But when he checked for the Salvetti address her name had practically jumped out at him, and the impulse was too strong to ignore.

He remembered her better than most of the other jurors, because she had looked straight at him for almost the entire trial, except when one of the witnesses was actually testifying. Most of the others avoided looking at him unless they thought he wasn't watching. But not that old biddy.

She had stared right at him, her mouth screwed around so that he knew right from the first that she was going to vote guilty. Before she even heard the evidence, he'd known from her face.

122

He'd been confident that he could get her to open the door, and it would have been a simple matter to throttle her. He liked a gun, but who needed a weapon with an old lady like that? And strangling didn't make any noise.

And then he'd had no answer to his knock so he'd knocked louder, thinking maybe the old gal was deaf. Christ, they must have paper walls in the place, the way the other broad came out and chewed on him for banging on the door.

Well, it didn't matter. The light was so poor she couldn't have gotten a good look at him and eventually Sophie Garabaldi would return from Bermuda or wherever the hell she was. He'd get back to her—providing they didn't catch up with him first—or this goddamned thing in his head didn't finish him.

There was the sign, barely readable in his headlights. HORSESHOE ROAD. He swung to the left and drove across the wooden bridge without noticing that the black water was within inches of the planking under his wheels.

Mousy had said there were no street numbers out here, but there were only five houses on the entire loop, and the names were printed on the rural mailboxes. Easy to read, Mousy said.

Mousy hadn't counted on a night like this. He might have to get out to read anything, Jory thought sourly. It occurred to him that Mousy had never evinced any curiosity as to what use the list would be put. Well, he'd learn before long, when the victims made it into the news.

Quite possibly he wouldn't get around to all of them. That big redheaded cop would realize it before anyone else, probably, when they started turning up dead. He'd figure it was Jory.

His alternatives—prison or hospital, and death regardless —were sufficiently bleak so that Jory simply refused to think about them, except in the momentary flashes he couldn't help. He would concentrate all his energies upon what he had set out to do.

The first mailbox showed up and he slowed to read the name. E. Lindquist. He drew on past it, noting the farmhouse lights set far back from the road.

With each box that wasn't the right one, Jory's irritation grew. Why the hell hadn't Mousy told him which one it was? He had to practically come to a stop to read the damned names, which might have attracted attention on a normal

123

night. He wasn't worried about that *tonight*, because there didn't seem to be any other traffic. He passed two mailboxes side by side: D. M. Roberts and C. W. Roberts.

Well, there were only supposed to be two more houses on the loop, so he couldn't be far away now. He drove half a mile before the next mailbox loomed out of the darkness.

A gust of wind sent a shudder through the small vehicle, and at the same time a black animal appeared out of nowhere, directly in front of him.

Jory swore and hit the brakes, sending the Volkswagen into a skid. It and the cow collided, and the muddy verge offered no traction. The cow bellowed in surprise and fright; for a moment he thought she was coming through the window on top of him, and then the car tilted and slid into a ditch.

It was, he learned immediately, a watery ditch.

Obscenities exploded in a violent outburst. The engine died. He twisted the ignition key and it caught again, but when he tried to back out of the ditch nothing happened. From the angle of the car, he judged that the rear wheels were probably off the goddamned ground.

Jory threw open the door and crawled out, through icy water and squishy mud. It wasn't deep, but it held the stolen car fast.

One thing he was sure of, he wasn't going to drive it out of there. He plunged back into the turgid dark water, reaching across the seat for the shotgun, making sure the .38 was still in his jacket pocket. There was also a roll of small tools under the seat; he had to reach underwater to find them, discarding the rag that wrapped them before those, too, were crammed into a pocket; the flashlight from the glove compartment he would need to keep from falling into the ditch again.

Too bad Richards-Salvetti's husband wasn't a traveling salesman. He'd like to find her home alone. He transferred his fury at his predicament to Kay Salvetti; it warmed him to think of the possibilities when he found her.

He swung the light up at the next mailbox: S. Case.

Christ, why hadn't Mousy just told him to come in from the upper end, and it would be the first house?

There were lights out across the field; they seemed a long way off. They had to be the Salvetti place, and Jory went doggedly on.

At the mailbox that verified that he'd reached his destination, he turned off the flashlight. He didn't want anyone to look out the window and see him coming. He didn't want Kay Salvetti to be prepared.

It was a long driveway, lined by trees that whipped in the wind without doing anything to cut the force of the rain driven into his face and down his neck. There were frequent puddles. Not that it mattered; he was already soaked.

His head hurt. He'd have to take another one of the capsules before long. There were only three of the strong ones left; he'd have to find some more soon.

He reached the yard at last, waiting for a barking dog, but there was none. If they had a dog, it was inside. It didn't worry him much; the .38 would take care of anything smaller than an elephant.

It was a big house. Two stories, old-style farmhouse. Lights on the lower floor.

And a car parked in the backyard.

Jory began to feel better.

The baby's temperature was rising.

Donna read the thermometer uneasily. One hundred four point eight.

Maybe she'd better call Kay, she thought. She'd given him as much of the liquid aspirin as the directions said were allowable, and it wasn't helping. It might be only his teeth—he did chew on the nipple of his bottle more than he sucked for the milk—but with a temperature of almost one hundred five he seemed sick enough so his parents ought to know about it.

Denny had dozed off and on, but always in her arms. Whenever she tried to put him down he whimpered so pathetically that Donna scooped him up again, whispering soothing words, cuddling him against her breast.

He was heavy enough so he made her arms ache, but she liked the feel of him. He smelled of soap and maybe baby powder, and there was something about his helpless dependency that brought out a strong maternal urge.

Donna brushed her cheek against the top of his head, feeling the warmth through his hair. "You know what you've done to me, sweetie?" she asked softly. "You've made me want a baby, too."

She grinned ruefully. Well, there was only one way to get one, and that included finding a man who didn't make her want to run when he touched her. If there was such a man.

"Mama," Denny begged, and Donna shifted him to a position more comfortable for her tired arms.

"I wonder if you'd like to have your face washed with a nice cool cloth?"

But he fought in rage and struck out at her with small fists when she attempted to bathe his hot cheeks.

"Okay. No more amateur methods. We'll call your mama," she said, and headed for the phone.

Kay had left the numbers on the pad beside the phone, both the one at the senior Salvettis' and the doctor's. It was going to be awkward dialing and holding the baby at the same time, but she knew he'd yell if she put him down and she felt so sorry for him she was reluctant to do that.

She never dialed, however. Because when she lifted the receiver to her ear she knew at once that it was dead. There was no sound at all.

Darn. It wasn't unusual for the phones and the lights to go out during a bad storm, and this was the worst of the season, after a relatively mild, dry winter. She stood in the bright, silent kitchen, listening to the frenzy of the wind. The old house creaked and groaned, which wasn't especially alarming because her own home was of the same vintage, and it, too, complained at night, even when there wasn't a storm.

The cedar trees lashed against the side of the house like fingers across the windowpanes. With a sigh, Donna replaced the telephone in its cradle.

Well, she couldn't call Kay. But probably they'd be home before long, anyway.

She walked through the lower floor of the house, jiggling the baby, singing softly to him. He seemed to like being sung to; she wondered if Kay soothed him that way. She couldn't walk around with him for long, though, her arms were pulling loose at the shoulders, she thought.

Somewhere outside something banged sharply, as if a garbage can lid had blown into the side of the house. She'd parked her car under an apple tree; she hoped none of the branches came down and damaged it.

His head pressed into her neck, Denny gave a small snore.

Donna smiled and hugged him gently. He was so sweet. But he was breaking her arms and her back. Maybe she could put him down for a few minutes.

Not all the way back upstairs. There was a big chair in the living room; she could wedge a straight chair in front of it and he couldn't roll out. If only he didn't wake up when she put him down.

This time the baby was limp. He lay as she placed him, not stirring. She wasn't sure whether to cover him or not; he was practically burning up with fever, yet this end of the room was cool. She put the blanket loosely over him, and turned away.

She was hungry. The Salvettis had told her to help herself to anything she wanted to eat, pointing out a few specific

127

things. She turned on lights as she went through the house, in the dining room and the kitchen-family room. It would be fun to have a house like this, to choose the colors and the patterns and the fabrics to decorate it.

To share it with a man?

Donna made a derisive sound and opened the refrigerator. Maybe she'd been ruined forever by that terrible man, but she didn't think so. She just hadn't met the right man yet. Twenty-four might be late to be still looking, but she had an aunt who hadn't found her lover until she was thirty-eight, so there was still hope.

She took out lunch meat and mustard and mayonnaise and made a sandwich, thinking about Aunt Rose. Lover was what she had found, for she hadn't married him, she was only living with him. Donna's mother, Rose's sister, was scandalized.

Donna poured a glass of milk and bit into the sandwich, chewing thoughtfully. Well, she wasn't scandalized. Oh, she personally believed in marriage, and she didn't think you needed to try sex with someone first to see if it would work out—she *knew* it wouldn't for her, because she'd feel so guilty about it the entire thing would be impossible. But Rose was old enough to make her own choice, and she'd made it. She didn't want to give up her freedom and her independence.

I'd give mine up if someone asked me, she reflected. If the right man asked me. She reopened the sandwich and added more mustard. Well, not *all* of it. But she'd like to share her life with someone, someone who respected her as a person as well as turned her on physically.

Maybe the trouble was that every guy she'd gone out with wanted her to go to bed with him before they even had a chance to get to know if they *liked* each other. For some people making love was like scratching an itch, but Donna couldn't feel that way about it. First she'd have to like him, and then love him, and then feel that they were going to make a permanent commitment to one another, old-fashioned as that idea was, and then maybe she wouldn't feel that panic of remembering Russell Jory's face looming over hers, his breath on her face, his hands ripping at her clothes, hurting her—

Why the devil was she letting herself get off on that track?

Well, if she thought about having a family, it meant finding a man, and obviously just any man wasn't going to be good enough. It certainly wouldn't be fair to the man, either, to get

128

married just so she could have a cute baby like Denny. She'd have to love him and want to go to bed with him.

And he—what about the man? She supposed everybody in Redwood County knew she'd been raped when she was a kid. They hadn't used her name or her picture in the paper during the trial, but in a small community everybody knew everything. As many of them as could crowd in had been in the courtroom, and of course all the kids knew it. They'd all liked Larry, they were all horrified by his death, and they knew Donna if only because she ran around with Kay Richards, who was one of the prettiest girls in the senior class.

How much would it matter to a man who might otherwise want to marry her, to know she'd been raped? Some guys, no matter how promiscuous they'd been themselves, wanted a girl who was a virgin when it came time to think about marrying her. It wasn't Donna's fault that she wasn't a virgin—in fact, she *felt* like a virgin—but she couldn't claim to *be* one.

Apparently it hadn't bothered Wally Salvetti. He and Kay seemed to be very happy.

Surely there's another man out there, somewhere, who wouldn't hold it against me, and who wouldn't think because it happened to me once that I'm ready to do it with *anybody*, she thought.

She finished the sandwich and the milk, and rinsed out the glass in the sink before putting it into the dishwasher. Then she selected a big red apple and bit into it, enjoying the spurt of juice and the crispness of the fruit.

Denny slept on, undisturbed by the wind and the whipping branches that brushed across the windows. She touched his forehead, very lightly, and felt as if her hand had been scorched, he was so hot.

Donna stood looking down on him, frowning. If only the phone hadn't gone out, so she could consult with someone about him!

The storm sounds intensified until she'd have sworn someone was trying to get into the house. Doors and windows rattled, and every so often something blew across the yard and hit the building with a crash or a clatter.

Of course, for all the remodeling they'd done, it was still an old house. She knew about old houses; she'd lived in the same one all her life, and her father had grown up in it, too. The doors didn't fit snugly unless you packed rags or insulation

129

around them and the windows would move noisily in the wind.

Why didn't Kay and Wally come home? They'd said they'd come early, but it was now nearly midnight. If they'd tried to call home and didn't get through they'd know she was stranded, without a phone. Surely that would hurry them up a little.

She finished the apple and threw the core into the fire, where it sizzled and spat before it began to turn brown. She put another log into the fireplace, glad Wally had brought plenty of wood in for her.

The firelight threw flickering shadows across the baby's sleeping face. Was it contributing to the color of it, too, or was Denny as bright a pink as it seemed?

It made her uneasy to be cut off here with a sick baby.

Of course she wasn't completely cut off. Not really. Her Pinto sat right out there in the yard. Maybe, if Kay and Wally weren't there by midnight, she'd consider taking the baby over to her mother for advice. She'd feel better, if she couldn't get Kay or the doctor, if her mother took a look at Denny. Or, if all the phones weren't out, she could talk to either Kay or the doctor about him.

Denny stirred and whimpered.

She bent over him, checking his diaper. Wet. So much for peace and quiet; she'd have to take him upstairs now.

Donna lifted him again into place against her shoulder. If she had a baby, she wouldn't have the nursery so far away from where she kept the baby when he was awake, she thought.

He cried, but only fitfully, when she put a clean diaper on him. There was a faint fine rash across his chest, barely visible in the artificial light.

Did babies have rashes when they were cutting teeth? She couldn't remember hearing anyone say so, but when he was so hot to the touch it wasn't surprising if it came out in a rash. Maybe she'd better take his temperature again.

This time the silver line climbed so high that she was fully alarmed. One hundred five and two-tenths. Surely that was too high to ignore any longer, and the measures she'd taken weren't helping.

If Kay didn't come home in another ten minutes, she'd bundle him up and take Denny to her mother's. Surely Kay wouldn't object to that, under the circumstances. She'd leave a note explaining what she'd done.

Donna moved around the nursery, picking up a diaper bag (already filled with necessities) and the thermometer. She'd put in the last of his bottles, too; although he didn't normally eat at night, he'd had very little to eat today and he might want it. And blankets to wrap him in—he wore one of those sleepers that almost rule out the need for covers, but she didn't want to risk getting him chilled. She knew that sometimes they packed people in ice to reduce their fevers, but somehow it still seemed dangerous to let a sick baby get chilled.

With the diaper bag slung over one shoulder, and Denny over the other, Donna made her way back downstairs. She hoped she wouldn't have to go, that the Salvettis would come home before the end of the time she had set as a deadline. The wind was intensifying and the house creaked and groaned in the storm's fury.

She went to the front door and peered through the small viewing window. There were no lights coming up the long driveway, no lights anywhere.

She turned away from the door, jumping when something fell inside the locked study. Surely a window hadn't blown open in there, so that the rain was coming in? But no, the windows were the same as elsewhere in the house; except for the new patio doors in the dining room, everything was old. The casement windows had to be pushed up to open them.

Maybe she ought to go in there and check, though. It would be a shame if anything were damaged that she might have prevented.

Donna hesitated, and the baby moved fretfully in her arms. No. She didn't know why, but she didn't want to open that door, and she turned and walked back to the living room, to the warmth from the open fire, to wait out the remaining few minutes she had allotted before taking Denny to her mother.

She did not see the knob turn on the study door, slowly, silently, only to be released when the latch refused to open.

Christ, didn't anybody leave anything unlocked anymore?
Jory muttered under his breath as he beat his way against
the wind, around the big house, looking for a way in. It
was an old house, he'd expected there would be loose windows or unlocked doors—when he was a kid nobody in
the country ever locked their doors—but the place was secure.

Even the shades and draperies were drawn so that
he couldn't see inside. How many people were in there?
Kay Richards Salvetti had a husband and a child. Mousy
had said there was a child. The husband was a druggist—he might provide access to narcotics, Jory thought
angrily. The pain was there, behind his eyes, eating at
him.

Killing him.

But not yet. Not before he'd evened the score.

A druggist. One of those intellectual, nonphysical types,
Jory pictured him. Not a hunter, the way so many men in this
part of the country were. He wasn't likely to have a gun. But
even if he did, it wouldn't bother Jory.

Salvetti would be an amateur when it came to killing
anyone.

Jory was a professional.

Yet he wasn't getting into this goddamned house.

He returned to the car parked in the backyard, risking the
use of the flashlight, keeping it turned carefully away from the
windows.

The Pinto was a pale blur in the rain and the keys were
gone. All right, the distributor cap, then. He lifted the hood
and removed the cap, tucking it into his pocket along with the
nearly empty vial of codeine. He put down the hood and

made his way on around the house, using the flashlight now, until he found the window he wanted.

No shades or curtains here; from the look of it they were remodeling this room, it was full of junk.

He chose a sturdy screwdriver from the pocketful of tools and went to work on the window.

She might have known they wouldn't get away by eleven. The party was still in full swing, and Sy had just brought out another gallon of wine. Kay refused with a smile, and Sy swung on to Connie, who held out her glass for a refill.

The kids had mostly fallen asleep by now, Stephie on Angela and Sy's king-sized bed, two of her cousins across the hall in the guest room, and Chuckie, Jeanette's youngest, lay sprawled across a couple of cushions in one corner of the living room.

Charlie, Connie's husband, accepted more wine, then walked to the front door and peered out into the night. "Boy, is it getting nasty. We may all elect to spend the night instead of driving home, Angela."

"Plenty of room; we'll dig out the sleeping bags and put all the kids on the floors," Angela said, unperturbed. "Connie, see if there are any of those little crackers left, and the cheese—the cheese is out on the counter."

Kay pushed herself out of the enveloping chair. If she couldn't leave immediately—and Wally was still in animated conversation with two of his brothers—the least she could do was call home and see how Donna was making out with Denny. She hoped his fever had gone down and he was sleeping peacefully.

She dialed her home number, but nothing happened.

Phones out? Well, it wasn't unlikely, not during a storm like this, when they'd been without rain or wind for weeks. Nothing to get excited about, but she didn't like the idea of Donna being unable to call if Denny got worse. Just in case she'd misdialed, she tried again.

Wally had spotted her, and the expression on her face brought him out of the circle of males to cross the room. He put a hand on the back of her neck, ruffling her hair.

"What's the matter, hon? Denny worse?"

134

"I don't know. The phone seems to be out." She held the receiver for him to listen. "Maybe we'd better go, honey."

"Okay. Just a few minutes. I wanted to try that new cheese Ma was talking about. You want to round up our coats?"

"You're not going already, are you?" Jeanette demanded, pausing with a tray of crackers from which Wally absently plucked a few.

"Yeah. Denny wasn't feeling good all day, and now the phone seems to be out."

"You left him with a good sitter, didn't you?"

"Donna Malloy. Sure, she's competent. But I'm holding down the store tomorrow; I wanted an early night anyway," Wally said, taking upon himself the onus of responsibility for their desertion. "I *am* beat, and I think Kay is, too. If she's going to be up half the night with a sick baby, I think she deserves a boot toward home."

Kay gave him a grateful smile. Wally enjoyed his family, and he didn't mind all these command performances for birthdays and anniversaries, but he also knew when she needed rest and privacy. He grinned back. "Grab our coats. One bite of this cheese—or maybe two—and we'll go. I'll tell Ma good-bye."

No one ever left without specifically telling Angela good-bye.

Kay collected their coats, paused to sample the cheese Connie proffered, and made her way through the gesticulating Salvettis toward her mother-in-law. All the Salvettis, even Wally, talked with their hands. That was because, Wally had once said, everybody talked at once, and the only way you could get any attention was to wave your arms around.

There was the expected chorus of "Going already? It's early yet!" but Kay kept moving. Wally bent over to kiss his mother on the cheek, then turned to help Kay into her coat.

"Good night everybody! Good night!"

Sy walked with them onto the porch. He was a small man, considerably smaller than his wife. He was going bald, but it didn't bother him. Everybody knew baldness was a sign of virility, he said. He had fathered eight kids, so nobody could question his virility, and he'd have been capable of fathering eight more if his incubator hadn't broken down. (Angela had had a hysterectomy nine years before).

He clamped a fatherly hand on Kay's shoulder. "Let Wally bring the car up to the walk; no sense in both of you getting soaked. And next time you bring that Denny, eh? He's a corker, that one is."

"He is," Kay agreed, smiling. "He's going to be walking soon."

"And then he'll keep you busy. I remember Wally, when he started to walk. It went right from walk to *climb*. Couldn't keep him out of anything, like to drove his mother crazy. Listen, you take good care of that boy. And thanks for coming tonight, you know how much it means to Angela to have you all here."

"I know," Kay said. Maybe someday she'd be grateful to have Denny and his wife and children come on her birthday. "There's Wally. Good night, Sy. Thanks for everything."

She ran for the car, sliding in beside Wally, turning to wave back at Sy who still stood on the porch, the windy rain blowing over him.

Wally was grinning. "Like pulling teeth to get away from them, isn't it? But they're a good bunch. I'm glad you're more relaxed with them now. At least you seem to be."

"I told Connie tonight," Kay said, "that I can't have any more babies."

He put a hand on her knee and squeezed. "You feel better, now that someone knows?"

"Yes."

"I thought you would. Judas, there's a tree down across the street. Can I get around it or am I going to have to back up?"

It was a small tree, blown diagonally, so that Wally had to drive over the tip of it. Kay huddled in the seat, her feet outstretched to the warmth of the heater. She *was* tired; she hoped Denny would be asleep and all right, so they could go right to bed.

They were not prepared, in spite of the limbs and the entire tree they had seen across the roads, for Little John Creek.

Wally swung off the River Road onto the upper end of Horseshoe, and abruptly slammed on the brakes, sending the car skidding slightly.

"What's the matter?" Kay demanded, straightening up, but already she could see. In the headlights the dark water flowed over the bridge, and there was debris building up against the railings still above the flood, debris that could very well take out the entire bridge if the spate continued.

Wally swore softly. "I can't drive over it. I wonder if the other bridge is still passable?"

Alarm surged through her; Kay forgot that she wanted to sleep. "What if it isn't?"

"I don't know. Let's find out before we consider alternatives." He shifted into reverse and the car lurched backward up the incline.

Kay clutched at the edge of her seat. They had to be able to get home. What if Denny was worse? Would Donna know what to do with him? She leaned forward, trying to see through the driving rain as they moved ahead.

The bridge at the lower end of Horseshoe was no better. Even walking across it would be a dangerous undertaking.

A truck rumbled toward them, headlights blazing, and pulled to a stop. National Guard, Wally thought. It must be getting bad. He rolled down his window and looked up into the face of the driver, a young man in fatigues.

"No through traffic back that way, sir," he stated. "We're supposed to shut off everything between here and the main highway."

"I live on Horseshoe Road," Wally told him. "We've got a sick baby at home; we need to get across."

The youth shook his head. "I don't think there's any way to do it. We've got units removing people from the lowlands, and orders to keep out all traffic along the river. Your place on high ground?"

"Yes. I'm not worried about the place. But the baby may need a doctor." Wally was aware of his wife's strained, pale face beside him. "Maybe I'll go across the bridge on foot, then. I don't suppose you've got a rope, have you?"

"Sure. You want a lifeline? I can let you have that. I can't spare anybody to go with you, though."

"Okay. Just give me the rope," Wally said, with a calm he didn't feel.

Kay sat rigidly as the rope was handed over, and the Guard truck moved on in the direction from which they had come. Wally backed and filled to turn around, and followed after the vanishing taillights.

"Wally . . . it could be very dangerous."

"You want me to go back to town and wait until the flood goes down? Or get to Denny?"

She swallowed. "If only we'd been able to talk to Donna—"

137

"Well, we weren't. And we won't be. If the flooding's bad enough to bring out the Guard and close off roads, it might be days before they can get the phones fixed. We can't leave Denny that long without knowing what's happening." He pulled into upper Horseshoe for the second time, leaving the lights streaming out across the swirling, angry stream. "Get me the flashlight."

Silently, she handed it to him, and he jammed it into his jacket pocket.

"Okay. I'm going to fasten the rope to the front bumper. I think the bridge is still solid enough to walk across, hanging onto the railing, but if it goes I'll have the rope to haul myself back on." He wasn't certain he could do it, if that water was as rough as it looked, but he didn't know what else to try. "Now. You wait here until I get all the way across. Then I'll untie the rope and let it free, and you haul it in on this side. Then drive back to Ma's and get some of the guys to come back out here. By the time they get here I'll have had time to get to the house and see how things are, and I'll drive Donna's car back here to the bridge. If we have to, we'll rig up some way to get Denny back on this side. Or if he's okay, I'll go on home with him and you can stay at Ma's overnight; we'll work out what we need to do in the morning."

An instinctive protest rose in her throat, and Kay caught it back. This was no time to be a baby, to expect things of Wally that he couldn't do.

"All right," she said quietly.

For all that it was warm enough to melt the snows that were causing a flood, it was damned cold. Wally's hands were icy by the time he'd secured the rope to the bumper and then to his belt. When he stepped into the water he couldn't control the sharp, painful intake of breath.

The tug of the water was incredible. Something moved by it struck him a glancing blow on the thigh, and then he was in water up to his waist, struggling to move across the wooden structure. He'd never have kept his footing without the railing; he pulled himself along it with both hands, willing forgetfulness of the cold and the discomfort.

Behind him Kay stood in the rain, silhouetted against the headlights. He turned and waved, which was a mistake; he was nearly swept off his feet, and from that point on he concentrated solely on getting across Little John Creek.

Once he slipped and went down, the water surging to his

chin; it was so icy he could hardly draw in the air his laboring lungs demanded. But at last he reached the other side and struggled up the bank.

His fingers were too numb to untie the knotted rope. After a few moments he gave up and groped for the pocketknife he always carried. Even getting that open was an accomplishment, but he managed it, and began to saw on the borrowed rope.

..................Saturday, January 19

The note was anchored to the kitchen table with her empty milk glass. Donna glanced around to see if she'd thought of everything. Maybe some graham crackers for Denny, in case he could be persuaded to chew one. She knew babies didn't starve from missing a couple of meals, but it bothered her that he'd refused everything but a few swallows of milk.

She didn't see any way she could lock the house behind her, not without locking herself out permanently. Wally had keys, of course, but it was possible she might want to get back in.

Her inner debate was limited. Denny was fiery to the touch; when he roused, his blue eyes were glazed and sick. She didn't dare wait any longer to seek help for him.

She left the kitchen door unlocked and went out, running across the space between porch and car. Denny whimpered softly as she put him down on the seat.

The car refused to start.

Donna sat for a moment, listening to the rain on the roof, the wind in the tops of the cedars, and Denny's struggle against the blankets she'd wrapped around him.

What was the matter with the car? It had been fine on the way over here.

She wasn't the least bit mechanical. All she knew about a car was how to drive it, not fix it.

What next, then? Go back into the house and continue to wait for the Salvettis to come home? Or take off on foot?

Taking a sick baby out in a car was one thing. Carrying him out in the rain was something else. Yet Kay and Wally should have been home by this time. Maybe something had happened so they couldn't get here. In a storm like this it wasn't unusual for trees to blow down across the roads, things like that. It might be hours yet before they showed up.

Frustrated in his efforts to free himself of the confining

blankets, Denny wailed. It was a thin cry, far different from the vigorous, angry protests of a healthy baby.

Out across the fields, Donna saw the yard light at the next farm. Case's place, wasn't it? The same place she'd gone that night Jory had attacked her and Kay . . .

Someone was home, or they wouldn't have the yard light on. Maybe their phone was working and she could get through to the Salvettis to tell them about Denny, or to a doctor.

She had to have help. She was seriously concerned about the baby, and she didn't dare leave him here. How far was it to Case's place? It didn't seem far, although of course she'd have to go by the road, not across the field.

Her own coat was an all-weather one, but she'd have to do something about Denny. The blankets wouldn't protect him from the rain at all.

Garbage bags, she thought. Big plastic garbage bags, she could put Denny, blankets and all, inside of one, and fold the top over his head, just making sure he could breathe all right. Surely Kay used the same type of can liner that her own family did.

It took her only seconds to find them. The kitchen seemed very brightly lit after the darkness, a snare, luring her to stay here in the safety of the house.

But Denny wasn't safe here. Denny needed a doctor.

Donna got him into the bundle of plastic bag, and once again went out into the night. The rain slashed her face, but once she started walking the baby quieted down and rested against her. The diaper bag slapped against her side as Donna slogged resolutely down the driveway to the road.

Jory tripped over something, moving across the room, and froze, listening. On a night like this, with things blowing around, they might take it for an outside sound.

There was a crack of light around the door; he turned on the flashlight again so he wouldn't knock over anything else, and made for the door.

There was someone on the other side of it. He stood and heard the faint whimper of a child.

Were there only the two of them? The young woman and the baby? Exultation sent a gush of warmth through him, and the pain was receding somewhat as the codeine he'd just swallowed took effect. He had the shotgun, and he turned off the flashlight and stuck it in his pocket before he reached for the doorknob.

It was locked.

The son-of-a-bitching door was locked.

Inside the house? Why would they lock an inside door?

Rage exploded within him, so that for a moment he almost lost control and shot his way through the door. Then reason took over. He'd cut the phone line, but if by any chance the husband was home, if he had a weapon—damnedest country, practically everybody kept a gun of some kind, some of them even had racks built in their pickups to carry hunting rifles—no, it wouldn't do to give notice of his presence. Not before he knew how many there were.

All right. There was an enclosed back porch, and while the outer door was locked, he knew he could get in there. Maybe either the door or one of the windows opening from the porch would be unlocked.

He retreated across the icy room, his resolution hardening. It didn't matter how many obstacles they threw in his way, he'd get around them. Jory threw a leg over the windowsill and dropped to the ground. He cracked his head against some unseen projection and had to stand still until the pain receded. He swore steadily, hating the Salvettis with an intense hatred.

The back door was not only unlocked, it stood ajar.

He stiffened, wary, fading back into the shadows to consider the situation. There were lights in the back part of the house, now, and a broad yellow band streamed out across the porch, illuminating the corner of a chest freezer and a pair of rubber boots.

Jory moved out into the open, then pushed cautiously at the door.

He knew, even before he spotted the note, that the house was empty. He could feel it.

He moved the glass and stared down with rising fury at the note.

Dear Kay:
Denny's fever is up to 105.2°, so I'm going to take him to my mom. If the phones aren't all out, we can at least contact the doctor. Anyway, Mother's a lot better equipped to make guesses about a sick baby than I am. Hope this is okay.

Donna.

Jory read it through a second time, the tension growing in his body until at last he hit out with one fist and shattered the glass that had anchored the note. He didn't even notice that it had cut his knuckles.

Kay Richards Salvetti hadn't even been in the house. Only her child was here, with a sitter, and now even *they* were gone. How? He'd disabled the car.

Profanity, mindless, uncontrolled, erupted from his throat. He moved through the house, leaving muddy tracks on the pale gold carpeting, jerking open cupboards and drawers, overturning smaller pieces of furniture in sheer rage.

He went up the stairs, knowing there was no one there—surely the sitter hadn't *walked* away on a night like this?—but yielding to the urge to make sure. He opened the jewelry box on the dresser in the master bedroom, decided there was nothing of sufficient value to be worth the risk of getting rid of it, and threw it on the floor.

The bathroom, then. Again he rifled through the bottles and vials, dumping everything into the lavatory. A druggist,

146

for crissake, you'd think he'd have more stuff here than Band-Aids and Pepto-Bismol. One prescription, and that for an antibiotic. Nothing. *Nothing!*

He'd been right about one thing, although there was no satisfaction in it. Salvetti wasn't a hunter. There were no guns.

Well, the house was empty. But they'd be back, Kay Richards and her druggist husband.

When they came, Jory would be waiting for them.

Her arms ached until she thought she would be unable to go the rest of the way without dropping the baby. And just as she reached the end of Stan Case's driveway, the yard light went out.

Somewhere along the way her rain hood had blown off, and the hair was plastered to her skull while icy rivulets ran down her face and neck; her glasses did little more than contribute to her general feeling of blind helplessness.

She didn't bother to try to avoid the puddles, when she could detect them. Her feet were soaked. Nothing she did now was going to make any difference. Denny cried steadily, but as if he didn't really expect any relief, occasionally bobbing his head so that it struck her under the chin.

She half-fell up the back steps. There was still a light inside; Casey must have just come in from the barn. Donna had been raised on a farm; she knew barn visits this time of night meant sick animals or calving.

She didn't even have a hand free to knock. She could no longer support Denny with one arm, so she kicked and called out.

"Please. Please, help me!"

She saw him coming, a tall, well-built young man. She had seldom seen Casey since that night when she and Kay had come to him for help; but her father and brothers knew him and they sometimes bought or traded livestock.

His wife had died several years ago in an automobile accident; he had a seven-year-old daughter, Paula, who had been in Donna's first class a year ago. She had felt oddly uncomfortable with him the time he'd come to Family Night with Paula, but he had acted as if he didn't remember her coming to his house late at night, bleeding and crying. He talked to her about Paula, just nice and friendly, and after a while she didn't feel uncomfortable anymore.

He turned on the outside light, then swung open the door.

"Who is it?" He stared down at her, then reached to take Denny in his plastic cocoon out of her arms. Donna almost fell, again, following him into the warmth of the kitchen. "Donna Malloy?" he asked, looking over at her as he began to peel the child out of his confining wrappings. "What's happened?"

She sank into a chair without waiting for an invitation. "I'm taking care of the Salvetti baby, they've gone to a party. He's sick, he has a terrible fever—and the phone's out, and then my car wouldn't start."

Casey's dark eyes took in her bedraggled condition, then reverted to the baby. "He's hot, all right. Here, take it easy, fella, we'll get you out of there."

"His temperature was over one-oh-five when we left the house. That's hot enough to need a doctor, isn't it?"

He ran a hand through brown hair as wet as her own, and wiped the moisture on his jeans. "Pretty hot. I think Paula's got that high once, and we had her in the hospital overnight. She was older, though. I don't know if that makes it better or worse."

"I don't know, either," Donna admitted, and grinned ruefully. She felt better already, now that the responsibility was not entirely her own. "Is your phone still working?"

"Don't know. I'll check it." He handed Denny to her, and moved to the wall phone. "Nope. They're probably all out. Hell of a wind, it's bringing down a lot of trees, I think. Well, I'll get the pickup out and run you into town, or home. That where you want to go?"

"I left a note saying I'd gone to my mom's. Of course my car is still sitting there, so they won't know what I've done. If you could get me to a phone, though, or home, I'd appreciate it."

"Okay. Just a minute, I'd better tell my ma where I'm going. I'll be right back. There's coffee on the stove, there, if you want some."

It was all she could do to get up, holding Denny, but the thought of coffee was irresistible. She felt the baby's head. Was he a little cooler than he had been? Well, no point in rechecking now, he'd only fight it, and there was nothing she could do except get him to a doctor, anyway.

She juggled the baby while she poured coffee, then sank back down into the chair to drink it.

Mrs. Case came to the kitchen door, wearing a bathrobe and slippers; she'd obviously been asleep.

"Poor baby. Where'd you say his folks are?"

"At a birthday party for Wally's mother, I think it is. His temperature just kept going up and up, and I thought one-oh-five point two was too high to ignore any longer. They were supposed to be home over an hour ago, but they hadn't come so I thought I'd better try to get help."

The older woman nodded. "Casey will get you some." She moved aside to let her son through the doorway. "People shouldn't go away and leave a baby when he's sick."

"He wasn't nearly this bad when they left," Donna said. Denny had leaned against her chest and fallen asleep again. "I guess I'll have to bundle him up again, but not inside the plastic bag. I think it was too hot for him, the rash seems to be worse. Could he have a rash just because of the fever?"

"More'n likely. Haven't you got anything to put on your head, son?"

Casey, in the act of pulling on his rubber boots, grinned. "Sure. I got a nice knit cap, and it's sopping wet. So's my head. So what difference does it make? I'll drive right up by the back steps, Donna, be just a minute."

She had, she realized now, deliberately avoided Casey over the years, because she couldn't see him without remembering how she had first met him. It wasn't her fault she'd been raped, everybody said that, including the police, who had been very kind. But she had felt guilty, dirtied, by Jory's assault, and somehow the fact that Casey knew what had happened to her made her want not to look at him.

But that was stupid. Casey didn't blame her for it. He was a nice man, and she was glad he was here to help her again.

His pickup was old, like the one her brothers drove around the farm to haul feed; it smelled of good alfalfa hay and cow manure, which didn't bother her since she was used to it. Casey reached out to help her get the baby onto the seat, and she slid in beside him.

Donna dug into her jeans pocket for a dry Kleenex to wipe off her glasses. "I don't know why emergencies always happen when the weather is so terrible, and I'm on my own," she said.

Casey had a good grin, the kind that didn't make fun of you. "Maybe it's that if you weren't alone and there wasn't a storm, it wouldn't *be* an emergency."

She made a sound of chagrin. "Of course. I'd just have gotten into my own car and driven Denny to the doctor, wouldn't I? Anyway, I'm glad you were home tonight."

"I'm home most nights. Milking cows, it's hard to get a day off. They're my dad's cows, actually, and his farm, but when we had to put him in a rest home Paula and I moved back out here. Since my wife died I've had to have a sitter for Paula after school anyway, and this makes it easier for all of us."

"And you hold down a job, too, besides milking?"

The headlights seemed very pale, scarcely outlining the edges of the drive and the road, but Casey drove with the confidence of one who knew every fence post. He had thick, curly dark hair and a rather beaky nose, but Donna thought he was attractive.

"Yeah, I'm doing carpenter work for Omar Construction. It's slow this time of year, though, so I'm not a steady. If Dad's not better by spring we'll probably sell the cattle, but Ma thinks he'll be able to take over again gradually. He had a stroke, you know, but he's getting better."

Denny squirmed around, trying to crawl onto her lap. "Mama," he piped.

"Yes, honey, we'll find your mama. I wonder if there's any chance she's come home; I've been gone quite a while."

Casey eased up on the gas. "You want to go back that way first?"

"No. Keep going. I'll feel better if my mom sees Denny, and maybe our phone's working so we can contact the doctor. I'm sure Kay will want to talk to him, anyway."

A moment later, Casey's booted foot slammed on the brake. "Damn, we're not going across that!"

Donna stared in dismay at the twisted remains of the lower Horseshoe bridge. The water of the normally placid creek was so wide the headlights didn't even reach the other side.

"Maybe that's why the Salvettis haven't come home. Maybe the other bridge is out, too."

"Could be. We'll go back and take a look. Maybe we'd better see if there are any other phones working on the Horseshoe." He backed around to return the way they had come, and as they watched a slender eucalyptus tilted and slid into the swollen stream, the bank washed out from under it.

Neither of them said anything. It was only too clear that this was not an ordinary storm, and that the probability of a widespread phone outage was great. They were lucky there

151

was still power, Donna thought, and wondered if Kay and Wally were frantic about their son.

When they saw the second bridge, Casey drew in a deep breath. "Well. Looks like we're trapped until the water goes down. I'll take you back to our place, and see if Ma can do anything for the baby. He seems fairly perky right now." He glanced down at the child, who was attempting to pull himself up by hanging onto Donna's coat. "Okay?"

She considered and made a reluctant decision. "I think maybe I'd better go back to the house. I mean, if Wally should get through some way that's where they'll expect me to be. And the note I left says I went home, so they won't know where to look."

"Mama!" Denny insisted, and Donna hugged him to her as the truck turned and headed back into the wind.

Casey obediently turned the pickup into the Salvetti lane, driving more by instinct than by sight. He pulled around the stalled blue Pinto and halted at the back door.

"I'll take a look at your car and see if I can figure out what's the matter with it," he offered. "The keys in it?"

Gratefully, Donna dug into her pocket for them. She draped the plastic sack over the protesting little boy and made a dash for the house, pausing to wipe her feet on the mat on the porch.

As she stepped through the doorway into the lighted kitchen, she became immediately aware of several things. Her note was no longer on the table but on the floor, and there were red splatters on it. Broken glass crunched under her feet, and she turned at a harshly drawn breath to look into the muzzle of a shotgun held by a man who was, for a few seconds, only vaguely familiar.

"Come on in," the man said very softly, "and don't shut the door. Who else is out there? Is he coming in, too?"

Recognition was gradual, a paralyzing thing. Denny struggled to be put down, and Donna almost let him slip out of her grasp. She was not aware of beginning to move her head, almost imperceptibly, from side to side in negation.

No. No, it couldn't be *him*. He'd been sent to prison for life, he couldn't be here in Kay's kitchen pointing a gun at her—

"Step over that way," Jory said, gesturing with the gun. "And don't make any noise. I don't want to kill you yet."

Yet. She was frozen in an agony of horror, but the word registered. *I don't want to kill you—yet.*

Denny pushed against her chest with all the force of his baby arms, and she went down with him, onto her knees to keep him from falling. The diaper bag slid off her arm onto the floor, beside the note with its bloody flecks.

She heard Casey's feet on the back steps, then crossing the enclosed porch; she wanted to scream a warning but with those dreadful pale blue eyes upon her she could not utter a sound. The pain that tore through her was as great as it had been nearly eight years before; it was as if simply by looking at her Russell Jory violated her body and her mind. *Yet. Yet.*

Oh, God. Oh, God, she thought, *please don't let it happen again. Please.*

"Donna?" Casey blinked in the bright light. "Your distributor cap's—"

Jory gestured once more with the shotgun. "Come on in, mister. Stand right over there against the wall, and don't make any sudden moves unless you want to buy it right now."

Casey's jaw dropped. "What is this? What's going on?"

Jory sidled toward the door to kick it shut.

"Shut up and stand still. Put your hands up by your shoulders."

"Who the hell are you? What do you want? We've got a sick baby here and—"

Jory made no attempt to reach Casey. Instead, he swung the shotgun in a vicious arc that struck Donna's glasses and sent them skidding across the vinyl floor.

She flinched as the frames bit briefly into her nose and temples, then watched aghast as Jory brought down one foot upon them, twisting the glasses into a mangled heap.

"You want me to ram this down her throat next time, you keep it up, man," Jory warned.

Slowly, Casey lifted his hands to the level of his shoulders and held them there.

Until he knocked her glasses off, Jory didn't realize who the baby-sitter was.

Her hair was different, short and almost straight instead of long and curled. But it was the same girl, all right. Donna Malloy.

She hadn't worn glasses the other time.

The baby crept into the broken glass and cut his hands; he sat back, now, extending bleeding palms, and began to cry.

Casey made a movement toward the child, but Jory waved him back.

"Hold it, buddy. Right there. Just stay put."

"The kid's bleeding; it can't hurt to let us get the glass out of his hands," Casey urged.

Jory ignored the plea. "He is Kay Richards's kid, ain't he?" he demanded of Donna.

She still knelt on the floor, her throat working unproductively as she tried to speak.

"Her name's Salvetti now," Casey said. "Kay Salvetti."

"Yeah. But her name was Richards, and you're the other one. Malloy." There was satisfaction in the rusty-sounding voice.

Casey looked from one to the other of them, trying to interpret this. "The other one what? Donna, you know this guy?"

Her brown eyes were wide, unprotected-looking without the glasses. "He—he—" If he touches me again, I will die, she thought.

Denny leaned forward and put his weight on his hands, attempting to creep, and screamed in pain. This time Casey ducked down, quickly, to scoop up the child and set him on the edge of the yellow-tiled counter.

"I told you, man—" Jory began, but Casey was already holding the baby's hand, extracting a glass splinter.

154

Tears ran down the little boy's cheeks, but he sat still while his injuries were ministered to.

"I need some Band-Aids," Casey said.

"Tough shit. Do I have to put a slug through somebody to convince you this is no joke?" Jory asked, flat-lipped.

Casey straightened, holding Denny still with one hand. "No, you don't. What do you want of us?"

"I don't want nothing of *you*. *She's* going with me, her and the kid. You can stay here alive, like down the cellar, or you can stay here dead. It don't make no difference to me."

"No—" Donna managed the one word, a choked, painful one.

"What do you need with the baby? I'll put him in his crib," Casey offered. "He's no good to you, whatever it is you want from us."

"The kid goes. And I don't need you. She can drive me, after we put the distributor cap back in her car. Her and the kid, that's all I want."

Donna struggled again with the terrible pain in her throat. "I can't. I can't drive, you've broken my glasses. I can hardly see across the room, let alone ahead of a car! I'm so nearsighted I'm practically blind."

For a moment Jory was disconcerted, but not enough to give Casey a chance to move. His mouth flattened into an ugly line.

"Okay. You, you'll have to drive, then. With the end of this baby right up against the back of your neck."

"All right," Casey agreed. "But leave Donna and the baby here."

"Listen, you son of a bitch, don't keep bugging me or I'll put a hole through you big enough so you can stick your head in it. I don't need no suggestions from you, understand? There's a pad over there by the phone. Write a note on it. Write what I say."

Casey considered that, fully aware of Donna's terror, far beyond what he would have expected unless she knew the man. He reached for the note pad and the pen beside it. "OK. What do I write?"

"Write this: 'I got your kid.' And sign it 'Jory.'"

For a few seconds Casey didn't move to obey. Oh, Jesus, that was it. Jory. Russel William Jory, who'd been on the front page of the paper for weeks after he killed that boy and raped the girls.

"Write," Jory said through his teeth.

"Sure," Casey said, and did as he was told, balancing the no longer weeping baby with one big hand braced against his stomach. Then he turned back to Jory.

"You can't drive out of here, you know. The bridges are both washed out, there's a flood."

The pale face contorted in building rage. "Don't give me that crap, I just drove in here."

"Maybe you did, but the bridges are underwater now. We just tried to get out to take the baby to a doctor," Casey told him.

Jory hesitated. They might be telling the truth—certainly there'd been enough rain to float an Ark—but he didn't trust anybody. "Well, we'll just go take a look. Come on, move." He reached into his jacket pocket and tossed the distributor cap at Casey, who caught it in automatic reflex. "Put that back where it belongs, and you drive. She sits in front with you, the kid goes in back with me."

For a second Casey hesitated, then lifted Denny in his left arm. "Wrap him up, Donna."

She obeyed, stumbling to her feet, reaching for the diaper bag as well, looping it over her shoulder. It was a nightmare returned, only worse, because this time she knew what it could be like, and she knew she wasn't going to wake up and find it a dream.

Jory gave Casey no opportunity to try anything. None of that grabbing the gun barrel shit, he wouldn't get close enough for that. And to make it perfectly clear he spelled it out. "You try anything smartass, and I'll kill 'em both. Easy as squashing a bug."

Casey glanced at Donna, but she was in a state of shock; the words might not even have registered with her. "Whatever you say," Casey agreed, and led the way out into the night.

Wally had once been lost for two days with a buddy, in the Trinity Alps when an unseasonable snowstorm caught them far from camp. He had thought then, for a time, that he might freeze to death.

He hadn't been any colder then than he was now. He clamped his chattering teeth together and resolutely ignored his feet. Kay had obeyed orders; as soon as he'd let go of the rope, she had reeled it in on the other side of the swollen creek and left for town.

It wasn't a long walk, only a miserable one. He could see the lights from his own house winking through the trees. The thought of clean, dry shoes and clothes, of the warmth of the open fire, urged him on at a quick pace.

The headlights were a welcome sight. Wally stopped and waved his hands in the accepted signal to stop.

The car swerved around him without slowing, however, leaving him staring after it with mixed feelings. He hadn't had a good look at it, he knew only that it was a small light-colored vehicle. Well, some woman who was afraid to stop, he supposed.

"You won't get far, lady," he observed aloud. "You can't cross that bridge except the same way I did."

He turned and trudged along the road and into his own driveway. There were lights upstairs in his and Kay's bedroom as well as in the bathroom. He hoped that didn't mean Denny was worse. The thought quickened his step.

Donna's Pinto was gone and there was a familiar-looking pickup in its place.

What the hell? Wally ran up the steps and into the kitchen and stopped dead still.

Broken glass, and blood. He recognized it at once as blood, even as he stooped to pick up the note that had blown off the table. The written message only half-registered, since it seemed to have no relationship to the mess before him. Gone to Malloys? But Donna wouldn't have created such a disaster scene.

He took a step toward the phone, even though he knew it wasn't working, and lifted the receiver to confirm it. Dead. And then he saw the note pad, and the tiny, bloody handprint on the yellow counter top.

Denny's hand. Denny's blood.

And the note.

Jory.

Oh, Christ.

His first anguished thought was for his wife. It would kill Kay, it would literally kill her if anything happened to Denny.

He lifted his head and shouted. "Donna! You here?"

The house was empty. He knew it was empty. But he ran through it, opening doors, turning on lights in the few rooms that had remained dark, seeing the open window in the study, the muddy footprints on the carpet, the medicines dumped into the bathroom sink, and back to the kitchen and the broken glass and that bloody baby handprint on the counter.

Wally ran for the pickup; he remembered now whose it was, that Stan Case's, from down the road. If only the keys were in it—

They were not.

He forgot he was cold. He forgot he was tired. Wally ran, back toward the submerged bridge, praying more earnestly than he had ever prayed for anything in his life.

"Don't stop!" Jory growled from the backseat, and punctuated his order by poking Casey in the head with the muzzle of the shotgun.

"Who was it?" Donna asked, turning her head even though she could see nothing beyond the black pane of the car window.

"Wally Salvetti," Casey said. He swerved, grateful Wally hadn't stepped out in the middle of the road where this joker would have forced him to run the man down or get his head blown off.

Donna bit her lower lip and tasted blood. Her mindless prayer continued, automatic, yet without real hope. Behind her Denny began to fuss, but when she started to turn around Jory jabbed at her with a brutality that betrayed his frustration.

"Keep going," he said.

"Salvetti wouldn't be walking if he'd been able to drive over the creek," Casey said.

"If he got across it, we can," Jory told him. "Keep going."

One look at the turbulent flood changed his mind, however. He didn't know how the hell Salvetti had crossed it, but he had no desire to drown. He couldn't even count on getting himself across the water, let alone taking the kid and the girl with him.

Once more the shotgun bit into Casey's back. "Turn around. Get us on another road, get us out of here."

"I told you. There is no way out of here, not until the flood goes down. The road makes a half-circle, that's why they call it Horseshoe. It crosses the creek at both ends. There is no other way out."

Jory gestured angrily to the east. "There's got to be a way out there, that way!"

"There's nothing there but hills. And beyond the hills are

159

mountains." Casey spoke slowly, as if to someone not quite bright—or rational. "Between here and the base of the hills are just fields. Pasture, for cows, and then some woods. That's all."

Vituperative fury boiled out of the man who held the gun. "Don't give me that crap, there's got to be a road going east, and you'd damned well better get us on it, man!"

Casey turned the Pinto and drove back the way they had come, wondering what the hell he ought to do next. The man was a lunatic, and logic wasn't going to have much effect on him. Maybe when Salvetti saw the mess, and found the notes, he'd think of something. He'd better think of something, or they might all be dead before long.

"I can't take you on a road that doesn't exist," Casey said. "There's one main highway cuts through the hills going east. One. That's all, for maybe a hundred miles. And we can't get to it from here, we have to go back out on the freeway to reach it. You figure out a way to do that, and I'll follow orders."

Jory leaned forward, the gun barrel resting against the side of Casey's neck as he peered forward. "There! What's that? Ain't that a road?"

"It's a lane. An access road, so I can haul hay to my cows on the back pasture. It doesn't go anywhere, it's a dead end."

"Turn! Goddamn you, turn in there!" Jory commanded, and Casey turned.

"Just like the old days, eh, Lieutenant?" Andy Sleder said, grinning. He swung the car around a corner, avoiding an idiot in a black raincoat who was crossing between crosswalks, practically invisible in the rain.

McDuff inhaled, then relaxed when the pedestrian jumped for the safety of the sidewalk. "Yeah. Like the old days. How the hell have you managed to keep your driver's license?"

"Why do you think I became a cop? Shall we go Code Three?"

"Cool it, Andy. The flood isn't going to be impressed by sirens or speed. Who do we have out in the Salmon Creek flats?"

"Guidotti. I talked to him just before you came out. They're moving everybody out, got four National Guard trucks out there. You want to check it out?"

"Not if they have it under control."

"Guidotti said it would be pie except for one old couple way up the end of the road. They live on high ground, but will be cut off before morning and the old guy's got a bad heart and she's crippled with arthritis. They were going to try to get through with a four-wheel drive to bring them out."

"Ernie Snedson," McDuff remembered. "They'll probably have to hog-tie him to get him to leave his place. He's got chickens and rabbits and a goat. We went through this once before. He insisted he had to stay with them. We told him if he was cut off we couldn't do anything for him, can't even get a helicopter in there."

Sleder negotiated another sharp corner. "What did you do with him?"

"Loaded him and his wife in the back of a truck and brought them out. The flood closed the road for twelve days. When the water went down his rabbits had all drowned, and half his chickens were washed away. The rest of them made it

161

through, and the goat was stuck in the crotch of a tree. Old Snedson tried to sue the county for the loss of his rabbits and his chickens. Judge threw it out, of course. We took up a collection to buy him a pair of rabbits and a box of baby chickens. Let's take a look at the Big Bend, see how bad it is."

"I hope to Christ we ain't going to be completely shut off from the outside world again," Sleder observed. "My wife never got dressed for three weeks. Said what was the use, she couldn't leave the house and nobody could come in except by boat. Uh-oh."

They had both spotted the blinking red lights ahead that meant a patrol car was stopped on the highway. They slid in behind it, peering through the slashing downpour.

A uniformed CHP officer walked back to bend down to Sleder's opened window. "Hi, Lieutenant, Andy. Looks like we're going to have to close the bridge before morning. Some drunk ran over into the river and we're fishing him out."

"Dead or alive?" Sleder asked.

"Well, he's yelling his head off, if that's any indication. Shitty night, isn't it?"

"Beaut. See you later," Sleder said, and put the car into gear. "Just think," he said to McDuff as they pulled out around the CHP cruiser, "if VonDorn was pulling his weight you wouldn't have had to come out tonight."

"I'd probably have come out, anyway," Mac said, noncommittal.

Sleder gave him a sideways look. "How long think he's going to hang on, the way he's going?"

"Until he gets his pension. Evers won't fire him, not after all these years in the department. Swing out along River Road, let's see how Little John's doing."

"Right you are," Sleder said, and gave it a little more gas.

"There's no sense in you going back out there, Kay," Sy told her as the men prepared to leave. They were supplied with rain gear and blankets in case Wally had to bring Denny out, and at the last moment Angela produced a fifth of whiskey.

"Wally might welcome it," Angela said. "And he's right, Kay, you're already cold and upset, and going back out there won't help. Besides, they need the room in the cars, unless they take three instead of two. There's nothing you can do for Wally."

"If he brings Denny out, Denny will need me," Kay said. "I want to go back with them."

"She's right about the room. We'd have to take an extra car." Sy patted her cheek in a paternal way. "Don't worry, Wally's a grown man. He'll take care of things on the other side of the creek, and if he needs us, we'll handle anything on this side. No matter what, we'll let you know right away. Now come on, be a good girl, take off your coat, and Angela will give you a glass of whiskey. You look like you could use it."

She argued further, but it was of no use. She was left behind. She stood at the window looking after the departing lights with a sense of bitter frustration. *Be a good girl.* As if she were a child.

She waved away the drink Angela offered. Anger provided the needed warmth, and her mother-in-law read it in her face.

"Don't be upset with them. This is for the men, Kay, they'll do what needs to be done. Denny will be all right."

"You can't know that," Kay said, her expression stony.

Angela's dark, fleshy face shifted into sympathetic planes. "No. You're right, I can't. It's one of those stupid things people say when they don't know what else to say. Still, there's nothing we can do but wait until they come back. Come on, we'd better make some sandwiches, and Connie, get the big coffeepot out again. They'll need it if they all go

163

running around in the wet. Take off your coat, Kay, and help us. It will give you something to do."

She didn't want anything to do, but she went with them, Wally's mother and sisters and sisters-in-law. She knew they meant well, but she was seriously concerned about Denny. Heaven knew how long the phones had been out, and if Donna had tried to get Denny to a doctor she couldn't have crossed the creek. Probably it had been impassable for hours.

She shouldn't have left him. If he wasn't well enough to go along, she should have stayed home with him. It wasn't a valid excuse that the Salvettis would have been critical if she'd done that. Denny was her child, and only she could decide what was best to do regarding him.

This was the last time she'd knuckle under to Salvetti opinion when she knew they were wrong.

She began slathering mayonnaise on the bread Angela put out, and beside her Connie added slices of cold ham.

She looked at the clock over the sink and wondered how she'd stand it for the hour it would certainly take to reach Wally and then get back to her.

"Sorry, sir, River Road's closed to through traffic," the Guardsman said.

"Now, wait a minute." Sy ducked his bald head out into the rain. "My son went across the upper bridge to get to his house because he had a sick baby there with a sitter, and we're to meet him on this side in case we have to get the baby out. He's Wally Salvetti, on Horseshoe Road."

The Guardsman was young and uncertain. "I don't know, sir. I was told not to let anybody onto River Road, and I don't think it's possible to get onto Horseshoe."

Sy made a sound of exasperation. "Look, who's in charge here? If my grandson needs medical attention, we're not going to let a little water stop us."

"It's more than a little, sir. I don't know where Lieutenant Harvey is, but there's a sheriff's car right up the road. I can check with them. If they say it's okay to let you through, then I guess it is. But I can't do it on my own."

They were allowed to crawl along the road for fifty yards, when they were again stopped by a massive figure in a black raincoat and uniform cap with a dripping brim.

"Sorry, sir. No traffic allowed. Didn't the Guard tell you?"

"Who is it? Pat McDuff? This is Sy Salvetti."

There was an immediate, even unexpected, interest.

"Yes, Sy, what's up?"

Sy told him. "So Wally wants us to meet him on this side of the creek—we want, at least, to be able to tell my daughter-in-law that the baby's all right. Or, if he isn't, to get him and Wally over so we can get medical help for the baby."

McDuff bent over to peer in the window. "She with you? Wally's wife?"

"No, she's back at our place. But she's anxious, you know."

"Sure. Well, if she's there with your wife, she's safe enough

165

then." There was an oddly personal note to his voice, Sy thought, but he was concerned only with his errand. "All right. Go ahead, but keep it slow. Little John's over its banks, and the bridges are impassible. If Wally thinks the baby needs to be gotten out, let us know and we'll handle it. Don't try to cross by yourselves, we don't want any more casualties."

"Had some already?" Sy asked. He was eager to be gone, Wally would be waiting, but this cop was an influential one and they might need his help.

"Oh, yes. Flooding's bad the entire west side of the county—good thing we've got an ocean to dump it into. If we only had a way to dump it faster we'd be okay."

The men all laughed, and Sy pulled ahead, seeing the headlights of his son's car following behind.

Within a few minutes they saw why the River Road was being closed to traffic. Black water licked at the paving and, in a few low places, flowed across it into a well-filled ditch on the other side of the road.

"For God's sake," Connie's husband Charlie said from the back seat, "how are we going to know when we're at the bridge? You can't tell anything with all that water over everything."

"Kay said Wally had a flashlight. He'll be watching for us," Sy said.

"There! There, someone's signaling from the other side right now."

"He's yelling something," Sy said. "Wait'll I turn off the motor so maybe we can hear."

It was not until both cars, lights still cutting weakly through the night, had been silenced that they could make out Wally's shouted words.

"Dad! Get the police! Denny's been kidnapped!"

"But I gotta get through," the kid said. "I have to take my girl home or her folks will kill us both."

"Sorry, fella," McDuff told him. "There's no way you can get through. There's water over the road. I suggest you find a girl friend to leave her with, or take her home with you. This is one time her folks are going to have to be broadminded."

"But there isn't even any place to turn around," the kid said. He was only about sixteen, probably hadn't had his license for more than a few months.

Andy Sleder materialized out of the gloom. "If you can't back that thing up, boy, you got no business being out with it."

"Back it up all the way back to town?" the kid asked, but he was already shifting into reverse.

The two officers, large and small, looked at one another in the glow of the headlights. All vehicular lights seemed subdued tonight, filtering through the god-awful weather.

"Well, you seen enough, Mac? The Guard's got it under control, so far as traffic's concerned."

"Yeah. We're fools to be out here when we're officially off duty, I suppose. But . . ."

Mac left the words dangling. . . . But Bill VonDorn, who ought to be in charge, was pickling his brains and nobody knew whether he was capable of making a rational decision or not. Maybe in the morning—but at this time of night it was doubtful. And as long as Witwer knew he was out and around, it would be McDuff he'd turn to for orders, not VonDorn.

"Come on, let's get in out of the wet. We'll check in with Witwer and see what the overall situation is; maybe we can go home."

"Right. I can't wait to slide into bed with that nice warm

167

little woman," Sleder said. "I feel like my feet are froze clear to my ass."

Up the road the glowing taillights suddenly blossomed with white centers as the backup lights came on.

"Salvetti's coming back. Maybe we better wait and see if they found young Wally all right," McDuff said. "We can't get much colder anyway."

He was thinking about the flooding, which after all was a more or less routine problem. They had flooding to some degree every few years, and three times in McDuff's seventeen years with the department it had been major flooding. He'd been relieved when Salvetti said his daughter-in-law was safe at his own place. He hadn't taken time to do anything with the list of names, names of people Jory had threatened when he was sentenced. Not that he really thought anything was going to happen, but he didn't want it on his conscience if it did.

He was not prepared for Sy Salvetti's agitated voice and frightened face when the brake lights flared and the vehicles rolled to a stop.

"Lieutenant McDuff—we need help! Wally says the baby's gone, he's been kidnapped. There was a note, nothing about ransom, just that he has the baby—Jory. That Russell Jory!"

Oh, Christ.

McDuff remembered the first time he'd been kicked, with vicious intent, in the balls.

He felt somewhat the same way right now. "Jory," he said aloud.

"And the girl's gone with him, Donna Malloy. She was baby-sitting. And Casey's pickup is in the yard, too, and there's blood and broken glass in the kitchen, and Wally's standing back there waiting—"

Sy sounded as if he were about to cry.

And Donna Malloy, too. Beside McDuff, Sleder muttered something profane.

"Okay," McDuff said. "Okay. You back up there, another quarter of a mile and you can turn around and get out of the way. We'll handle it. Andy—"

"I'll check in with Witwer," Sleder said. "We're going to need some help."

And that, McDuff thought bleakly, was the understatement of the century.

Why didn't they come? Or call, or something?

It was over an hour now. The coffee steamed in the big pot, the sandwiches sat under their plastic wrappings, waiting.

The women waited, too. Jeanette flipped on the big color TV, hesitating at the station carrying a late movie.

"Not that," Connie said quickly, and Kay knew why. The story involved a couple who had lost a young child to leukemia.

Denny didn't have leukemia. In all likelihood he was only cutting teeth, and tomorrow he'd be fine. While Wally would be lucky not to have pneumonia, wading through that water up to his waist. That was probably why it was taking so long; he'd been cold and wet and he'd have changed into dry clothes and got out his rain gear before he came back to the creek.

Jeanette switched to another channel and got the tail end of an announcement about the National Guard. "Must be worse than we thought if they're calling out the Guard. But we know Wally got across the creek all right; he'll see to Denny. Kay, why don't you sit down and rest? You look ready to collapse."

She was, but it made her nervous just to sit. "Maybe they'll have to get the Guard to help. They can get someone across even if it's flooded, can't they?"

"Sure," Connie said soothingly. "Is that the news? Leave it on, sis, let's see what's happening."

"This is a special bulletin brought to you by KSIX," the announcer said. The kids had monkeyed with the controls and the color was out of adjustment; he was a seasick pale green. "Motorists are urged to stay off the roads. All rivers in the area are at or near flood stage, and many secondary roads are underwater. National Guard troops are evacuating families along the banks of the Big Bend and the Hupa, particularly in the Salmon Creek flats area; the Red Cross has set up emergency quarters for the evacuees in the Municipal Auditorium. Highway One-oh-one is passable, but is covered with water to the depth of about a foot at the North Shore underpass south of the city. Sergeant Witwer of the County Sheriff's Department requests that travel be restricted to emergency vehicles only. Telephone service is out in several areas, and it is also asked that use of remaining equipment be for police and National Guard so far as is possible.

"Our reporter Phil Drummond reports major problems in the Horseshoe Road area, and there is no, repeat *no*, through traffic either there or on the River Road. We don't yet have the full story on the emergency, but we understand that sheriff's deputies are on the spot and that reinforcements have been called for. We will bring you that story as soon as we have details. And now, back to our late-night movie, *The Monster from the—*"

The screen went blank and Jeanette drew back from it. Her two oldest, Gary and Cathy, uttered protesting shrieks. "Hey, Ma, let us watch the monster movie!"

"Go watch on the set upstairs," Jeanette said. Her face was troubled. She was ten years older than Connie, the missing link between her sister and her mother, pretty, but putting on weight through the breasts and hips. She turned away from the set, but Kay forced herself to speak.

"Let them watch. If there's a newscast we'll want to see it, anyway. They said something was wrong in the Horseshoe area. Maybe we'll find out what's keeping our men."

Connie shot her a quick glance and concurred. "Leave it on low, Jeanette. Kay's right. We want to know what's happening. You may have to move into town for a few days, Kay. Until the water goes down."

"Plenty of room here," Angela said, shifting her bulk in one of the recliners. "We still have the crib in the front bedroom upstairs."

Kay didn't reply. What were the major problems the announcer had been talking about? Surely they didn't consider it a major problem that the Horseshoe loop was cut off; that had happened several times within her memory. People who lived in the country kept a good supply of food and fuel; it wasn't really an emergency to be cut off for a few days, not unless someone was seriously ill.

Wally would surely be here before long. And there was no

reason to think Denny was seriously ill. He'd run a fever before, several times, and it hadn't lasted long.

Still, she'd feel better when she knew for sure. The kids sat on the floor in front of the television, avid attention upon the monster movie, and she tried to let it engage her own thoughts. Yet all she could think of was Wally, wading that black and swollen creek, and how long it was taking him to get Denny and bring him out.

McDuff stood on the creek bank, shouting across to the sodden figure on the far side. He had a pretty good idea how Wally Salvetti must be feeling, yet the man was controlling himself well. No outward panic, only an urgent plea for help and a readiness to do whatever should be required of him.

"Anything to indicate how long ago Jory was there? At your place?"

"No." Wally threw his voice into the wind. "Nothing. We left the house about six-thirty; it could have happened anytime after that. Young Case's truck is there, though. Maybe his family will know when *he* went over; that might give us a clue."

"Okay. Well, there's no telling whether or not Jory's still on the loop, or if he got over the creek before the bridge went under. He may still be trapped somewhere on the loop. We can't get a helicopter in there in the dark and with this wind, but we've got a man rounding up a rubber life raft from one of the Guard rescue units. I think we can get across to you. Are any of those trees sturdy enough to tie a line to?"

"Yes. I'll secure it if you get one across," Wally replied.

"Okay. Hold on, we'll get to you as soon as we can." McDuff turned away from the dark figure illuminated by the headlights of two vehicles. There was no time to waste on sympathy, no time to consider his own guilt in this mess. Two young Guardsmen met him with serious faces, ready to help. "Can you get a line across to him?"

"Yes, sir. Right away," one of them said, and he left them to it. Andy Sleder loomed up beside him. "I'm going across as soon as they get that damned raft here," McDuff told him. "I

172

want a man to go with me, and the shotgun out of the squad car."

"I'm going with you," Sleder said. "Let's take every gun in the goddamned county, and this time blow the son of a bitch out of the water."

They strode toward the black-and-white, McDuff reaching for the hand mike before he'd even closed the door.

"Yes, Lieutenant," Witwer's voice responded.

McDuff cleared his throat. "Jory has the Malloy girl and the Salvetti baby. He may be trapped on the Horseshoe loop, or he may have gotten them out ahead of the flood. Put out an APB on him. We don't know about the vehicle he's driving, but it may be a light blue Pinto registered to Donna Malloy. Andy and I are going across the creek as soon as they get us a raft, and I'll want a lab crew at the Salvetti house as soon as it's feasible to get them over there. In the meantime, I want every officer I can get. Roadblocks both ends of the county and on Chilton Pass. Notify the CHP and the city police, and pass the word to the Guard—no heroics if they spot him, just let us know. He's a killer, so let's not give him a chance to practice. If you can, get a squad car at each end of the River Road. Phones are out on the loop, so you won't be able to reach us once we cross, but I want everybody in the county watching for him. And you'd better get onto that list you got from Judge Verland—contact them all. Chances are he won't be going after anyone else while he has the girl and the baby, but get to them, anyway. I'll check in with you before we take to the water, maybe ten minutes."

It was closer to fifteen minutes before the line was secured between trees on opposite banks of Little John Creek and the yellow life raft ready to go. They would have used life jackets if there had been any handy, but McDuff refused to wait for them to be brought. Even minutes might count.

Witwer came on the air immediately, sounding different. "We were too late, Lieutenant. When there was no answer at Judge Verland's I requested a check by a city patrol car. They just called in."

McDuff waited, his bulk filling the front seat of the car, while Sleder crouched on the far side of it, listening.

"They're both dead. Shotgun, close range. Both the judge and Mrs. Verland."

McDuff thumbed the mike. "Okay. I read you. Get to the rest of them. I'll leave one of the kids from the Guard on the radio."

"Ten-four," Witwer said, and Mac replaced the mike.

"Okay," he told Sleder. "Let's go after the fucking bastard."

"Lieutenant! Wait a minute!" The tall figure dodged between vehicles, running to the edge of the creek as they clambered into the raft while a pair of guardsmen attempted to hold it steady. "What's going on out there? Is it true? There's been a kidnapping?"

"I don't know yet what there's been," McDuff said. "And if there *has* been a kidnapping, we don't want it on the air. Not yet. Wait until we know something, and we'll give you the story. But don't endanger any possible victims by a premature report, Drummond." He waved a hand, and the Guardsmen released the bobbing little craft, playing out the rope that was attached to it.

Phillip Drummond stood looking after them in frustration. The flood was always a story in this country. KSIX would report on it in detail. But a kidnapping was something big; they'd carry it on the network stations; it could go nation-wide.

He watched the receding raft with the hulking figures in it, squinting to see who waited on the far side to meet them. "Who is it? Who's been kidnapped?"

Nobody answered, and Drummond swung around to yet another Guardsman. This one was very young and excited, and Drummond edged him off to one side.

"Who was that over there?"

"Wally Salvetti," the kid said. "Jeeze, it must be terrible to have your kid taken by a guy like that."

Drummond's voice sharpened. "A guy like what? Who? Who is it?"

"Jory, they said. Remember him? Jory?"

175

Drummond's whistle held its own element of excitement. "Russell William Jory? No kidding, is that who it is?"

"They said Jory," the kid replied. "Hey, look, what are you—?"

But it was too late. Drummond was already gone.

"I can't go any farther," Casey said, the strain showing in his voice. "The lane ends right here, and this car wasn't designed to drive across fields. Especially after the kind of rain we've had the past few days. We'll sink out of sight."

Jory's breath was warm on the back of Casey's neck. "What's out there? Ain't that some kind of building?"

"It's an abandoned barn. The roof's fallen in, it's no shelter. And the lane doesn't go past it. There's just grazing land beyond it, and hills. It's miles out on foot, if that's what you're thinking. You'll never make it. Not with a sick baby and a girl who can't see where she's going. Why don't you just go back—"

A vicious jab from the gun barrel brought his words to a halt. "When I want your advice, I'll ask for it, and I ain't asked yet. Go on, drive up to the barn."

"I told you—"

"Drive," Jory said through his teeth.

Casey swallowed audibly and wondered if he'd get a bullet through the head if the car bogged down. It wasn't a road, it was only a grassy lane, and holding all the water that it did now, it was greasy and slippery. The Pinto slid sideways; he gunned it and overcompensated, grazing the fence on one side of the lane before he could straighten it out. And then he was through the gate and moving on the tufted pasture; he braked beside the barn.

It could hardly have been called a structure anymore. It had scarcely any roof left, and only parts of the walls, which leaned away from the prevailing winds. He'd been intending to tear it down and use the lumber for something else, but it was one of the things he hadn't gotten around to.

"Now what?"

"Get out," Jory said. There was a savagery in his voice that

177

brooked no argument. "Turn off the lights and give me the keys."

Silently, Casey obeyed.

They climbed out into the wet darkness. Denny began to whimper again when Jory passed him over to Casey, and Casey patted him reassuringly. "It's okay, fella," he said, and wondered what good it did to make such a clearly false statement. He doubted that it even soothed the baby, let alone anyone else.

Jory brought out his flashlight and swung its beam across the tumbledown barn. The weathered wood was nearly black in its wetness; a door hung crazily ajar on one hinge, and he reached out with the hand holding the flash to pull it open.

It opened into a small lean-to, more nearly intact than the main part of the barn. There was a little moldy hay on the dirt floor, and the roof offered some shelter. Jory stood aside and gestured them ahead of him.

Donna stumbled over the sill, going in, and fell to her knees. Jory planted a foot on her behind and shoved her the rest of the way in; she sprawled against her already injured hands.

Jory's light swung in Casey's direction. "Take off your belt, and fasten her to that stanchion, or whatever it is. Hands behind her back."

The diaper bag had slid off Donna's arm; Casey stepped on it, moving after her, and it slithered to one side. Denny continued to emit an unhappy wail.

"Shut that kid up," Jory said.

For a few seconds there was no sound but Denny's plaintive voice and the drumming of rain on what remained of the roof.

"How do you suggest we do that?" Casey asked quietly. "He's sick, and he's tired. Let Donna take him back to the house."

Donna listened as profanity rolled off Jory's tongue, corrosive as acid. The roving light showed Denny's small tear-stained face, and for a moment Donna's own predicament took second place to his.

Jory was a madman. He was quite capable of killing a small child because he cried. His milk, she thought, maybe he'd take some of the milk. Maybe it would quiet him.

She groped for the diaper bag. The milk was cold, of course, but maybe that wouldn't matter too much. She knew Denny was learning to drink out of a cup; she'd seen it in the

178

dishwasher, one of those weighted ones that don't tip over when the baby sets it down. So probably Kay didn't heat the milk she put into his cup.

Her fingers trembled—with fear? or cold?—so that it was all she could do to get the cap off the bottle. Since Jory was flashing the light around the walls of the lean-to, she worked virtually in the dark. Casey stood, hands at his sides; she saw them clench and then deliberately relax, and knew he was as helpless as she was.

Denny made a hiccuping sob, and Donna drew him close to her on the moldering hay. It wasn't actually wet, but the dampness of it worked through her jeans as she knelt on it.

She forced herself to concentrate on her small charge, to suppress the terror that threatened to overwhelm her. The immediate need was to calm Jory, to keep him from killing anyone because the baby cried.

To her relief, Denny sucked hungrily on the plastic nipple. She cradled him against her, blinking when the light suddenly swung toward her.

"What're you doing?"

"Giving him a bottle." Her voice wavered, but at least this time she'd managed to speak. "He's hungry."

Jory stared down at them, then made a movement toward his jacket pocket that sent her adrenaline surging again. It wasn't a weapon he produced, however, but a capsule. "Take the top off it. Dump this in it."

Uncomprehending, for a moment she did nothing.

"What is it?" Casey asked.

"Something to shut him up," Jory said. "Here, you do it. Take the thing apart, and dump the stuff in the milk."

Donna and Casey stared at one another in the half-light.

"If that's an adult dose, it's too much for a baby," Casey said slowly. "It could kill him."

"Listen, you fucking jerk," Jory said, and there was no mistaking the menace in his tone. "I had a bellyful of you. I ain't going to keep making threats, I'm just going to shoot you."

Silent now, Casey reached for the bottle and then the capsule Jory tossed to him. There was no way of getting close enough to get past that shotgun, and no way he could avoid following orders. He tried to spill some of the minute particles that were inside the capsule, but he didn't dare spill enough so that it would be obvious. God knew what it was, or

179

how dangerous, but it couldn't be much worse than Jory with a gun in his hands.

Denny had begun to cry again when the bottle was taken from him. He accepted it when it was passed back, unaware of the additive.

There was no sound except the baby, sucking, and the rain on the shingled roof. And once more the fear invaded Donna's mind, insidious, crippling.

She tried to pray, but she couldn't even do that. The warmth of Denny's small body began to come through to her; she held him, and she waited.

"I found it this way," Wally said. His face was white under the kitchen fluorescents, and his hand shook as he moved it across the lower part of his face. "There's Denny's handprint on the counter. He's hurt."

McDuff stepped carefully around the broken glass, and looked down at the note, and the tiny handprint beside it.

"Probably a superficial cut; maybe he crawled into the glass. Any sign Jory was in any other part of the house?"

"I think he came in through a window in the study. It was jimmied open, only the door was locked into the front hall from there. And when I got here the back door was standing wide open, so maybe—I don't know. He—he was upstairs. All the stuff out of the medicine chest is dumped into the sink. Like he was looking for something."

"Oh?" McDuff looked at him thoughtfully. "You know what was in there? Could you tell what might be missing?"

Wally made an effort to pull himself together. "There couldn't be a mistake, could there? I mean, I thought this Jory was serving a life sentence—"

"He's out on parole," the big cop told him. "Since day before yesterday. Or I guess it's the day before that, now. See if you can tell what he took from the medicine chest, will you? Andy will go up with you."

"We didn't keep much of anything," Wally said. "No drugs. You think he was looking for drugs?"

"Could have been." He wasn't known to be a junkie, though. "What about the pickup out there? Who's it belong to?"

"Casey. Stan Case, lives on the next place down."

"Okay. We'll check with everybody on the loop. How many are there? Half a dozen families?"

"Four, besides us. The Roberts brothers, the Cases, and the Lindquists."

181

"We'll talk to all of them. One of them may know something. It would help to know if he's on this side of the creek or if he got out. As soon as it's daylight and we get some extra help in here, we'll search everything. The houses, the outbuildings. It would help if you'd make a sketch for Andy, show the houses, the barns, everything."

"Daylight?" Wally echoed. "But that—that's hours away."

"I'm sorry," McDuff said. "But in the dark, in a storm like this—chances are we couldn't see anything, couldn't find anything, even if we had the manpower to do it now. Which we don't. We're calling in our reserves, but with the flooding we need a lot of them to rescue people in outlying areas, and there will be trouble with traffic on the roads, too. Soon as we can see, though, we'll have searchers out if we have to pull in the fellows from the college, the police science students. Wherever Jory went, he's left a trail of some sort." He thought bleakly of Judge Verland and his wife, and hoped the rest of the trail wouldn't be as bloody. But Salvetti didn't know about the Verlands. "We'll find him."

"Why did he take Denny?" Wally asked. "What did he hope to gain by taking our baby? He didn't leave a ransom note—" He stared at the impassive face of the redheaded officer. "You don't think he took Denny for ransom, do you?"

"No point in guessing about that," McDuff said, and turned away, squatting to read the story in shattered glass and drops of blood. He'd have the lab boys in here, but he knew the lab wasn't going to be the answer on this one. It wouldn't matter whose blood was on the counter, and whose spattered on the note the Malloy girl had written.

What would matter was whether they could get to Jory before he killed them both. And maybe Case, too, if he were with them.

"He's taken Denny," Wally said, and his voice cracked so that he had to start over again. "He took Denny to get even with Kay for testifying against him, didn't he? He doesn't intend to ask for money to give him back. He doesn't intend to give him back."

McDuff stood up and faced him, then. "Possibly. But I will make a guess, after all. I'll bet he won't do anything before he knows that your wife is aware of the situation, Mr. Salvetti. I'll bet he wants to make her suffer, and until he can be sure she knows he has the baby, he won't do anything. I'll bet even further than that—I'll bet he'll want to see her, to talk to her. And if he makes a move in that direction, we've got a good chance of getting your baby back."

Wally wanted to believe that, but he couldn't, quite. "But he has Denny as a hostage. You couldn't—shoot him, or anything. Not while he has Denny."

"I have at least fifteen men," McDuff told him very softly, "who can put a bullet between his eyes at two hundred yards. Even if he's holding the baby. Without hurting your son. But we'll face that when we come to it. Let's find out what the neighbors know, if anything. That'll put us a little closer to knowing what we have to do."

Wally stared after the two officers as they walked out of the kitchen, checking out the rest of the house. Shoot him? While he was holding Denny?

Oh, God. Oh, God, what was he going to tell Kay? *How* was he going to tell her? Maybe Sy had gone back to the house already, maybe she already knew, and she'd need him, she'd need him worse than she had ever needed anybody, and he wasn't there.

The pain in his throat was so terrible that he thought he could die from it. He stood there, carefully not touching any of the broken glass, and listened to the men moving about in the other room, and thought about Denny, and Kay.

Something was wrong. Something *had* to be wrong, or Wally would have come by now. Kay looked at her watch, the beautiful watch Wally had given her for her birthday last year, in celebration, too, of the birth of their son.

Sy and the rest of them had been gone for two hours. Which meant it was two and a half hours since she'd left Wally on the creek bank.

Why didn't someone come? No matter what was wrong, why didn't they let her know?

The monster movie had ended. Jeanette prodded at her son with the toe of a silver slipper. "Okay. You kids go up to Gram's room and stretch out on her bed. You've been up late enough."

"When we going home?" Cathy asked, and then shot a look at Kay. "Are we going to stay until Uncle Wally gets here with Denny? How much longer will he be?"

"We don't know. Go on, go get some sleep."

"There's coats all over Gram's bed," Cathy protested.

"Then move them."

"I don't want to go to bed with *him*."

Her brother rolled over and sat up, twisting his face into a sneer. "I don't want to go to bed with *her,* either."

"It's a king-sized bed, and you can each have plenty of room without touching each other. There's an afghan in the closet, you can cover up with that. Now don't argue."

They got up, squabbling, shoving one another, but too tired to work up to anything much. Kay sat dully, her apathetic gaze on the screen. She shouldn't have left Wally out there, she should have driven to the nearest house and called, and then gone back to wait for him. Surely Sy had made contact with him by this time. So what was wrong?

The announcer's face came on the screen, adjusted to a

warmer shade, a soft magenta. He was a good-looking young man with hair that looked marcelled. He leaned forward, as if to come in closer contact with his viewers.

"Good evening. This is Phillip Drummond of the KSIX news staff, bringing you a late news report. Because of the emergency situation in Redwood County tonight, we will be staying on the air past our usual sign-off time, and we will continue to bring you bulletins as the news comes in."

The waiting women all stirred in their chairs. Kay's lethargy was gone. If something major had happened maybe he'd tell them what it was.

"Virtually all rivers of Redwood County west of the mountains are in flood stage tonight, and we will have reports on specific areas where law enforcement agencies and the National Guard are evacuating those whose homes are in danger from the flood waters. First, however, we have news of serious import to our North Bend area viewers."

The handsome face became more intense, and again he leaned into the camera.

"This reporter has learned that Russell William Jory, who was convicted in this county seven and a half years ago of murder and rape, was paroled from San Quentin earlier this week."

For a moment the name had no impact, and then Connie gasped. Kay paused in the act of brushing back her hair, frozen except that her hand slid slowly down until it covered her mouth.

"Sheriff's department spokesmen refuse to comment on the situation at this time," Drummond continued, "but there is speculation that Jory is involved in the dual slayings of a prominent North Bend judge and his wife earlier this evening, and in the kidnapping of two and possibly three county residents, including a small child. The names of the victims are being withheld pending notification of their families, but we will bring you all details as soon as they are available.

"And now Tom Stokes will fill us in on the flood situation—"

The anguished cry torn from Kay's throat covered the following words. She started to rise, her eyes wide and distraught, and then slumped back in the chair, gasping. Not Denny! Not her precious Denny! Oh, God, no!

She was surrounded by shocked white faces. It was Jeanette

who spoke first, reaching out with her hand to turn down the volume, then moving toward her sister-in-law with a choked cry. "He didn't say it was Denny, Kay!"

Kay lifted glazed blue eyes in which tears were beginning to form, and her quiet words were more painful than if she'd screamed them. "But it is Denny," she said, and then dropped her face forward into her hands and wept.

"They left here a little after midnight," Geneva Case said. Her stunned eyes moved from the two police officers, the tall one and the smaller one, and then to young Wally Salvetti who looked like death warmed over. "The baby was sick, had a high fever. Casey was going to take the girl to her mother's. But they never got there?"

"The bridges are both out," McDuff told her. "So they probably went back to the Salvetti house because they couldn't cross the creek. Which means they're probably still somewhere on the loop. Where could they hide?"

Mrs. Case licked her lips. "There isn't much of any place. I mean, everybody's home, I think, and there's only the five houses. Of course everybody's got barns and chicken houses and the like, but you wouldn't think anybody'd want to hole up in those, this kind of weather."

"How—how sick was Denny, Mrs. Case?" Wally asked with an effort.

"Well, his temperature was about one-oh-five. He was real fussy, but I don't think it was dangerous. I remember Casey running a fever that way once or twice. But the girl wanted to get him to a doctor."

And now the baby was out there somewhere, maybe cold and wet. Nobody said it, though everybody thought it. But the weather was the least of Denny Salvetti's problems.

Geneva Case curled her fingers around the edge of her bathrobe, pulling it closer to her neck. "And you think some man kidnapped them? All three of them? I don't think Casey would be an easy one to do that with."

"It's Jory," Wally said. His eyes were becoming red-rimmed. "Russell Jory. He said he'd get even with them all, everybody who had anything to do with sending him to prison—he's hitting at Kay through Denny—"

"Jory!" The woman took a step backward, as though she'd

been dealt a blow. She didn't read the newspapers much, they were all too depressing, but she remembered that name, all right. Couldn't hardly forget it, the way the trial had gone on for weeks and everybody talking about it. But mostly, of course, she remembered the night those two poor girls had staggered in here, bleeding, crying, after what that man had done to them. "But they put him in jail—he escaped from jail?"

Nobody answered. McDuff started to run away. "We'll check with your neighbors, make sure none of them saw or heard anything suspicious. Is it all right with you if we search all your outbuildings?"

"Yes, yes, of course. There's the milk barn, and the hay barn—and the chicken house, and a toolshed, but it's not big enough for much—I'm here all alone, officer, except for my granddaughter. She's only seven."

"Lock all your doors and windows. Leave your yard lights on. Chances are he won't come here, but play it safe. Don't let anyone in unless he identifies himself. Our men will do that, or the National Guard."

She felt bereft when they had gone. Dear heaven, what would she do if anything serious happened to Casey?

She didn't know much about firearms. But her husband and son both hunted, and Casey had a target pistol. She didn't suppose any of the guns were loaded, and she wasn't sure she remembered how they did it, but she trudged toward the bedroom to get them.

If that Jory showed up here, she'd do what she had to do.

Only what about Casey? That girl and that poor baby, and Casey. Lord God, she thought, don't let anything bad happen to my Casey.

They found the abandoned Volkswagen, nosed into the ditch. Andy Sleder noted the license number, to be checked out as soon as they got back to the radio.

"Could be one Jory stole," he observed. "No blood in it, anyway, that I can see. Maybe he didn't shoot this guy."

"If it was Jory's, that means he and Case and the girl and the baby left in Donna Malloy's car. A light blue Pinto. That right, Mr. Salvetti?"

"Yes," Wally confirmed. "What are we going to do now, Lieutenant?"

"There's not much we can do until daylight, I'm afraid. None of the Horseshoe residents saw or heard anything suspicious, and there's no way of tracking in the dark, even if the rain hadn't already washed out tire tracks. If they were trapped by the water, they may have taken to the hills. If they did, we'll find them. We're going back and I'd suggest you come with us. Your wife will need you, and there's nothing you can do here anyway."

Wally's throat worked. "I—I can't go back to Kay without Denny."

McDuff touched one massive fist to the younger man's shoulder. "Come on. You've done all you could, you're wet and tired, and getting wetter and tireder won't help. Your dad's still waiting for you, and if you get some rest you might be of some use to us come daylight."

They moved together, then, not speaking. Kay, Wally thought. How could he tell Kay?

She already knew. Her slim body, held so rigidly in control, crumpled against him when he walked through the front door. Her fingers dug into his arms, even through his jacket, demanding something he didn't have to give.

"Is it true?" Angela asked over her daughter-in-law's blond head. "That Jory? He has Denny?"

Wally tried to speak and could not. His wetness was soaking into Kay's clothing, but he couldn't disentangle himself. They clung together, drowning, unable to save themselves.

"That's what the note said," Sy told the circle of white faces. "Jory said he had him. The Malloy girl is missing, too, and young Case from the next farm." He shed rain gear and for once Angela paid no attention to the drip on her carpet. "God, get us something to drink, and get Wally out of those clothes—he'll have pneumonia for sure. Kay, honey, don't—"

She didn't appear to hear him. Tears streaked her pretty face as she lifted it to Wally's suffering gaze. "He'll never give him back. Never. He's taken him for revenge."

Wally struggled through the pain to produce something affirmative, however small. "Lieutenant McDuff doesn't think he'll harm him, not without knowing for sure that you're aware Jory has him. He thinks Jory will want to see you, and he says when that happens, they'll—they'll get him."

Hands moved around them, drawing off Wally's wet clothes, urging drinks on them. Kay brushed them all aside, still attempting to cling to her husband. "I shouldn't have left him home tonight, I should have stayed with him—"

"Honey, it wouldn't have made any difference. Then he'd have taken both of you," Wally pointed out. "Kay, please, drink whatever that is Ma has—"

"I don't want it," Kay said. "I want my baby, I want Denny!"

Sy spoke quietly to his wife. "Maybe you better call the doctor. Give her a shot and knock her out or something."

"No!" Kay's voice rose, tinged with hysteria. "You can't put me to sleep so I won't know what's happening! What are the police doing to find Denny?"

Sy put a hand on her shoulder. "They're doing everything they can, Kay. Honest to God. They've got roadblocks all over the county, and in the morning, as soon as it's light, they'll have cops crawling all over the place, and they'll find them."

"In the morning?" She stared at him, wild-eyed. "When it's light? What about now? What are they doing right now? Is

190

everybody just going to bed and forget about it until daylight?"

"Nobody's forgetting about it," Sy assured her. "But going to bed and getting some rest is sensible. They told Wally he wouldn't be of any use to them unless he did. He's exhausted, Kay, he can't keep on going even if there was anything to do, not if he plans to walk all over the hills tomorrow with the police. Don't make it harder for him by having hysterics, girl. We know how you feel, we all feel the same way, but let's be as practical as we can."

Kay stared at him, hating him, hating them all. Even Wally. Wally wouldn't have gone out without her tonight, so she'd had to leave Denny, and Jory found him—

The unfairness of that hit her like a blow, a blow that at least partially restored her sanity. No, don't blame Wally. It wasn't his fault any more than it was hers, and there was no doubting his agony matched her own.

She began to cry again, but this time she wasn't noisy about it. Tears washed down her face, unchecked, and she didn't bother to try to wipe them away.

When Angela put something to her mouth she drank, not caring one way or the other what it was. She didn't remember being helped up the stairs to the front bedroom—the one with the crib—and was only vaguely aware when Angela unzipped her dress.

"I'll do it, Ma," Wally said, and they were left alone. The two of them, when there should have been three, and in Angela's house, not their own.

Wally's fingers were icy on her flesh, but she didn't care about that, either. Her new dress was tossed carelessly over the back of a chair, her shoes dropped where they fell.

The bed was cold and unfamiliar; she was shaking and she couldn't stop. Wally bent over her, brushing her forehead with his lips. "I'll be back in just a minute, honey. I'm going to take a hot shower, or I'll never get over the chill. I won't be a minute."

She lay, rigid as a board, listening to the rushing water across the hall, hearing the subdued voices and then the car doors slamming out front. They were going home, all the others. Home, to their safe warm houses, their families intact, their children safe. Home to sleep, and probably to thank God it wasn't any of their babies who'd been taken.

Denny. Denny. The anguish cut through her with the searing quality of flame. Where was he? Had Jory already killed him, left his tiny body somewhere along the road? No, no, it couldn't happen that way. God wouldn't let things happen that way, not to a little baby. He wouldn't.

He let things like that happen all the time. An icy, rational part of her mind told her that. Every day, babies died. Some of them were killed in accidents and some of them died of illness, and some of them were murdered. Every day.

Not Denny. Oh, please, not Denny.

The running water stopped. Downstairs a door slammed.

Jory. Russell William Jory. Why had they let him out of prison? How could they not have known that what he had done once, he would do again?

Rage against those unknown officials responsible for Jory's release made hot inroads in the chill that had enveloped her for the past several hours. How would they like it if *their* families were kidnapped, killed?

Jory had killed a judge and his wife. Judge Verland, it had to be Judge Verland, the man he had threatened in the courtroom. Kay hadn't liked Judge Verland; he seemed to her a cold and unsympathetic man, although when the time had come he had commended the jury for their verdict and had imposed the strongest sentence within his power to order.

Life. Life, and it had been less than eight years, and they'd set the madman free to kidnap and to kill. He'd killed the Verlands. What had he done to Denny?

Wally padded across the room, wrapped in one of his father's robes, which strained across his shoulders and chest and barely met at the front. He dropped it on the floor and slid into bed beside her, reaching up for the light switch.

Unlike their bedroom at home, it wasn't completely dark when the lights were turned off. There was a light on the corner that filtered through the shades.

The bed was crowded; they'd forgotten how small an ordinary double bed was, after their years in a larger one.

Kay didn't move. She might have been made of stone as Wally put a hand on her stomach and moved it upward. "Try to sleep, honey. Ma's going to wake me at six, and I'll join the police as soon as it's light enough to see anything. We'll find him."

She said nothing. He curled his arm around her body, drawing her closer to him, resting his cheek against her hair.

"Kay," he said. The need to evoke some response from her was strong.

"He might already be dead," Kay said unexpectedly, her voice choked. "My baby might already be dead."

In the silence they heard a car go past on the street, and then Wally told her very softly, "He's my baby, too, Kay. Don't shut me out. We both love him, and we're both afraid. But it's worse to go it alone. Let me in, let me share it, whatever it's going to be."

For a few terrible seconds she seemed to stiffen even further; and then, with a broken cry, Kay turned and pressed against him.

Wally held her while she cried, and after a time her breathing quieted and she slept in his arms, her breath warm on his cheek.

He almost wished he'd taken some of whatever his mother had given to her, so that he could sleep, too. But he was afraid it might make him groggy and stupid, barbiturates often did that, and he needed to be alert in the morning.

He had to help them find Denny.

The Fitzpatricks heard it on the 6 A.M. news.

Sara sat frozen to her chair in horror, her meal forgotten. It wasn't an impossible nightmare, it was true. Jory had come back, and he had killed people, and kidnapped a little boy and those others.

Tim, too, forgot his breakfast, although he'd already eaten most of it before the news came on. His mouth flattened, and his head nodded almost imperceptibly. He had known it. He'd expected it.

And he was ready for Jory.

He got up from the table and began to pull on his barn boots over two pair of heavy socks.

Sara's words emerged jerkily, a squawk of protest. "Where are you going? What do you think you're going to do?"

"I'm going to help search," Tim told her heavily. "They're looking for that baby and the girl."

Fear was a smothering blanket. "But that's what the police are for, let them do it!"

He pulled on the second boot and straightened, facing her. There was a light in his eyes that made her catch her breath. "For crissake, woman, didn't you hear it? There's a major flood going on, and the cops and the Guard are all out there trying to save people's lives. It would take all the cops they got for a job like this, even if there wasn't no flood. They'll need volunteers."

"No. No," Sara said. "They didn't ask for volunteers. It's a job—" She stopped, unwilling to say *for young men,* and groped for a different ending to her sentence. "For professionals. You might get hurt."

"You think I care about that? To get the man that killed Larry, you think I'd sit home warm and dry on my backside while somebody else does it? I don't care about anything else but getting him."

194

Sara seemed to shrink inside her skin. *Care about me,* she wanted to cry, but the words refused to be spoken.

Tim pulled on a jacket and then the rain suit that covered everything but his hands and face. He picked up the thirty-aught-six.

At the last minute he turned back and stooped to kiss her awkwardly on the forehead. "I got to go," he said.

Sara continued to sit at the table after he had gone, her hands clenched in her lap. Maybe they'd send him home. The police couldn't want him, a middle-aged man with a bad foot. She hoped he wouldn't do anything foolish if they told him to go home.

It had been a long time since she'd cared passionately about anything. She could see it now. They hadn't even tried to start living again after Larry died. They'd gone through the motions, but they hadn't cared about anything. They'd stopped going to church, or having people over for dinner or an evening of cards. Tim had even lost interest in the farm that had been his pride and joy, next to Larry. It was a small place, because a farm was a lot of work and it didn't pay enough to live on, so he just had what he could take care of and work at the mill, too. And when one of the cows died Tim hadn't bothered to replace her but just kept on milking the other three.

It's a punishment, she thought. We acted like we was dead, too, and now maybe we will be.

Because if anything happened to Tim, it would kill her, too.

After a long time she got up and began to clear the table, but she left the TV on, in case there was another news bulletin.

Water had begun to spill over the top of the dam on the Big Bend about 4 A.M. At a quarter of six in the morning the earth-works construction, battered by debris that included gigantic logs and stumps of incredible proportions, began to leak.

Twenty minutes later the message went out by radio: "She's going, get everybody out of the way!"

The water gushed forth, sweeping with it everything in its path—trees, rocks, earth, vehicles, and people.

Two isolated homes were lifted off their foundations as if by a gigantic hand and smashed into kindling-sized bits, occupants fighting for survival. One family had enough warning to make their terrified way to higher ground, where they clutched one another and huddled together to await rescue.

In the other house, the young people had been drinking heavily the night before. They had no electricity and therefore no radio or television; they did not hear the warnings, and they were still sound asleep when the corner of their frame dwelling was struck by an eighty-foot Douglas fir that had been uprooted by the flood.

Their kitchen, uncleaned for weeks, vanished underwater. Three ancient vehicles, parts spread about as two of them awaited repairs, slid sideways into the riverbed.

The long-haired, unshaven youths pitched from their beds into icy, swirling water. Four of them died without ever realizing what was happening to them. The other three were thrown free of the house when a corner collapsed and the wall split; one was struck on the head by a stump eight feet in diameter and was sucked under.

The remaining two managed to catch hold of the branches on a tree that might have been an arrow shot from a mighty bow; its speed was swift and there was no stopping it. They rode it down for some miles before it was possible to get to the bank and climb, battered and bleeding, to a chilly refuge.

The flood roared on, the noise of it deafening, taking everything in its path.

It reached the flatlands and began to devour the farms and small homes as it slowed only slightly in its race to the sea.

"He's been a busy son of a bitch," Andy Sleder said. "You want to read the reports, Lieutenant?"

No one would have known how little sleep either man had had the previous night. McDuff grimaced over the proffered pages. "No, condense it for me."

"Well, we don't know if we've got the whole story yet, but what we have sounds like our boy Jory, all right. He visited his sister in San Francisco Thursday afternoon, looking for money and a car. She didn't have either one, so he left. Next thing he turns up in Stockton, busts the head of an old man named Kevin Rutledge, eighty-two years old. Neighbor found him thinks there used to be a handgun in the house, but it's gone now. The arrogant bastard left his fingerprints on everything—he don't even care if we know it was him!"

McDuff sipped bitter coffee, watching Sleder through the curl of cigarette smoke that hung between them. Sleder took another deep drag and went on.

"He took the old man's car and abandoned it at a service station on 101. Before that, though, there's a chance he met another victim. Girl name of Lucy Olivera was raped and shot to death in her cabin; the neighbors say she was known to hitchhike and there was an old car at her place around noon on Friday, could have been the one Jory stole from Rutledge. Killed her dog, too. No fingerprints there, so we're just guessing."

McDuff nodded, his face impassive.

"Well, the old car gave out on him and he got a lift with this kid Jerry Hornecker. Shot him and left him for dead in a ditch in Rattlesnake Canyon, but a trucker found him before he bled to death. They did surgery on him last night and he's in stable condition this morning. He'll need a lot of plastic surgery to make his face as good as it was, but they expect him to live."

"Jory's been a busy boy."

Sleder bobbed his head. The smoke writhed around him, giving him a Satanic air. "That he was. He came on up 101 and for some reason decided the Thunderbird he stole from the Hornecker kid was hot, so he stopped at the Redwood Inn to trade it in. Old guy there barricaded himself in the cellar after he saw Jory hide the Thunderbird in his garage; he heard him drive off with the Volks we found out near Salvetti's place. Old geezer wouldn't open the door until the officer shoved his identification through the crack to prove who he was."

"And then he came on into North Bend," McDuff said, "and found Judge Verland and his wife, and killed them."

"Yeah. Only he made one more stop that we know of. He's got a list of those jurors, Lieutenant, or a damned good memory. He made a try for a little old lady named Sophie Garabaldi, lives at the old Finch Apartments. She was walking the dog so wasn't there when he knocked on her door, but a neighbor saw him and figured he was a no-good of some kind and told him the old lady was gone on a trip. Garabaldi saw him but didn't realize who he was.

"So far as we can tell, he didn't contact any of the rest of the jurors, but it's a safe bet he intends to."

"If he can," McDuff said softly. "I'm hoping to Christ he's trapped out there on the Horseshoe loop. And I hope to the same Jesus H. that he hasn't killed those people yet."

"You going out there yourself, Lieutenant?"

"Right. Hold the fort, Andy. You can coordinate everything from here. How bad is the flooding since the Big Bend Dam broke?"

"Bad enough. They've called in National Guard units from three other counties, but it'll be a couple of hours before they get here. In the meantime I'm jerking every officer out of bed that I can reach."

"Yeah. Let 'em sleep next week, when the water's gone down," Mac agreed, turning away.

"If it goes down," Sleder muttered. "Keep in touch, Lieutenant. And good luck."

McDuff didn't answer. He sure as hell was going to need

good luck, if it wasn't already too late, to rescue that Salvetti baby and the other two.

He didn't even see Sandy Moennig when she passed him in the corridor, blond hair shining, face bright and smiling.

All he could see was Russell William Jory, and a little boy who didn't deserve to die.

What had seemed adequate shelter while Jory considered matters was not, after all, adequate. The roof leaked, so that no matter what position one sought, water dripped on some part of the anatomy. And after a time the cold began to get to him in spite of his effort to ignore it.

He hadn't dared turn off the flashlight—he didn't trust that Casey bastard, he had the look of a man who might do something crazy, given half a chance—and it lay on the stinking hay at Jory's side, aimed between Casey and the girl, so they couldn't move without his knowing it.

The stuff in the baby's milk had finally taken effect, so the damned brat stopped crying. He slept lying against the girl, who did not sleep at all, but watched Jory with wide, myopic eyes.

This wasn't going the way he'd planned it. Who'd have thought there'd be a fucking flood to screw things up? And he hadn't missed the significance of the lights moving around back there along the road and around the Salvetti house.

Salvetti had come home, and then he'd got the cops. They could even come out here looking for him anytime. Of course, he had three hostages, but this wasn't the way he'd intended to do it. He couldn't even demand a car and free passage out of here, because there was no way he could get them to ferry himself and three others across the goddamned creek without being vulnerable from every direction. He knew they'd promise him anything and blow him to hell at the first opportunity.

Well, he'd delay that opportunity as long as he could.

Jory watched the girl through half-closed eyes. She wasn't as pretty as the other one, the blonde, but she wasn't bad. She'd filled out some; he remembered her as having small tits and narrower hips. She was a woman, now, not a kid anymore.

If he had some way to secure that goddamned Casey, he could have some fun with the girl.

It was out of the question at the moment, though, too dangerous. So he entertained himself by remembering the other time, and then Lucy Olivera, who had fought most satisfactorily.

He wished now he'd killed Casey earlier, before the cops were around, when nobody would have paid any attention to the shot. Now he'd only attract attention. The lights were out at the Salvetti house, but he didn't know if that meant there was nobody around or not. Anyway, he couldn't chance bringing them out here, in case the cops had left anyone behind.

As soon as it was light enough to see, they'd be crawling all over this place, and he had to be gone. They'd find the car, there was no help for that, but *he* couldn't still be here. This crummy old barn wasn't where it was all going to end for Russell Jory.

He shifted his gaze and found that Casey was staring at him, too. Itching to get his hands on either the shotgun or the .38, no doubt. Well, it wouldn't happen.

The girl moved unexpectedly, leaning forward over the baby, and Jory's hand jerked on the shotgun beside him.

"What's the matter?" Casey asked softly.

"He—he's breathing so quietly," Donna responded. "I wasn't sure—you gave him too much, he's too small for an adult dose of anything—"

Her accusatory face was a pale oval in the reflected light, turned toward Jory.

"Tough shit," Jory said. He pushed himself up, getting to his feet. He didn't know what time it was, but he couldn't wait until dawn—when the hell was dawn, anyway? Seven, eight o'clock? It stayed dark late this time of year, especially when it was storming.

He moved to the sagging door and kicked it open, the flashlight hanging at his side.

Rain slashed his face, cold, black. And yet, after a moment, he found that he wasn't totally blind after all. For a moment he didn't credit what he was seeing.

Water? The whole goddamned field was covered with water? "Stay put," he said tersely to the watching pair, and stepped outside, where he could see the lights of the Case house, still blazing through the night.

The light glinted off water. Acres of it.

How was that possible? The goddamned creek couldn't produce that much water, no matter how hard it rained—unless . . .

He tried to remember the topography of Redwood County. Little John Creek must run into one of the rivers, the Big Bend, wasn't it? And there was a dam on the Big Bend, he remembered they'd been having a hassle about some stupid dam, when he was in jail awaiting trial. A flood control dam, high up in the hills—the papers had been full of it, as well as the story about Russell Jory, which was how he'd come to see it, since reading newspapers wasn't one of his usual habits.

Well, it didn't look like the flood control dam was working now. If the dam broke or something, would that cause the Big Bend to back up here along the creek?

He didn't know, but it looked like he'd better get the hell out while he still could. The only good thing was that nobody could follow tracks through this slop. . . .

He ducked back inside the shed. They were both sitting up, watching him. "All right. On your feet. We're moving out of here."

For a moment neither of them reacted, and Jory jerked the flashlight in a gesture of command. "Come on. Get up. Pick up the kid."

Casey rose first, and stretched out a hand to the girl, then bent to lift the sleeping Denny. Jory wondered if he *had* given the kid too strong a dose of the medication; the kid was as limp as wet string.

Not that it mattered. The baby was only the means to an end, and that end was Kay Richards Salvetti. She'd come, when he wanted her, whether the baby was alive or dead.

Donna bent to retrieve the diaper bag, and the bitch almost got away with it—with leaving the empty baby bottle there in the moldy hay.

He prodded her with the gun barrel—it was safe to do it with the girl; she was too terrified and not strong enough to wrest it away from him—making the blow hard enough to hurt. "Pick that up, too. Don't leave anything."

She obeyed without making a sound, only the hand that crept to her shoulder indicating he had hurt her.

Casey's indrawn breath when he saw the water was audible. The girl stumbled against him, her face upturned, questioning. "What is it?"

203

"Flood," Casey said. "Where is it we're going?" He hoisted the sleeping child onto his shoulder, adjusting the plastic bag that served to keep the baby dry.

"You're going to take that car," Jory gestured toward the Pinto, a pale blur in the surrounding darkness, "and run it in that gully. It's full of water now, it ought to cover the thing. And don't get any fancy ideas about driving away from us, unless you want me to kill them both right now. Give her the kid."

"He's too heavy for her, she's exhausted—" Casey began, but stopped when Jory's exasperated profanity began. "Okay. Okay." He transferred the child to Donna's arms. "The gully isn't that deep, though. It won't hide the car completely. And once I drive it in there, there's no way of getting it back out."

"Just head it over that way. I noticed there was a wide, low spot, and that water is moving this way. Right there, beyond those bushes."

Casey did as he was told. He was afraid the bastard was right; if the water rose only a little more it might well completely cover the small car in the ditch. The searchers would find it eventually, of course. Once it was broad daylight a car would probably show up from the bank, and if the wind went down a little they'd probably have helicopters overhead; they'd be sure to see it from the air.

For a moment he hoped it wasn't going to settle in the depression, but it did. He'd had to leave the door open so he could get out, and he was soaked to the waist as he struggled toward the higher ground.

As he turned to watch, the Pinto sank with a gurgling sound so that only a few square feet of the top remained visible.

"Up that way," Jory said, pointing to the hills that were as yet no more than deeper shadows to the east.

Casey took Denny back from Donna and fell into step beside her, walking across the soggy field, wondering how long it would be before the water covered this land, too.

He hadn't spent much time in this part of the country, when he'd been here before. But Jory remembered a few things. One was that on the flatlands the farms had dairy cattle. Another one that in the hills they ran beef stock, which foraged freely most of the year until it was rounded up to be butchered.

On the flatlands, they worked mostly with pickups and tractors. But in the hills, where they couldn't take vehicles except on a few roads, they used horses.

He didn't know a damn thing about horses, and he didn't think Casey had any, or he might have tried riding out in spite of his inexperience.

But he'd been up in those hills once—well, maybe not these exact hills, he wasn't sure about that—but somewhere near here. And a couple of times he'd seen cabins where the men sometimes stayed overnight when they were herding cattle or checking fences.

He'd broken into one of them, once, with a girl he'd picked up along the road. He was more interested in her than in the shack—that's all it actually was—and his impression of it was vague. But it was shelter, and he thought he could find one of them again. Probably Casey knew where there was a cabin, if only he could be induced to tell.

Jory prodded them ahead of him, toward the hills. It wasn't dawn, but there was a faint lightening of the sky and they could move without the light. Occasionally the girl would stumble and fall, and he had to admit she wouldn't have been up to carrying the kid, so he needed Casey for that. Which meant he couldn't kill him. Not yet.

The ground was rough and slippery. They climbed a fence—Jory kept well back while Casey helped the girl over and handed her the baby, then vaulted over himself—so they had no opportunity to try anything at close quarters. The hillside itself was still black, and the scrubby oaks and evergreens didn't provide much cover, although he knew that the growth was more dense higher up. He hoped to be far enough from the flats so they wouldn't be spotted when true dawn came.

The dull ache was back behind his eyes. He had only a few of the capsules left, a day or two at most of release from pain. Well, maybe that was all he'd need. They'd catch up to him by that time. Then he'd have them bring Kay Richards Salvetti, and let her see her child die before she bought it herself, and then—

Then he wouldn't hurt anymore, or be locked up anymore. He'd beat them all in the end, just the way he'd planned it, even if he didn't get through the entire list. He'd get the

205

important ones. Maybe he'd even get that big redheaded bastard of a cop, if he was lucky.

The climb was steep and her legs were shaking. She thanked God for Casey; she could never have done it carrying Denny. Donna slipped and reached for a low branch to right herself.

It was light enough to see their surroundings now. She'd never been up here, although her brothers had. Where did Jory think they were going? There was nothing, no roads, no towns, for miles and miles. They couldn't possibly go up over the hills and down the other side. This part of the slope was comparatively easy, but before long the grade would be steeper. There were deep gullies, and heavy brush, and rock outcroppings that were sometimes impassable. Where were they going?

She tried not to think any further than that. She didn't want to speculate on what Jory would do when they got there.

Denny dangled over Casey's shoulder; she could see his tiny face and one hand flopping loose. If Jory had given him to much of the drug for his system, how long would it take him to die?

At least he wasn't crying, he wasn't frightened. Maybe that was something to be thankful for. And if he did die because of the drug, well, maybe that was better, too, than whatever Jory planned for them all.

For a moment she thought of Kay. Did she know by now that Jory had Denny? God, I'm sorry, I'm sorry—

She stepped in a hole and went down on one knee, her ankle painfully wrenched. The diaper bag slid off her arm and she doubled over, taking a needed breath.

"Come on, get up," Jory said behind her.

Donna straightened, praying that the ankle was only twisted, not sprained so she couldn't walk on it. Yes, it hurt, but it wasn't serious. She reached out for the strap of the plastic diaper bag and yelped when Jory's foot came down on her outstretched hand.

"Forget the fucking bag. He ain't going to need it. Get going."

Casey paused above them, turning back to see what was going on. He drew in a breath, his gaze going beyond the dark figures below him as he saw the water. Slate gray and spreading over the familiar landscape so that if it hadn't been for the lights around his own place he might not have known where he was.

Donna swallowed hard against another outcry, nursing her hand, and then she, too, turned to look back.

Oh, God. Even without her glasses she could tell.

The pastures and the roads were gone. The remnant of the barn where they had rested was now surrounded by water, which inundated everything she could see for miles except for scattered houses and barns.

Nobody would ever find them. The Pinto was submerged, there were no tracks—even the ones she'd made, slipping and sliding, would be washed out by the rain before the police ever got here.

Only Jory saw the water with satisfaction. If he had to be trapped, then make it in some way that would slow the bastards down. Give him time to do things his own way.

"Move," he said, and Donna began to climb again.

Either Jory had gotten out before the bridges went, or he'd taken to the hills.

If he'd crossed the creek, there was nothing McDuff could do about it. Virtually every police officer in the county was on duty, and they were all watching for Jory. The National Guard had also been alerted and with their CB's and walkie-talkies they could get the word around pretty fast if anybody spotted him.

But McDuff was betting on the hills. And if that's where they were, they had to be on foot.

He left the inch-by-inch search of the Horseshoe area to a pair of younger men because he didn't expect them to find anything. If there had been tracks or clues, they were now washed out. And Jory's plans had had to be revised drastically if he were trapped; whatever he intended with the Salvetti baby, he hadn't accomplished it yet, and he wouldn't be taken—or even concerned—until he did.

Mac had a few words with VonDorn regarding how many men to pull off the flood duties to go after Jory. He wound up with four in addition to himself, and added two more volunteers from an emergency rescue unit, both of them willing to use their four-wheel drive vehicles for the search. These two, Calhoun and Zabaga, knew the territory well and they were tireless workers; they'd once assisted the sheriff's deputies in getting a wrecked car and four injured kids out of a four-hundred-foot-deep canyon, and McDuff respected their judgment and their intelligence.

The four department men were all crack shots.

He had hesitated only momentarily over the Salvettis.

They appeared, white-lipped, red-eyed, yet restraining their anguish.

"I'd like to come along, Lieutenant," Wally said. "I know

that country, too. I won't break a leg or do anything stupid, and I'll follow orders. Whatever you say. I just want to be there."

"It may mean just sitting in the back of a Scout, waiting."

"At least I'll be where I'll know, as soon as anybody knows. . . ."

Kay stood beside her husband, looking slim even in her bulky jacket. She wore slacks and boots, as well, and she was working to control herself. Only the tenseness of the hand curled around Wally's arm betrayed the extent of that effort; the knuckles were white.

"Lieutenant McDuff." Her tone was low, husky. "Could I go, too? Please? I promise not to interfere in any way, but the thought of simply sitting home waiting to hear—" Her voice broke briefly. "Please."

Ordinarily it would have been out of the question. Sort of the same principle as keeping the mother out of the emergency room when the doctor is pumping her child's stomach or suturing a nasty gash: there is simply no time to cope with a fainting or hysterical mother.

If McDuff guessed right, however, when they cornered Jory he was going to flaunt his hostages to force them to produce the child's mother. And it might make things safer, in the long run, and save a hell of a lot of time, if she came with them. The question was whether she was strong enough to sit tight and keep still.

McDuff's consideration didn't take long. He wouldn't do it for reasons of compassion—at this stage of things, he couldn't afford to indulge in compassion, because it might cost more lives, and he had enough wrong moves to his credit already—but he *knew* Jory wanted Kay.

"You might as well ride with Zabaga—he's the one in the yellow Scout. It's understood that you stay in the vehicle, say nothing, do nothing to interfere, no matter what happens."

The relief in their faces was more than he could look upon. McDuff turned away toward the unmarked car where a tough young cop named Danny Lowell waited behind the wheel. "Okay, let's get this show on the road," said McDuff, and the car was in motion before the door slammed behind him.

George Zabaga was in his late thirties, a swarthy and muscular man who looked rather like a Mexican bandit in an Italian-made Western. Kay was surprised that she could have such a thought at a moment like this, but it was a relief to think of anything that relieved, even briefly, her anxiety for Denny.

Zabaga accepted their presence matter-of-factly, waving them into the back of his Scout. "Coffee there in the thermos if you want some," he offered. "My wife always makes up a gallon when I go on these things; sometimes it's just about saved my life."

They settled into the backseat and buckled up with cold fingers. "You do this kind of thing often?" Wally asked, reaching for the indicated container. They'd been unable to drink anything before they left Angela's, but now the cold and the slight release of tension since McDuff had agreed to let them go along made the hot drink sound good.

"Whenever they call me," Zabaga said. He put the Scout in gear and fell into line behind a dark red Jeep, driven by Calhoun, and followed McDuff's lead car. Another unmarked police vehicle brought up the rear. "Of course it was never a kidnapping before. Usually it's getting a wrecked car out of some canyon, or rescuing somebody who fell over a cliff, something like that. How old is your little boy?"

Wally's hand trembled slightly as he held the plastic cup, filled it and passed it to Kay, and reached for a second cup. "Just over a year."

"I got two kids," Zabaga said. "Two little girls. Three and six."

He meant it as a gesture of sympathy, Kay thought. She warmed her hands around the cup, sipping cautiously. It was black, and she ordinarily used milk and sugar, but she drank it anyway. She needed it. Gradually the warmth of Wally's body began to come through to her along the length of their thighs. She was glad their driver didn't comment on Jory, or commiserate with them; it would only have made the situation more starkly real and more painful.

It was still dark. She didn't know how she'd managed to sleep at all, and she suspected Wally hadn't done more than doze through the night; certainly they had both been awake before Angela came to wake them an hour and a half earlier. She wished she had her own clothes, but getting to the house for them was out of the question, so she'd borrowed from Connie, and the boots were an old pair she'd left at Angela's months ago after some forgotten expedition.

The cars moved through the silent streets, stopping for

210

unnecessary traffic lights the first time, going through them after that when McDuff led the way. Twice they saw crews clearing debris from clogged drains, and in every low place they drove through water several inches deep on the city streets.

They were unprepared for the river. Kay drew in her breath as they approached the bridge on the freeway going north out of town; it was still above the level of the water, but not by much, and the flood licked around the buildings closest to it. The parking lot of the Sears store was a shallow lake, and the warehouses must be flooded for the river had risen several feet on their sides.

"I've lived here all my life," Wally said, the strain showing in his voice, "and I've only seen it higher than this once, in the bad flood in sixty-four."

"Will it get into our house, do you think?" For a moment, only a moment, Kay was distracted by the prospect as she imagined her pale gold carpeting soaked and muddy.

"The house is on a knoll," Wally reminded her, and fell silent. It didn't matter to either of them. All that mattered was Denny.

In spite of her determination to remain strong, to keep from showing her emotion in any way that might result in her being sent home, Kay was unable to prevent the prickling tears that blurred her vision.

Denny with Russell Jory; God only knew what the man was capable of, but a man who would kill and rape with such savage ease was more dangerous to her son than if he'd been thrown into a pit filled with wild animals.

It was impossible not to remember what it had been like, being raped by Russell Jory. She had told Wally about it—how could you marry a man without telling him something like that?—and the telling had been almost like being raped again.

And now Jory had Denny. And Donna, too. Had he abused her again, the way he had the first time? Her family must be going through the same thing she and Wally were, knowing what might be happening to her.

Donna wouldn't have been there if Kay hadn't decided to leave Denny home with a sitter. So there was one more thing to feel guilty about, she thought.

The caravan of which they were a part passed over the bridge and the swollen Big Bend and turned east toward the

211

imperceptibly lightening sky. The police thought Jory had taken his hostages into the hills, and that's where they were going. But what if they were wrong? What if Jory had gotten out? What if they were already out of the county by now? It might be weeks before they were discovered, before the Salvettis and the Malloys and the Cases knew what had happened to their children.

Kay made an involuntary sound of distress, immediately stifled. Wally's hand moved out to cover hers, but for once there was no comfort in his touch.

Perhaps there was no comfort anywhere, ever again.

They had to pause to rest. The climb had been a stiff one, and even Jory had to admit they couldn't keep it up indefinitely. He stared around at the hillside emerging from night, at fallen trees and gullies filled with underbrush, and the goddamned water seeping out of the goddamned ground so that it was like walking on a wet sponge.

Nothing seemed familiar.

He'd been up here, he knew they couldn't be far from the shack he remembered, but where the hell was it?

Too much had changed in nearly eight years. If they'd come in from the road he might have found it—he remembered where they had turned off the gravel road, and then back in on a trail that might now be completely overgrown.

The moment he called a halt the girl slid to the ground, resting her back against a fallen log. Casey sank to a sitting position on it, cradling the baby, checking to make sure he still breathed.

Christ, Jory thought. They could wander around forever and not find the fucking cabin. Except that they weren't going to hold up much longer. And he didn't like the way Casey was looking at him. Like a man thinking dangerous thoughts. Like a man pushed to sufficient desperation to try something foolish.

"The baby's really sick. He may die if he doesn't get to a doctor," Casey said, looking right at him. It was light enough to see one another clearly now. The rain had slackened to a drizzle but it scarcely mattered. Even Denny was unaware of physical discomfort as he lay in his deep, drugged sleep.

Donna turned her head, putting out a hand to touch the baby's exposed face, then looking up at the man who held him.

"Is that what you want?" Casey asked sharply. "You want him to die?"

"You're so anxious about the kid," Jory said, "you take us to that cabin."

"What cabin?"

"The cabin that's up here someplace. The one where those guys stay when they're moving cattle. It oughta be within a few miles of here. You want to get the kid in out of the weather, you take us there."

For a moment he saw only resistance on Casey's face. Then Casey looked around, getting his bearings in the cold gray light. "There's a shack up beyond Pacific Ridge. I think that's the next hill over, but I'm not sure. I haven't been up here for years. If it was clear so I could see the ocean I could tell for sure where we are, but I think we're quite a ways south of the shack. And I don't think anybody's using it anymore. It may even have fallen down."

"You find it," Jory suggested. He kicked at the girl's outstretched foot. "Come on, let's go."

Donna's mind barely registered the kick. Exhaustion was now added to misery and fear, but she stumbled to her feet. Casey offered a helping hand until they got over the fallen log and began to work their way farther up the slope.

Behind them, Jory stepped in a hole and swore. A glance back revealed that he'd apparently twisted an ankle, for he came on more slowly, favoring his left foot.

She spoke quickly, before Jory should again come within earshot. "Denny's cooler, isn't he? He's not worse?"

Casey murmured his reply. "His fever's down, but he's unconscious. Far as I can tell, though, he's breathing all right."

"Maybe they're looking for us by now," Donna said hopefully.

"Maybe. But unless we're damned lucky, they won't find us in time."

In time? "What do you think he intends to do?" she demanded, resisting a compulsion to look behind at Jory, to see how close he was.

"Whatever it is, it won't be good. The way I see it, we haven't got a hell of a lot to lose. If I get a chance, I'm going to try to take him. If you can make a break for it, run. Leave the baby, you wouldn't get far with him, and maybe as long as he's drugged Jory won't do anything to him."

"It wouldn't be any use. I really can't see very far without my glasses. I'd just get lost in the woods."

"It isn't all that far to a road from the cabin, if I can find it. There should be a path running to it, along the top of the ridge. Just go north, and eventually you'll hit road. Then go west until you come to some mailboxes and driveways. You can find a mailbox on the road, can't you?"

"Hey!" Jory's angry shout made them jerk guiltily apart. "Knock it off! Just keep moving!"

"Remember," Casey muttered, "be ready if I make a try for him."

Her dread was only increased by Casey's intent. What if he tried to "take Jory" and was killed for it? And what if she couldn't find the path, how long would it be before anyone came looking? For all she knew, the police might think Jory had been long gone when the flood came, and they were looking in entirely different places for him and his victims. There might not be anyone out in this brush until summer or even fall.

And Denny. Poor Denny, how long would he live without someone taking care of him?

She had fallen slightly behind Casey, and she could see the baby's face, hanging over the man's shoulder. Unnaturally still, heavily drugged.

Without knowing she was doing it, she began again to pray.

They came upon the cabin abruptly, no more than a tar-papered shack in a small clearing. Jory had been prepared to break into it, but there was no need.

Clearly it had been abandoned; the door stood ajar and a small cedar struggled for a start right through what had been a front step.

It was not as he remembered it. Smaller, and more rustic, and several windows were broken. Still, it was shelter of a sort and, what was more important, a reasonable place to make his stand. There were no trees within a hundred yards of it, and there were windows on all sides.

Unless they came at him from all directions at once, and he doubted they'd have enough men to do that, he had a chance of holding them off. And he would have, of course, the baby and the girl.

Casey was working himself up to something. Jory was sure

of that. Well, regardless, he'd have to put him out of commission shortly. He'd carried the kid here; he'd served his purpose. And unless the cops had anticipated him and come around by the road to meet him, a most unlikely premise, there was no one close enough to hear a gunshot.

He kicked the door open, then stood well back, motioning them ahead of him.

Donna went first, stumbling over a broken chair in the dim interior, then turning as the men followed. Casey came through the doorway and spoke to her.

"Here, take him, my arm's broke."

She accepted the child, and as Jory came through the doorway, Casey spun, lunging for the shotgun.

Jory had been anticipating him. He fired, his aim thrown off but not enough to make him miss entirely.

Donna watched in renewed horror as Casey staggered backward, a hand pressed to a spurting wound at the junction of neck and shoulder; he fell, crashing into a squat cast-iron stove in the middle of the floor.

The stovepipe popped apart as the stove moved under the impact; soot scattered beneath the remaining section suspended from the ceiling, settling on Donna's and the baby's faces.

Casey lay, stunned or mortally wounded she didn't know. For a moment she thought Jory would fire again, down into the helpless man as he had fired a second time at Larry, and she made a jerky, compulsive movement toward Casey.

"No, don't—"

"Get over there," Jory said, indicating the far side of the small room that comprised the whole of the shack. He'd hoped the place was still in use, that there might be supplies; there was nothing but trash. A mattress on the floor, well shredded by mice, yellowing newspapers, a few empty tin cans, a handful of old garments not worth taking back to civilization.

Donna half-fell onto the mattress, letting the limp and unconscious child slide from her arms. He was going to kill them. Why he'd made them climb all the way up here in the hills was beyond her, but it was clear that any rescue was going to be too late unless it arrived at once.

Jory had, for a moment, his back turned to her, as he peered out one of the dirty windows. Her decision was almost

215

mindless; she was not conscious of making it, she simply moved. Toward the fallen Casey, whose eyes were shut, and whose blood was welling out of the hole in his jacket in alarming quantities.

Donna crawled to him, looking about desperately for something to staunch the hemorrhage. Reason failed to inform her that it didn't matter, that they were all as good as dead anyway. The blood was soaking into Casey's jacket and dripping off onto the dirty floor, staining her hand when she touched him.

Jory glanced at her, uncaring, and then stepped to the next window, assessing his position. Donna scrambled back to the mattress, pulling out a handful of the cotton wadding that filled it, and she had packed a substantial amount of it inside Casey's jacket, pressing it into the torn flesh, before Jory spoke.

"Come here."

His tone had changed; she read it correctly and nausea swept over her.

No. No, not again. She couldn't endure it again. She gagged, turning away from him, moving instinctively toward the sleeping baby, although there was no logic in this.

His foot sent her sprawling toward the mattress; her teeth cut through her lower lip, and this time the blood was her own. Jory came down on top of her, knocking the breath out of her, cracking her head on something so that for a moment pain obliterated everything else.

When it eased she was aware of hard hands wrestling her onto her back and tearing at her clothes, of a knee thrust between her legs, of his breath on her face.

She fought. Fought blindly, instinctively, for her life.

"Go on, bitch. Make it interesting," Jory said, and it all happened again.

The searing pain, the tearing of tender flesh, and the screaming that erupted from her throat until that, too, seemed to rupture, as she fought against Russell Jory.

And lost.

Tim Fitzpatrick sat in his pickup and watched the procession that left the courthouse in the predawn rain. He had been there since Lieutenant McDuff arrived on duty, and he'd observed the arrival, too, of the young Salvettis. He didn't know who they were, and their names hadn't been mentioned on the news report, but he made the correct assumption that they were the parents of the kidnapped child.

He felt pity for them, but the emotion was not as strong as it might have been had the kidnapper been anyone else but Russell Jory.

For the first time since the news of Jory's release, Fitzpatrick was calm. He knew what he had to do, and he would do it. There must not be another arrest, another trial, another prison sentence, and another parole. No. If the state would not execute a killer, then it was up to the citizens to do it. Just the way the vigilantes did in the old days.

He saw McDuff talking to the young couple, and then waving them toward the yellow Scout. Even if the radio report hadn't said McDuff was in charge, he would have guessed it. Pat McDuff had a reputation, and they gave him the tough jobs. In a small town, you always knew which cop did what, and McDuff was frequently mentioned in the papers.

When the cars pulled out, on the one-way street going south, and circled the block to head north, Fitzpatrick was behind them. He stopped for the traffic light they all went through, but it changed immediately, and he didn't get far behind them.

There was almost no traffic on the streets except for a couple of emergency vehicles, so he didn't want to seem to be joining their procession. On the other hand, the way the roads outside of town were being flooded and blocked off, he didn't want to get far enough back so anybody would stop him from following them. Not, at least, until he figured out where they were going.

They must have some specific idea of where to hunt for Jory. They moved with purpose, and he recognized the significance of the Scout and the Jeep. Four-wheel drive, which meant back roads or rough turf somewhere.

The entourage slowed at a mass of blinking red and yellow lights: a pair of smashed cars, an ambulance, police cars. A uniformed officer showed briefly in the headlights of McDuff's lead vehicle; he bent his head toward the opened window, then waved them on. Fitzpatrick took advantage of the pause to attach himself to the rear of the train, and they drove out of the city.

When the first car swung onto the Pacific Ridge Road, Fitzpatrick's pulses quickened. Up in the hills, from where?

217

Out there along the flooded plain beyond Little John Creek? He had to stay with them long enough to see which way they went when they reached the top of the ridge.

He turned off his lights, and followed. Before long it would be light enough to see him clearly, but maybe they wouldn't notice him now. Give him time to determine their destination.

When they found Jory, he'd be ready.

The Guardsman posted at the turnoff was positive. Nobody had come out of the area in the past four hours except two families, one with a sick girl and another with an ailing grandfather. "If there was any chance they'd get trapped in the hills," the young man explained, "they thought they'd better move into town until the water goes down, to be near the doctor. Nobody's come out on foot. This is the only spot of flooding, right here, and it's only a few inches deep so far." He indicated the expanse of water over the roadway. "Everybody else up there is well above the danger level, and they all got plenty of supplies unless this lasts for more than a couple of weeks." Curiosity was evident on his face. "What's up, Lieutenant?"

"There's a possibility Jory's up there, along the ridge."

"Russell Jory?" Astonishment was written across the man's features. "I heard about him, on the news—got my transistor on—but what the hell would he be up there for? No way to get anywhere in a hurry, that's for damn sure."

"He may have been pushed toward the hills when Little John flooded. How many families up here?"

"Oh, seven or eight, besides the two that left."

"Well, Jory's dangerous. If you see anything suspicious, don't try to do anything about it but report in. And warn any of the residents you see."

"Those ridge runners are a trigger-happy bunch," the Guardsman said. He grinned, rain streaking his face. "Anybody that eats government beef regular isn't going to stop at shootin' a varmint like that."

"He has hostages," Mac said. "And he's a killer several times over. Don't take any chances."

"Well, good luck. I hope you get the son of a bitch," the Guardsman said, and snapped them a salute, stepping back so they could go through, and wondering why the pickup that brought up the rear was running without lights, but what the hell. It was none of his business. He wished he could go with them. Running down a killer would be more interesting than sitting here in the rain waiting to tell everybody they couldn't go through unless it was an emergency.

He went back to his truck and lit a cigarette and wished he hadn't already drunk all his coffee.

The Ridge Road went nowhere. Like its counterpart down on the flats, Horseshoe Road, its only function was to provide access to a few scattered homes and ranches. To the east of it, the hill country became steeper and wilder, impenetrable except on foot or horseback.

Maybe, McDuff thought with a growing uneasiness, wild enough so that it was impossible that Jory and his captives would have made it. A sick baby, a young woman who wasn't used to climbing in the hills, and Case.

For a time he'd been puzzled by the inclusion of Stan Case among the hostages. The fact that he'd just happened to be on the scene wasn't sufficient justification for his inclusion; not when a man like Jory was calling the shots.

And then it occurred to him that Case might have been needed to carry the Salvetti baby. That almost had to be it; Donna Malloy would have all she could do to get herself up that mountainside. She wouldn't have lasted long enough carrying a twenty-seven-pound child. And if Jory himself had done the carrying he'd have found it considerably more difficult to control the girl as well, since he was undoubtedly still carrying the shotgun he'd used on the Verlands.

And in that case, the other man was safe until he got where they were going. Until he'd carried the child as far as Jory wanted him carried. That accomplished, Jory might very well kill him.

He quickened his step through the drenched woods, feeling the ground give spongily under his feet, occasionally being slapped in the face with a wet branch that everyone else had ducked under. It was still dark under the trees. It was a relief when they passed through a cleared spot, even though it often meant there were fallen logs to climb over or ravines to work around.

Daylight, and the rain slackened off to a drizzle he scarcely noticed. He hoped to Christ they got to Jory before he killed anyone else.

And if he wasn't right? If he'd guessed wrong all to hell and

219

gone, where would they find the bodies? Maybe, with half the county underwater, they never would find them. If Jory simply wanted to dispose of them, there would be dozens of possibilities.

But he didn't think he'd guessed wrong. If he'd only wanted to kill, Jory could easily have left them all there in the Salvetti kitchen. The fact that he hadn't seemed an indication that he had something more in mind, some exquisite torture planned for Kay Salvetti and, maybe, the Malloy girl.

His walkie-talkie suddenly crackled. They heard Danny Lowell's voice, from where he stood guard over Kay Salvetti and the equipment they hadn't been able to bring any farther into the woods.

"Lieutenant McDuff."

"Yeah, Danny."

"They found the Malloy girl's car, the blue Pinto. Run into a gully on the back of Case's place, covered with water. Preston went down and checked it out. No bullet holes he could spot, no sign of anything except that it was deliberately run into the gully. Keys still in it."

"Good." McDuff's response was short, but elation surged through him. He was right! Jory had taken to the hills. "We're getting close to the lower shack. We'll be in touch."

"Ten-four," Lowell said.

They were close, but getting there was not a quick matter. As Zabaga had guessed, the deep ravine that had to be crossed was filled with small waterfalls and, between them, enough deep water to preclude easy passage. Well, that was all right. If it was difficult for them to cross, it would be even more difficult for Jory and his hostages.

He hoped, with a deep, passionate hope, that the others were trapped on the other side of the ravine. That they were at the abandoned shack. That Jory had not killed any of them yet.

"There's a tree down across the gully," Zabaga said, gesturing. "Up there. We can walk across it."

McDuff glanced back at Wally Salvetti. He was silent, not joining in any of the conversation, but he maintained the pace and responded immediately to suggestions or orders. McDuff waved him on ahead, and Wally followed after George Zabaga, his hands thrust deep into his jacket pockets, his face set and gray.

The fallen tree was not easily traversed, since it lay on a

slant and the branches were on the far side, too far away to do anyone any good. Zabaga went first, relatively surefooted, half-running when the slope became too much for him, scrambling through the cedar boughs on the far side.

Salvetti hesitated for a moment, looking down at the rushing water a dozen feet below, then grasped an out-stretched root to haul himself onto the tree trunk. McDuff saw him swallow, then spread his arms for balance and start down the tree; he made it across, only to fall into the brush on the other side.

McDuff and the other two cops, Hanks and Bruder, followed him over. Zabaga was already climbing higher on the ridge, angling south and east, while Wally Salvetti disentangled himself from the underbrush.

With the slackening of the rain and the growing light, they could now see, not the ocean that would have been visible in good weather, but acres of floodwaters where there should have been farmland. A hell of a climb to here, if Jory had indeed forced the others to it.

Zabaga had paused on top of the ridge, and when they joined him they saw why.

The shack was barely visible through the trees, centered in a small clearing a hundred yards below them. No chance of sneaking up to look in a window without being seen, McDuff observed. And no indication that it was anything but totally abandoned.

"I can edge around the other side of the clearing," Bruder offered, "and see if it looks like anybody's climbed the hill."

McDuff nodded, and the officer began to work his way down the slope. The rain might have washed out any tracks, but as soft as the ground was, there were bound to be traces somewhere, under the trees or in other protected areas, if three people had passed within the past few hours. He didn't think they'd have attempted the climb in the dark; it would have been almost impossible to accomplish.

Hanks unslung the heavy, scoped rifle he carried. He was very young, with peach fuzz across his upper lip where he was trying to cultivate a mustache; out of uniform, anyone would have taken him for about seventeen years old.

He was a crack shot.

"Want me to go up and around the other side, Lieutenant?" he asked calmly.

"Yes. Let me know when you get there, where you can see

the cabin door. And remember, if Jory's in there, so are the others. We don't want anybody hurt."

Hanks nodded. He peeled a stick of gum out of a package and unwrapped it, carefully stowing the paper in his pocket before he moved off, chewing slowly.

In spite of the cold, there was a beading of perspiration on Wally Salvetti's forehead. He glanced at McDuff and kept his voice under control. "What do you want me to do, Lieutenant?"

"Nothing, unless you're specifically told to do it. Stay out of the way—up there under that tree would be a good place. We may have to act fast when the time comes, and we won't have time to worry about you being in the way."

Wally nodded, then licked his lips. "What if—what if they aren't there?" The cabin was dead, deserted-looking.

"If they aren't there, we go on up to the next ridge and the other cabin, and hope they're there." And God only knew what, after that, if they didn't find Jory.

But the Pinto had been submerged in a ditch, right up against the foot of the hills, McDuff thought. They were up here somewhere.

Salvetti moved off obediently, to stand beneath the concealing limbs of a massive cedar.

McDuff hunkered down to wait.

He knew where they were going now. Tim Fitzpatrick was glad when they turned off the main road, because it was almost full daylight and he couldn't follow them much longer without being detected. He eased his own pickup onto the side road, falling back, no longer afraid of losing them. He knew the country well, he had hunted over it for thirty years, and there was nowhere they could go now except to the end of the road.

It was no more than a trail, really, and they couldn't go more than a few miles with the two unmarked police vehicles. After that, they could push on for another five or six miles with the four-wheel drives, if they knew what they were doing.

He stopped short of the turnaround where he knew they'd leave the police vehicles, and stepped out, reaching back into the cab for his rain hat and the thirty-aught-six.

He stuck the extra shells into the pocket of his jacket, and began to make his way along the edge of the woods.

222

It was just as he'd expected: the two unmarked police cars left behind and tracks leading out across the hillside. Fitzpatrick backtracked to the pickup and passed the empty cars, then shifted down and followed the tracks.

He almost overshot and ran right into the Jeep. If it hadn't been empty, he might well have been detected and sent packing. As it was, he maneuvered off the trail and parked, not particularly caring that when the police returned they would see the pickup. By then, he hoped, it wouldn't matter.

The Scout showed yellow through a stand of leafless maples. Avoid that, too, for there were two people there. He passed by, well within the woods, glimpsing them only briefly. The young woman, he assumed, and an officer left to monitor the radio.

They must believe that Jory had holed up in the old abandoned shack. Fitzpatrick gave no thought to how they'd come to that conclusion; he simply expected Jory to be there.

He had no trouble following the trail, for in addition to footprints in the soggy earth there were broken twigs and even a few damaged branches. Not that he needed to follow the prints, because there was only one place they could be going.

His bad leg throbbed painfully, and his limp became more pronounced, but he refused to think about it. Seven years in jail for killing Larry. That's all they'd done to Jory. Seven years, against all the rest of Larry's life.

Well, it couldn't be allowed to happen again. Fitzpatrick paused for breath and to ease the stitch in his side, and then went on again until he saw them, squatting under a tree, waiting and watching the cabin below.

Someone whimpered.

For a moment Donna wondered if she were doing it herself. She thought she couldn't survive, either physically or mentally, another assault such as the first one had been. And, indeed, she had been only partially conscious for some time, since Jory had hit her with his fist after she bit him.

She felt engulfed in scalding pain, and she didn't have to investigate with her hands to know that she was bleeding. Not seriously, at least she didn't think so, not enough to die from it, but oh, God, how she hurt!

Casey. Casey was the one who was bleeding to death.

Had Casey moaned?

She rolled her head, willing her vision to clear, and lay still in the new position until her eyes focused as well as she could expect without her glasses.

The mound that was Casey remained as she had last seen it: motionless and silent. Was he still breathing? It was impossible to tell.

Jory, where was Jory?

For a moment she had the wild hope that he had gone, but no, there he was at a window, the shotgun in his hands.

The whimper was repeated.

Not herself. Denny. Denny was rousing from his drugged sleep. Not dead, then. But he might be better off, poor baby, to have died in sleep than from whatever else Jory planned for him.

Donna became aware of the cold, the chill of the mattress with its smell of mildew, the nakedness of her own lower limbs. She raised on one elbow and groped for her clothes. Her underpants were a bloody scrap, and useless, but she drew up the jeans and saw the spreading stain on the mattress beneath her. She wished desperately that she had her glasses; she felt blind and more helpless without them.

Jory was absorbed in the view from the window, paying no attention to her pathetic movements. When Denny stirred, she crawled toward the baby.

He wasn't awake, but he was obviously uncomfortable, for he squirmed and pushed out with his hands against the confining blanket that still wrapped him. His cheek was warm to her hand, but not, she thought, abnormally so. His fever was surely decreasing.

He was undoubtedly wet, but since she had no way to change him there was no point in verifying it. And if he woke fully he'd certainly be hungry, and she had no way to appease that, either.

A muffled exclamation brought her around to stare fuzzily at Jory's back. Did he see something out there?

Oh, God, she thought, please let someone find us.

But how likely was that? Who would guess he'd have brought them up here in the foothills? Why had he? What did he intend to do?

She didn't see Jory's sudden thrust with the gun barrel against the window, but she heard the shattering glass and the blast that followed, leaving her ears ringing.

"You out there, pig?" Jory yelled, but he was standing to

one side of the opening, no longer looking out. "You out there?"

There was an answering shout after a delay of some thirty agonizing seconds. "We're here, Jory! You're surrounded. Put down the gun and come out with your hands up."

"Fuck you, pig!"

Donna lay on her stomach on the bloody mattress, an arm outflung across the child, holding her breath. Think, she had to think. How could she help? Briefly, she forgot how battered she was, because suddenly, miraculously, there was a chance. Maybe not much of a chance, but better than she'd thought a few minutes ago.

If only Casey had waited until now to make his try, when there were police out there. But no, Jory couldn't have raped her with Casey sitting there, he'd have had to shoot him even if Casey hadn't tried to jump him. And now Casey . . . she wouldn't think about Casey, not yet.

"You can't go anywhere, Jory! Make it easy on yourself, come out!"

The vituperation that flowed from Jory's mouth would ordinarily, in itself, have been enough to make her feel sick. Today, however, she was past that. Dear God, if she could only see decently, maybe there was something lying around that she could use as a weapon, anything to distract Jory enough to give the police an opportunity. . . .

Jory leaned forward, putting his mouth close to the window opening. "I've got the kid in here, McDuff! You want to see him?"

What was he going to do? Something terrible, he had some purpose in bringing them all this way, but she didn't understand what it was. If he only wanted to kill them, why hadn't he already done it?

"Give us the baby," McDuff shouted back.

"Oh, hell, yes," Jory muttered. He turned swiftly to bend over the drugged child, ripping him out of the cocoon of blankets, brushing Donna aside. And then, holding the baby against his own chest, he opened the cabin door and stood there, using Denny as a shield. "Go ahead and shoot, pigs! Kill the kid if you want to!"

Among the waiting men at the edge of the forest, it was Wally Salvetti who first realized that there was something wrong with the small figure in yellow sleepers. For a petrified

225

moment he was convinced that Denny was already dead, for he dangled inertly from the man's encircling arm.

The other hand held the shotgun, and while it would have been difficult for Jory to fire it while holding the child, no one discounted the possibility of it.

Young Hanks spoke softly into the walkie-talkie. "I can take him, Lieutenant."

"No. Hold it." McDuff shot a glance at Salvetti, whose fists were knotted impotently at his sides. He raised his voice to carry across the clearing. "What's the matter with the baby? How do we know he's still alive, Jory?"

"Oh, he's alive! You just got to take my word for it!" Jory shouted back, and retreated within the cabin without ever presenting himself as a reasonable target.

He looked at Donna and grinned.

For a moment she didn't credit her senses. Was her vision distorted that much because she'd lost her glasses? But no, he was close enough so she could see the gleam of his teeth. He was insane, she thought. There was no telling what he intended to do; there need be no logic in it. She remained crouched on the mattress, the shred of once-white nylon beside her a bloody reminder of Jory's brutality.

They were out there, the police, with guns to rescue her. Yet she could not put aside the conviction that Jory could continue to do just as he pleased with her, regardless of the police.

He reached the mattress in a few steps and dropped Denny against her; her arms closed around him automatically, and once more he whimpered.

"Keep him out of the way," Jory said, the smile gone, and again he yelled from the window, this time careful to stay out of sight. "Come and get him, pig!"

Donna stared desperately around the small room. There was a window on each side, but except for the one Jory had broken they were all nailed shut. There would be no getting through one of them, anyway, not before he could shoot her in the back.

She might, if Jory were occupied at one of the other windows, get Denny through the broken one, though.

Would the men outside be able to rescue him without being shot, if she did?

And would she be signing her own death warrant?

Astoundingly, Jory seemed to relax. The tension went out

of his shoulders as he leaned against the wall, although the shotgun remained ready for action, propped beside him. He took the .38 out of his pocket and checked it over, making sure it, too, was ready to use.

There was nothing she could use, nothing. No forgotten tool or weapon, no way out. Yet she eased Denny onto the mattress and tried to be ready for whatever she might have to do. Don't think about the pain, don't think about the continued bleeding, don't think about poor Casey. . . .

Casey moved.

Only his hand, and she didn't think Jory saw it; he was checking one of the windows now.

Donna watched, scarcely daring to hope. Casey wasn't dead. He was coming around. But unless he roused enough to act surely and swiftly, he might only induce another attack if Jory noticed him.

The silence in the clearing went on for too long, and then McDuff shouted again. "Jory! What do you want?"

Once more Jory's lips stretched in what might have been a grin. His back was to Casey and he swung the shotgun into position again. "Bring her up here! I want to talk to her! That Kay Richards!" He'd forgotten for the moment what her married name was, but it didn't matter. They'd know who he meant.

And out on the hill McDuff knew he'd been right all along. This was what they'd been leading up to. Jory wanted Kay.

Wally Salvetti dropped to his knees and edged forward, although still within the area designated for him. "Lieutenant, what's he want? Why does he want Kay?"

McDuff spoke quietly into the small hand mike. "Danny, bring Mrs. Salvetti up. Jory's asking for her."

"Ten-four," Lowell said, and it was again silent on the hillside. The rain had stopped, although the sky was still dark and there was no wind blowing. Nothing to interfere with Hanks's shot when the time came; maybe he should have let him fire before, when Jory stood in the doorway, but the angle hadn't been good. Hanks had now maneuvered into a better position, so that if Jory emerged from the doorway a second time he'd be ready.

"We've sent for Mrs. Salvetti," McDuff called. "Do you have the Malloy girl?"

Jory responded readily. "She's here."

"Is she all right?"

227

"She's just peachy keen," Jory shouted. "Why don't you send somebody in to see?"

Donna tried to ignore what was going on, the shouted words, Jory's presence. She edged perceptibly nearer to Casey, thankful now that Denny remained more or less in his drugged state; at least that way he wasn't so likely to draw Jory's fire, nor need her own attention.

Casey groaned, but the sound of it was covered by Jory's voice. Donna stretched out a hand and touched his, finding it cold and unresponsive.

If only she could warn him, could make him understand that he should not do anything to excite Jory's interest.

But his eyes were closed and he did not react to her touch. She continued to crouch beside him, though, with her hand over his, waiting.

"Lieutenant," Wally Salvetti said. "He wants her to try to get Denny back so he can kill her, doesn't he?"

His face was gray with fatigue and apprehension, yet he spoke in a steady voice.

McDuff didn't look directly at him but continued to watch the cabin. "Probably."

"What are we going to do? I don't want to lose my wife as well as my son. There isn't really much chance of getting Denny back, is there? He—he knew you'd find him eventually, he's just been sitting here waiting, hasn't he? So you'd bring Kay to him."

"He hasn't won yet, Mr. Salvetti. I've got two men here who can put a bullet in whichever eye they choose, as soon as he shows himself."

"And what if he doesn't show himself, Lieutenant? What if he stays inside there and demands that Kay go in to him? She'll want to do it, if it's the only way to get Denny, but he'll kill her. I can't let her walk across that clearing to him."

"Hang tight," McDuff said, and then shouted his question at Jory. "Where's Stan Casey?"

Jory ignored that. He was making the rounds of the windows, checking the entire clearing, making sure nobody was trying to move in on him. They couldn't do it easily, because he could see out all four sides of the cabin at the same time, and there was a lot of open space to cross.

Somehow Donna forgot that her earlier prayers had been

228

disregarded. There was still a chance, if Denny didn't rouse too soon, if Casey could be kept quiet, if she herself did not anger Jory again. She rested her head against Casey's shoulder, her hand warming his, and prayed for them all. She knew she was hemorrhaging, she could feel the wet warmth between her thighs, but it was difficult to worry about it. If she stayed very still, Jory might forget she was there.

She closed her eyes to rest.

"Send her in here!" Jory shouted. "Let her come and get her kid!"

"No," Wally Salvetti said, almost under his breath. "No, he'll kill her."

Kay's fair skin was so translucent that the bruises of fatigue were blue smudges beneath her eyes. Her breast rose and fell rapidly, but she gave no other sign of agitation.

"What does he want of me?"

"He probably wants just what your husband said," McDuff told her quietly. "To get you within range so he can shoot you."

There was no apparent reaction to this, except puzzlement. "But how can he hope to get away with it? He's surrounded by armed police officers, isn't he?"

"Maybe he doesn't hope to get away with it. Maybe he's decided to settle for just taking as many people with him as he can. Including the Malloy girl and you."

"Is she in there, too? Donna?"

"We haven't seen her, but he says she is."

"Then you don't know whether she's . . . alive or not."

"That's right."

"And what about Denny?" Her tone hadn't changed; only the flutter of a pulse at the base of her throat added emphasis to her question.

"We only saw him for a moment. It's possible that he's unconscious; he may have been drugged. Jory went through the medicine chest at your place, and in a couple of other places before he got here. He may have had sedatives."

Kay considered the implications of that. "And you don't know for sure that Denny's even alive."

"Not for sure," McDuff admitted. "But my guess is that he is, simply because Jory wanted him for bait. To get to you. You'd hardly knowingly risk your own life for a dead child."

229

Kay looked at her husband for a long moment, then swallowed and faced McDuff again. "What do you want me to do, Lieutenant?"

Jory prowled from one window to the next, and if there had ever been humor on his face it was gone now. What the hell were they doing? Why had they brought Kay Richards up and then moved her back in the woods? Why were they *all* back in the woods? If they thought they'd get the kid out of here without sending Richards in, they had another think coming and that was for damned sure.

Behind him, the baby let out a long, thin wail.

He jumped, almost angry enough to fire the .38 he had taken up in exchange for the shotgun. Damned kid, they should have given him some more of the stuff that kept him quiet. He couldn't stand kids, never could. They were even worse than women, whom he'd hated as far back as he could remember. His mother, his teachers, the neighborhood women who didn't want him around their worthless, bitch daughters—and the ones who'd testified against him in court who were responsible for the seven years he'd spent in prison. . . .

He'd showed Malloy who was boss, all right. He'd whipped her into submission, taken all the fight out of her.

He hadn't noticed when she crawled across the floor to where Case lay, but she was done in. She looked like she'd passed out; he had nothing to fear from her.

Shit, he had nothing to fear from anybody, did he? This goddamned thing in his head was what he had to fear—going into a hospital and having some fucking doctor cut into his head, and people sticking him full of needles, and making him take all kinds of crap so he wouldn't ever know what he was doing—

It wouldn't happen, Jory reminded himself. They'd carry him out of here feet first.

But he'd take Richards with him.

Frustration erupted in a string of bellowed obscenities. He cupped his hand to his mouth, beside the broken window, and shouted across the clearing.

"Come on, pig! I ain't got all day! If Richards wants to see her kid alive, send her in here in the next five minutes, or I'll toss him out there in pieces!"

He could no longer see any of them. How many were there

anyway? Out of sight meant they'd worked around, getting into position for something. Jory made a rapid check through the other windows and saw nothing. Not even the trees were moving; the rain had stopped and there was no wind and he suddenly felt as if his nerve ends were coming through his skin.

What the fucking hell were they doing?

The reply came from a different direction, although the voice was still McDuff's.

"Bring the baby out, Jory. Mrs. Salvetti is here, let her see the baby."

"No way! You saw him, you know he's here. Let her come in and get him. That's one minute, cop! One minute!"

"Send the Malloy girl out, then! Or Case! You don't need them all!"

Jory glanced down at the pair on the floor and spat. "They ain't in any condition to come. That's a minute and a half!"

"That's only one minute to now," McDuff corrected. "Let's not rush things, Jory."

"Hell, I ain't got a watch. I have to guess. And when I guess it's five minutes, I'm going to shoot the kid, so she better not waste any more time! Come in and get him!"

Behind him, on the floor, Casey stirred, and Donna quickly lifted a hand to cover his mouth. He opened his eyes, which stared into hers at a distance of six inches: alert, cognizant.

Relief flooded through her, and she touched a finger to her lips. Quiet. Wait.

She withdrew the hand from his mouth and let it rest against him; after a few seconds she realized what she was feeling through the nylon of his jacket pocket.

A book of matches.

Excitement began in a thin trickle. Scarcely moving, she maneuvered her hand into Casey's pocket and extracted the matches. He watched her, then glanced at Jory, who was yelling something out of the broken window.

"All right," they heard McDuff call back. "She's coming in."

Almost simultaneously, a variety of things happened.

Denny screamed, a sound of rage and frustration that nevertheless brought a surge of hope to the watchers around the cabin.

Kay Salvetti stepped out of the shelter of the trees and

began to walk directly toward the cabin door. She knew the vest they had given her to wear would protect her from a bullet in the body, but if Jory chose to shoot her in the head there was no way *that* could be protected.

She also knew that her son was still alive.

At the same time, Donna Malloy lit one of the safety matches and held the flame to the edge of a torn newspaper almost under Jory's heels.

For a few seconds the tiny fire seemed undecided; and then it blazed up and ate its way across the accumulated debris.

The stuffing from the mattress lay scattered on the floor, and the flames greedily included that, too, in their feast.

At the far end of the mattress, Denny, awake, wet, and hungry, hauled himself onto hands and knees and lurched off toward the door, which now stood halfway open.

Jory's attention was entirely focused on the young woman walking slowly toward him. Let her get close, let her even get a look at the kid, and then he'd give it to her. Her, and the kid, both. There was no way he could miss at this range.

He didn't know where the cops were, but they wouldn't get their crack at him until after he'd killed them both. He had plenty of shells for that—Richards, and the kid, and Malloy, and maybe another one for Case, interfering son of a bitch. He'd like that big redheaded bastard McDuff, too, although he didn't expect to be that lucky.

His finger eased onto the trigger and he waited for just the right moment.

And then, suddenly, Kay wasn't moving anymore, because a man dashed out of the sheltering trees. He was solidly built in an old green rain suit, and he ran as if there was something wrong with one leg, but the son of a bitch carried a rifle like he meant to use it.

At the same moment, Jory smelled smoke and heard Denny's plaintive "Mama!" right behind him.

Men yelled. "Who the hell?" "Stop him!" "Get the hell out of there, you'll get your head blown off!"

But the newcomer kept coming, and Jory couldn't get them both with the first shot.

He fired.

Kay Salvetti felt the blow—no pain, only the blow—against her shoulder; she staggered, and fell.

Jory had no time for the baby at his feet, other than to kick blindly out at him. That crazy bastard with the rifle was drawing on him; Jory swiveled in the doorway, and fired again, and the man, too, went down.

Jory never had a chance to fire the third shot.

Glass showered over Donna and Casey on the floor; they were rolling, now, to escape the flames they had loosed, rolling together, scrambling to hands and knees, clinging to one another.

Danny Lowell had fired through the window to the west, putting his bullet neatly into Jory's right ear.

McDuff's caught him in the left temple.

And Tim Fitzpatrick, firing even as he fell, took Jory right through the belly.

Donna and Casey stared in disbelief.

Jory lay curled forward, eyes wide open and blood gushing from his mouth and over the hand pressed to his stomach. They watched as the .38 slid from his fingers onto the board floor.

Donna moved convulsively toward the baby, but Denny was already clambering over Jory's feet, his face red with crying, making his way toward his mother.

"Get out," Casey said thickly, but even as he gained his feet he saw that it wasn't necessary. The fire had burned itself out on newspapers and cotton batting; the mattress continued to smolder slightly, but posed no immediate danger.

Casey helped Donna to her feet, and by that time the men had reached the doorway. They all looked down at Jory. He was not a pretty sight.

Donna turned her face away, and Casey pulled her head against his shoulder and held it there.

In the clearing, Wally Salvetti bent over his wife. "Kay? Honey?"

She raised her face, dazed. "Denny?"

"He's okay," McDuff said, and swung the baby into Wally's arms. "How bad you hurt, Mrs. Salvetti?"

She looked blankly at the spreading stain on her jacket. "I don't know. Not very much, I think." She choked on a sob, then gathered her son to her. They sat together, the Salvettis, holding onto each other.

Donna and Casey worked their way around the fallen Jory—no one had bothered to cover him and his dead eyes stared at nothing—and out into the clearing. The rain had begun to fall again, but they didn't notice.

Donna was aware of Casey's large warm hand enfolding

her own, and she drew comfort from it. She was also aware of Kay Salvetti, sitting on the ground with a demanding child in her arms and blood on her jacket.

Their eyes met across the child—Donna's and Kay's. And something passed between them, unspoken, yet vital.

He did it again. . . .

Yes.

I'm sorry.

The barrier between them had ruptured, spilling out warmth and compassion. They might never again enjoy the close relationship they had once known, but they would never again be completely alienated from one another, either.

Denny writhed in Kay's arms, pushing in protest against her. "Eat, eat," he demanded.

Donna spoke with an effort. Weariness slurred her words. "There were graham crackers in the diaper bag. I think one of the deputies found it."

"I'll get it," Wally said quickly, and rose to his feet.

For a moment the two young women stared at one another, each fully aware of the anguish the other had suffered.

"Thank you," Kay said softly. "That's inadequate, but— thank you."

Donna swayed and immediately Casey brought an arm around her. "I think we'd better go sit down."

They made their way into the edge of the woods and a seat on a fallen log; Donna closed her eyes and tried not to think about anything except the arm around her, the shoulder against which she leaned.

McDuff had covered the intervening yards in a few steps, and reached for the man in the rain suit. He couldn't immediately place him, although he knew he'd seen the man before.

"Who the hell is he?" George Zabaga demanded, working to staunch the bleeding in the injured man's side. "Where'd he come from?"

"Fitzpatrick," McDuff said, out of the subconscious. "It was his boy Jory killed."

Zabaga glanced at the cabin, then added McDuff's hand-kerchief to his own over the wound. "Well, I guess he helped even the score. You sit up, Mr. Fitzpatrick?"

Tim stared down at the mess of jacket, blood, and protruding bone. "Did I get him?"

"You got him," Zabaga confirmed. "Here, sir, can you put

pressure on this? We'll bring up the Scout and get you to a hospital."

"Tell Sara," Fitzpatrick said. "Tell her I got him."

"We'll tell her," Zabaga assured him.

The men parted to let McDuff through at the cabin door. He stared down at Russell William Jory.

"Nice shooting, Lieutenant," Hanks observed. He was pale, but composed.

"Yeah," McDuff agreed. "Get on that radio and let's get a couple of ambulances out here."

"They're on the way," Bruder said. "Calhoun called as soon as the shooting started. Everybody else okay, Lieutenant?"

"We could use one of those first-aid kits. Everybody seems to be bleeding, but Jory's the only fatality." And a bloody goddamned miracle that was.

Danny Lowell touched Jory's foot with the toe of his shoe. "Funny, isn't it? How small he looks."

"The only thing that made him big," McDuff said, "was the gun." He looked across the fallen man to the pair beyond him. "You two able to walk? We're moving up the vehicles, we'll help you into one of them."

Casey pushed himself off the log. "Thanks. Thanks a lot, Lieutenant."

"Any time," McDuff said. He turned away.

"Christ," he said to nobody in particular. "I could sure use a cup of coffee."

AFTERWORD

.... A judge's dilemma—

In a courtroom, you occasionally hear of convicted criminals pleading for mercy —but did you ever hear of a judge doing so? I have. I recently received a shocking letter from Los Angeles Superior Court Judge Harry Peetris. Judge Peetris was pleading for mercy—mercy from California's current sentencing laws. You probably won't like what Judge Peetris said in his letter anymore than I did but I think you might be interested in hearing it.

Judge Peetris, in his letter, spoke of a case which was recently heard in his court. A man was convicted of several brutal murders. The evidence was clear cut. The man was criminally motivated, cold-blooded, and completely without any human compassion. So, you say, what's the problem? The man obviously deserves the death penalty or at least life in prison without parole, right? What he deserves and what he gets under our current laws are two different things. Let's look at the details of this case.

This particular killer got started in 1966. His first victim was killed in his efforts to take over a prostitution business. The woman he killed was sitting in her living room. The killer placed a gun in her ear and pulled the trigger. Sitting on the couch witnessing this horrible scene was the victim's 15-year-old son. Despite the boy's pleas for his life, the killer stuck a gun in the young man's ear and pulled the trigger. After all, the killer said later, he couldn't leave any eye witnesses. These two murders went unsolved for ten years.

Up until 1971, the killer served time in prison for a parole violation. After he was released, you guessed it, he killed again. His victim was a cocaine dealer. Some people might think he did society a favor but nonetheless, he took another life.

Our enterprising killer thought he was becoming quite adept at his craft. So much so that he decided to go professional. Now a hired killer, his fourth victim got the familiar gun in the ear. This time he fired three shots but the woman somehow managed to live—even though she remained partially paralyzed and had to walk with a cane. Not wanting to jeopardize his professional standing as a hired killer, he returned two months later to finish the job. This time he fired the gun in her ear and in her eye. Then, just to be thorough, he fired at the back of her head and at her heart. The killer then jokingly said, "This time she's really dead." Somehow that's not too funny to me.

Most people would agree that this cold-blooded killer should be put to death. Unfortunately, not enough legislators agree with the people. As a result of an eleventh-hour bill passed last year, coupled with the Supreme Court's ruling against the death penalty, killers can now get off relatively easy. Let's look at what choices Judge Peetris faced in sentencing this professional killer. The judge thought the proper punishment would be death. The court ruling against the death penalty came during the killer's trial. The Supreme Court said there was no opportunity to consider mitigating circumstances. So much for the sentence of death. The next lesser sentence would be life in prison without parole. That punishment is available for kidnapping for ransom with injury, trainwrecking with injury, and other similar crimes—but not for the crimes committed by this killer. So much for life in prison without parole. The next lesser sentence would be to give consecutive sentences for each of the murders to be served separately instead of running at the same time. In this case, the killer would not be eligible for parole for 35 years. Unfortunately Section 669 of the Penal Code requires that all of the murder counts merge into one. As a result of our current laws in this case, this killer will be eligible for parole in five years and ten months. Life is cheap in California.

Judge Peetris is frustrated and angry. He believes he can't impose a proper sentence, can't protect witnesses and can't protect society. Laws are what they are because the legislators choose to keep them as they are. Legislators are who they are because people elect them.

Are you as frustrated as the good Judge Peetris or could you be one of the many Californians who vote without knowing how your State representatives vote on law and order issues?

Reprinted from Richardson's Report
The Leader
Oakdale, California

The National Bestseller by
GARY JENNINGS

"A blockbuster historical novel. . . . From the start of this epic, the reader is caught up in the sweep and grandeur, the richness and humanity of this fictive unfolding of life in Mexico before the Spanish conquest. . . . Anyone who lusts for adventure, or that book you can't put down, will glory in AZTEC!"

The Los Angeles Times

"A dazzling and hypnotic historical novel. . . . AZTEC has everything that makes a story appealing . . . both ecstasy and appalling tragedy . . . sex . . . violence . . . and the story is filled with revenge. . . . Mr. Jennings is an absolutely marvelous yarnspinner. . . . A book to get lost in!"

The New York Times

"Sumptuously detailed. . . . AZTEC falls into the same genre of historical novel as SHOGUN."

Chicago Tribune

"Unforgettable images. . . . Jennings is a master at graphic description. . . . The book is so vivid that this reviewer had the novel experience of dreaming of the Aztec world, in technicolor, for several nights in a row . . . so real that the tragedy of the Spanish conquest is truly felt."

Chicago Sun Times

AVON Paperback   55889 . . . $3.95

Available wherever paperbacks are sold, or directly from the publisher. Include 50¢ per copy for postage and handling; allow 6-8 weeks for delivery. Avon Books, Mail Order Dept., 224 West 57th St., N.Y., N.Y. 10019.

Aztec 1-82